The Voyageurettes

Their Tales & Legends

by Rebecca B. Barry and Susan A. Engebretson

Illustrated by Jack Kraywinkle and Jonathan A. Norberg

Adventure Publications, Inc.

Cambridge, Minnesota

Dedication

To our parents, Floyd H. Barnes and Betty A. Barnes, who showed us how to derive great pleasure from the simplest things in life with vigor and humor.

Special thanks to Patricia J. Bell, Lynn E. Noel (Lisette Duval Harmon), Chuck Jansen, Howard and Janet Stahlheber, Everette and Luella Cooley, and Charles E. Barry for their mentoring, assistance and patience, and to all the real Voyageurettes who are truly legends in our minds.

Karen Freidman	Joyce Maurizzi
Ramona Graupner	Candace Rapf
Margot Kincheloe	Corita Schilling
Tina Landreneau	Jacqueline Taxter
Tricia Longworth	Gail Whereatt
Sarah Magnan	Chris Zasada

Cover and book design by Jonathan A. Norberg

Table of Contents

Foreword
by Lynn Noel

"Said one of these men, long past seventy years of age: 'I could carry, paddle, walk and sing with any man I ever saw. I have been twenty-four years a canoe man, and forty-one years in service; no portage was ever too long for me. Fifty songs could I sing. I have saved the lives of ten voyageurs, have had twelve wives and six running dogs. I spent all my money in pleasure, Were I young again, I should spend my life the same way over. There is no life so happy as a voyageur's life!'"

(*The Voyageur*, Grace Lee Nute [St. Paul: Minnesota Historical Society, 1955], p. vi)

Who the heck are the Voyageurettes? Weren't all voyageurs men? What is a bunch of middle-aged women doing running around in the Canoe Country making fun of our history?

Having a helluva good time. And reenacting, in the process, far more history than they know. Lets look at what it means to be a voyageur, so we can join the Voyageurettes in their romp through past and present in the eternal landscape of canoe country.

The Voyageur Milieu

Like Camelot and the clipper ships, the days of the voyageurs were slow to come and quick to pass. Though U.S. history teaches little of our continent's French heritage, the Jesuits and voyageurs of New France reached far beyond the Pilgrims of New England. Canada's history is America's history too, especially in the Midwest. From Hennepin Avenue in Minneapolis to Duluth and Fond du Lac, from Marquette and Prairie du Chien to Dubuque, the names of great explorers ring out. Streets, towns and rivers speak the language of the voyageurs.

Jacques Cartier arrived in Mount Royal in 1534, 86 years before Plymouth Rock. Père Brebeuf built the first mission in Lake Huron in 1639, long before New England reached the Great Lakes. But in 1670, King Charles II of England granted "the sole trade and commerce" of the entire Hudson's Bay watershed to a "company of adventurers" calling themselves the Hudson's Bay Company. (The initials H.B.C., it was said, stood for either "Here Before Christ" or to at least one Inuit woman, "Horny Boys' Club".) By 1686, at the mouth of the Missinaibi River in James Bay, it was war with the French "pedlars" from Montreal in their light, fast birchbark canoes. The voyageur era of transcontinental canoe trade could be said to begin in 1731, when Sieur de la Vérendrye opened a chain of northern posts designed to carry the French beaver trade into the rich Western districts to rival the HBC. The Montrealers' territory already reached from the Gulf of St. Lawrence to the Gulf of Mexico, where Sieur de La Salle had claimed the whole Mississippi Valley for New France in 1682.

But when Montcalm engaged Wolfe on the Plains of Abraham in 1759, the fall of Quebec took the Empire of New France with it. In the (English) history books, the eighteenth and nineteenth centuries would belong to the great fur companies, the railroads and the Americans. The battle for the new country called America was fought over furs in the north and farmland to the south. The border dispute ranged right along the treeline, in beaver country. Its beating heart was at La Vérendrye's key post, first Grand Portage and later Fort William, in the Boundary Waters.

The true, brief heyday of the voyageurs flourished between 1803 and 1821, in the era of the NorthWest Company under Alexander Mackenzie. Lewis and Clark may get the credit in the States for crossing the continent, but Canada's sea-to-sea explorer reached the Pacific six years before the Americans. From 1789 to 1793, Mackenzie and his voyageurs paddled to the Pacific and Arctic Oceans on a transcontinental route that now bears his name as a National Heritage Trail across Canada.

The Alexander Mackenzie Voyageur Route has long been known as the "Voyageur's Highway." To follow it, load up your canoe at the Old Port of Montreal (the heritage route officially begins in Quebec City) near the roaring Lachine Rapids. Turn right up the Ottawa River, singing "En remontant la rivière" against the current in spring flood. At Mattawa, take "the most famous left turn in history" up the Mattawa River, poling and carrying over thirteen portages to the height of land at Portage la Vase. Carry though this two-mile swamp and snap your pole over your knee at the Prairie des Français before running ninety miles of the French River to Lake Huron in a single day. Hug the north shoreline past Manitoulin of the windigos and

Sault Ste. Marie of the priests, and brace your thirty-six foot canoe for the wind and waves of Superior. Six weeks from Montreal, you'll arrive at North West Company headquarters.

From the western end of Superior, there are only two routes to the North West. Grand Portage was la Vérendrye's original choice, at the foot of a nine-mile carry into today's Boundary Waters Canoe Area. But after the American Revolution, the Canadians found themselves on the wrong side of the border, and by 1803 Mackenzie's group had moved the NWC thirty miles north to the Kaministiquia River (the current historic site is nine miles inland from the original post). From the Grand Portage (Mackenzie's original route) or up the Pigeon River portage from Fort William, the Voyageur's Highway followed native trails through the Boundary Waters to Lake of the Woods and Lake Winnipeg to portages at The Pas and Frog Portage (Flin Flon). The longest portage in Canada is a 35-mile carry into the Athabasca watershed on the Clearwater River at Portage La Loche. From here to Fort Chipwyan, Alberta, the Pacific route runs up the Peace, over the Rockies and down the Fraser to Bella Coola, while Mackenzie's Arctic route traces his River from Great Slave Lake to Mackenzie Bay.

All this country could be reached through the Boundary Waters, and the voyageurs became the heroes of their own tales. The short, stocky, tireless men are famous as the cowboys of the canoe country. According to legend, they have six wives and five running dogs, they can carry hundreds of pounds at a dogtrot, they paddle three-ton canoes upstream. They can eat their weight in pemmican and drink a canoe full of rum apiece. Naturally, their exploits are larger than life. They are as large as their land.

But the Voyageurettes go them one better. For where are the women in this story? How did an entire continent, already populated coast to coast, get claimed and settled by individual white European men? And not to get too technical, how did there get to be little voyageurs? For the answers to these and many more questions, tongue firmly in cheek, one must ask the Maries.

Women in the Voyageur Era

Sue and Becky's Voyageurettes are an anachronism, pur et simple. But it's easy for any independent, adventurous woman to feel like an anachronism when she is presented with five hundred years of history in which she is invisible. Were there really women voyageurs? Bien sûr.

If we break down the term "voyageur" into smaller ideas, we can find a woman to match virtually every criterion of the definition. In the sheer strength category, the Chipwyan women in Alexander Henry's journals could pull a loaded York boat full of furs on rollers. For endurance, we have Louis Riel's grandmother, Marie-Anne LaJimodière, who paddled to Superior and rode horseback to the prairies with her husband. She was dragged from horseback in her ninth month and gave birth the next day. For distance at speed, the record-holder may be Lisette Duval Harmon, who with her husband Daniel and two daughters, aged eight and two, paddled from British Columbia to Vermont in ten weeks. They stopped for five days at Fort William: on the 19th of August Lisette delivered a son, John. On the 20th they were married in the chapel, and on the 23rd they resumed their journey, reaching the Harmon homestead in Vergennes, Vermont in mid-September. Harmon's journal says only, "Nothing untoward occurred." These women could give any power-paddler milieu a run for his money.

Experienced voyageurs became guides, with extensive knowledge of the canoe country. The Chipwyan Thanadelthur and the Shoshone Sacajawea, both "country wives" of voyageurs, have made it into the historical record as "guide and interpreter", as did many nameless native women along the routes. David Thompson's Métis wife Charlotte traveled with him throughout his famous mapping expeditions to the Rockies, bearing his children en route.

Were women restricted to "blue-collar" positions in the fur trade? Hardly. The Grignon sisters of Wisconsin had become two of the largest landowners in Green Bay by the 1840s. Juliette Kinzie, wife of an Indian agent, had the wherewithal to bring her piano with her in the same canoe to Portage, Wisconsin. Arguably the most famous woman of the fur trade, painter Frances Anne Hopkins, was the *bourgeoise* wife of Governor Simpson who gave her name to Fort Frances, Ontario (across from International Falls, Minnesota).

When Michigan's Madeleine LaFramboise was widowed in Mackinac, she took over his trading operation so successfully that John Jacob Astor made her one of his agents rather than compete with her. (She also had at least three husbands, giving her a running in the six-wives category, though there is no mention of running dogs.) Mme. LaFramboise, like Charlotte Thompson and Lisette Duval Harmon, was multilingual in at least English, French, Ojibwa and Cree. Lisette is cited as the main informant in her husband's extensive anthropology of the Cree. As the Métis children of native women and French-Canadian trappers, these three women and thousands like them were literally daughters of the fur trade.

But where is the camaraderie of the brigade? Can the jolly boatload of singing voyageurs translate into female terms? Not exactly, but there are precedents. We know of at least three instances of groups of women traveling in the canoe country. In the 1600s, "*les filles du roi*" (the King's Girls) were shipped over from France as mail-order brides. Many married voyageurs and some departed with them (though they did not always reach their destination together!). From all accounts of *les filles du roi*, each was a perfect Bambi to her Jean-Baptiste.

On the English side, in 1811-12 the HBC sent a Scottish group of colonists to counter the NWC influx. The women and men of the Selkirk settlers arrived at York Factory late in the season, and endured a grueling winter at Churchill before their York boats slogged upstream to the Red River colony in Winnipeg. Whether like Marie Sue or like the rest of the Voyageurettes, the Selkirk women must have had strong feelings about oatmeal.

In Winnipeg at the Forks of the Red in 1844, Marguerite D'Youville's Grey Nuns of Montreal founded a mission at Saint-Boniface which puts their journey along the Voyageurs' Highway. Boatloads of nuns traveled this route in the latter days of the fur trade. The curator of the *Musée de Saint-Boniface* reports that the *Soeurs Grises* had at least one major influence on voyageur culture, as they apparently worked hard to clean up the bawdier voyageurs' songs into the pure, sweet laments of love we know today. Even so do the Voyageurettes, with tongue in cheek, seek the higher and better selves in their friends the voyageurs.

Women who value the voyageur mystique have a dual challenge in seeking to reenact it. Modern, culturally European "woodswomen" identify with both halves of the fur trade split: we are white like the men and women like the natives. When we succeed in achieving this dual vision, it pops the fur trade into stereo. Such a multicultural, multigendered perspective can fuse the dualities that have been used for so long to define not only the fur trade era, but North American history itself. Strong, adventurous women long to put ourselves in the picture, to feel personally connected to a history in which women have been taught we are invisible (or identified as male). When men or women can empathize both with Lewis and Clark and with

Sacajawea, both with David and with Charlotte Thompson, we gain new dimensions to the history of our continent and our place in it.

Any modern canoeist longs for the era of the voyageurs. The landscape itself evokes them. When the mist rises on Saganaga Lake, you can see the stern of the great canoes vanishing in front of you into the fog. In the call of wolf and loon, you know you can hear them singing. These men are our history. What would it be like to join in that *camaraderie*, to paddle with them? We all talk to the past. These are the tales that we might tell, as twentieth-century women, around the campfire with Jean-Baptiste and Etienne Brule. The Voyageurette stories are not ABOUT the voyageurs. They ARE the voyageurs: if they were us.

In the exploits of the Maries, the Voyageurettes have captured both the *camaraderie* and the *joie de vivre* of the brigade. History is only the canvas on which they paint, and we should turn our attention from backdrop to brushstrokes.

C'est pas l'histoire, c'est une histoire (not history, but a story)

Sue's and Becky's work fits into the tradition of story rather than history. The Voyageurettes evoke the spirit of the fur trade era through storytelling, which can be a form of living history but can also be far more. Accuracy comes not in the "facts," which have to be stretched in the tall tale tradition, but in the style of the telling: each story creates its own internal reality.

Voyageurette stories use gender and anachronism like flint on steel to spark a laugh. Humor comes from contrast, and the voyageurs themselves delighted in contests and competition. The contest here is twofold: modern women against eighteenth-century men, and history against its modern counterparts. It's a classic contest where the underdog always wins.

In the face of the macho voyageur image, it can be hard to visualize women in canoes as strong, confident and competent. Countering that can turn extreme, as paddling women can be so busy being strong, confident and competent that we lose our sense of humor! It is the great gift of the Voyageurettes to be willing to laugh at themselves by laughing at tradition while respecting it. The Marie stories grow from a joy in paddle and portage as deep and true in women today as in the men of old Montreal who left the farm to seek their fortune in the great canoes.

These stories are true campfire tales in the tall-tale tradition. They evoke Paul Bunyan and his Ottawa Valley cousin, Big Joe Mufferaw, whose boots dug the Rideau Canal by "commuting" to his girlfriend in Kingston. Either Paul or Big Joe certainly would have driven a cat sled in the Iditarod if he'd thought of it. After meeting B.B. Légume (whose translation is gloriously literal), it's obvious that John Jacob Astor was the L.L. Bean of his time. The larger-than-life "king of the fur trade" certainly would have appreciated Bean boots, though plaid pants are easier to see on Mackenzie.

Naming by opposites, like calling a chipmunk "Giant," is true to the Ti-Jean tradition in French Canada where the tallest guy is Ti-Jean (Little John), the smelliest is Sweet Violet, the ugliest Handsome, &c. In this context, the diminutive -ette is perfect for the larger-than-life figures of Marie Becky, Marie Sue and their colorful companions. Each has a well-defined role with a cameo caricature, just like the voyageurs. In the place of the braggart, the ladies' man and the know-it-all, we have the athletic ballerina, the oatmeal-hater and the naturalist. Who hasn't fallen into one or more of these roles in a canoe trip? They make the best stories, as well they should.

Becky and Sue have done men as well as women a service by putting a woman's face on the voyageur era. These tales remind us that the values of the voyageurs transcend gender as well as time. Camaraderie, companionship, *esprit de corps*, valor, adventure, love of a song and a challenge, and above all a sense of humor: these are as vital to the human spirit in women as in men. Voyageur values are as essential now as then. This is not how it happened then. This is how it happened now. Every storyteller knows that when you tell the story, you tell how it should have happened. *Vive les Voyageurettes!*

—Lynn Noel
"Lisette Duval"

Lynn Noel is a geographer, bilingual singer and storyteller, and professional voyageur. In her alter ego as NWC fur trader Lisette Duval, she has spent ten years retracing the Voyageurs' Highway from Vermont and Montreal to the Rockies, the Mississippi and the Mackenzie, earning national awards in both Canada and the U.S. for heritage education. Lynn is the author/editor of *VOY-AGES: Canada's Heritage Rivers* and is currently researching a biography of Lisette Duval Harmon.

Des circonstances particulières ont donné lieu à la constitution d'un groupe de femmes unique en son genre. Tous les goûts sont dans la nature.

A peculiar set of circumstances produced
a unique group of women.

1

How the Voyageurettes Came to Be

Marie Sue first opened one eye, and then the other, and stretched out on her feather bed in her cabin next to the Opecheekeen Outpost overlooking the fording place on the Rock River. She lay quietly in the dawning light for several minutes making up her opinion about matters and things in general. She thought about all the milestones she had already passed in her life. She had braved them all and now her life lacked zip, or so it seemed. Her offspring had grown up and were pretty much on their own and her husband continued to put in long months at work exploring and trading out on the prairie, leaving her alone most of the time.

Life around her cabin was not particularly exciting or challenging any more, either. The crown moldings that she had planed by hand had been installed in all three rooms for several months. The two clay flower pots she had managed to collect over the years had been sponge-painted, filled with pasque flowers and yellow buttercups and placed out in the sun by the front door. Both windows were now adorned with swags and matching tassels. In the evenings, she put a lit candle in a tin lard pail and placed it on the rough pine floor to provide dramatic up-lighting for her indoor plant. Just the week before she had assembled three dried flower arrangements using hot buffalo-hoof glue. They should last forever. All her hard work around the place was finished.

From high above the river, Marie Sue heard the honking of a flock of geese as they flew to their summer nesting places far to the North. Their many voices honking in concert brought forth an unexpected response. Immediately Marie Sue pined for a life closer to kindred spirits, with wild things. With wilderness! She wanted adventure—a little daring, some excitement—and shared experiences with others so later she could sit by the fire and reminisce with them about the best of times. Marie Sue knew she needed something more in life. Something more than sitting in front of her cabin in the shade of the shagbark hickory trees and watching other people have a good time. Most of all, she wanted to see what was beyond the rocky fording place she could see from her window, and what was past the bend in the river, and the bend beyond that one, all the way to the Far North. She needed to see for herself what was beyond the horizon.

Off in the distance she thought she heard voices. Soon, in her mind's eye, she saw eight men paddling their big canoe toward the Outpost next door. The men were cheerfully singing a *chanson*, their paddles in perfect time to their strong harmonies.

> "Down the river you can hear the windsong bearing tales of the voyageur,
> Bearing tales, oui, oui, oui; bearing tales, no, no, no,
> Bearing tales of the voyageur,
> Tales of lakes and of rushing rivers from the land we have never seen.
> From the land, oui, oui, oui; from the land, no, no, no;
> From the land we have never seen."

Marie Sue's heart skipped. Voyageurs! Real voyageurs, with their canoe heavily laden with bales of fur bound for the Rendezvous! They were dressed in their work frocks and brown pants with red woven sashes tied about their waists. Their caps sported brightly colored feathers or white ostrich plumes. They paddled so spritely, with wide smiles and hearty laughter! Marie Sue was captivated by their *joie de vivre*.

Marie Sue had heard of these traveling *voyageurs*, the experienced *hivernants* or 'winterers' who were employed by fur companies in their trading and transportation divisions. Every year they left home in early spring and did not return until the ice formed on the lakes and rivers of the North Woods. For months on end they lived a care-free life out in the fresh, clear air, singing their songs as they worked together in return for a few beaver pelts and a few items of clothing. They saw and heard wondrous wild creatures of the water and woods. They watched gathering storms, experienced their fury and relished the rainbows that came afterward. They saw the northern lights and stars high in the sky and watched the moonlight shimmering on the water. Theirs was a wonderful life!

For a few minutes Marie Sue thought about her situation. She assessed her current circumstance and generated alternatives. She mulled over her choices. Then she came up with a plan for going to the land where she had never been.

After breakfast Marie Sue went to trade for food with Francois L'Jewell at the Outpost. While checking over the early rhubarb in the food bin, she ran into Marie Rebecca. She said to her, "*Bonjour*, Marie!" Marie Rebecca said, "Halloo, Marie."

Then Marie Sue said, "Marie, are you tired of being bored, lonely and poor? For the past few years, I have felt stagnant—cooped up. I mope around my little cabin, waiting months on end for something interesting or exciting to happen. I do not want to lead the rest of my life regretting that I have not had more fun. So, I intend to take control of my life and make things happen. For a short period of time, I'm planning to take leave of my husband and family so I can experience grand adventures. How about you? Will you come along?"

Marie Rebecca said, "*Oui, biensûr*! But there is one small problem. How can we finance this adventuring? My personal funds for such things are a little low at the moment. For years I have wanted my own career and independent income to match my husband's. Maybe this would be a good time to have a job and make just enough money to go adventuring like the voyageurs do."

"Come to think of it, we could become even more successful than the big fur companies! Instead of having three major companies competing in the same territory and trading for identical goods, we can be the one and only company selling a variety of essential products especially for, *les femmes du pays*. You know, special products to take the drudge out of routine chores like cleaning, cooking and storing food. We could sell things to make life easier and more pleasant for busy people. We can distribute products to help ladies look good and feel better about themselves. We can combine a little business with adventure! We can paddle hundreds of lakes and rivers in the Canoe Country and make big bucks at the same time!" said Marie Sue.

Marie Rebecca said, "OK, that sounds like a plan!"

Then Marie Rebecca and Marie Sue went to wash their clothes at "The Point of Laundry Rock" down along the river. There they spotted Marie Margot and said, "Halloo, Marie," to her.

She said, "Halloo, Marie! Halloo, Marie!"

Right away the two Maries had the same thought. They said, "Marie Margot, are you tired of being bored, lonely and poor?"

She said, "As a matter of fact, yes, I am."

They said, "Then, join us! We yearn for fun and adventure and we desire freedom from life's dull routines. To finance our adventures we will start up a small business, and soon it will show a profit. We will paddle throughout the Canoe Country to the North and have challenging adventures in the wilderness!"

Marie Margot said, "What a creative approach! If we manage our income conservatively, we can shop to our hearts' content and pay in cash. That way we will avoid building up a huge trading account debit at the Outpost. Couple that with a keen understanding of economic indicators and making wise investment choices, we could end up as good role-models for other *femmes du pays* to copy in the future. Count me in!"

The three of them went to over to Jean Richard Simone's cabin for their fitness workout. There they saw Marie Chris.

"Halloo, Marie," said Sue, Rebecca and Margot all together.

She said, "Halloo, Marie; halloo, Marie; halloo, Marie," back to them.

Right up front they asked her, "Are you tired of being poor, lonely and bored?"

Marie Chris said, "Come to think of it, yes, I am. What's on your mind? I definitely need something different to do with my life. I'm ready to take on personal challenges and explore new horizons!"

The three other Maries said, "By all means, join us! On the way over here we did some demographics and market research and came up with a comprehensive business plan for North America. We are forming an innovative company which will sell quality products through a well-trained and highly motivated sales and distribution network. Right away our customers will have the opportunity to become distributors and true partners in this self-sustaining enterprise. We have many ideas ready to be implemented. We are going to call ourselves "The Voyageurettes." Very shortly we all will have enough disposable income to maintain a free-spirited life-style and have no financial worries, ever again. Then we can enjoy a happy life and devote our lives to serving others."

Marie Chris said, "This sounds wuuunderful! I can be packed and ready to go in fifty-seven minutes. Sign me up!"

This was the time of year that voyageurs from throughout the Far North spent six to eight weeks paddling south and east to the place called Grand Portage on Lake Superior where they were to spend an entire month in rendezvous with the *mangeurs du lard*, or novice 'pork-eaters,' who had just arrived in their huge 36-to-40 foot *canot de maître* or freight canoes all the way from Montreal. Each year the two groups of voyageurs from the east and to the west of Grand Portage met and exchanged trade-goods for furs and partied. When they partied, they drank. When they drank, they got drunk. When they got drunk, they argued. And when they argued, they fought hard and dirty. While they were drinking and arguing and fighting, they also told each other big lies about their horses, fast dog teams, fast canoes and fast women. Then they had to go back to work until the ice took on the lakes and rivers.

When the men left Grand Portage, their trip far north to Lake Athabaska took several months. They paddled the big 25-foot *canots du nord*, or 'North Canoe,' which weighed several hundred pounds and carried about three thousand pounds or more, in addition to the crew of eight. The voyageurs routinely portaged two ninety-pound packs-one hundred and eighty pounds total and sometimes carried even heavier loads. On the trip north, the voyageurs' *pieces* (packs) were filled with trinkets, beads, blankets, axes, knives, pots and pans and other goods to trade for furs.

Now, the voyageurs had big mouths, big muscles, and big heads. Too bad, they did not have big brains. The Voyageurettes, on the other hand, always used their brains. They did not paddle big *canots du nord*. Instead, they outfitted themselves with *canots leger* or light express canoes. Theirs were canoes with a difference.

"I have made quite a study of the voyageur's birch bark canoes," said Marie Chris. "They are fairly light and more durable than you might think. It is a real plus that they are made from readily available natural materials. However, I have heard that every night the voyageurs must spend hours working on their canoes, patching and mending holes and tears with pitch. I have an idea and I know a neighbor lady who is very clever and can help us. Here is my idea. Instead of spending hours patching holes in our canoes, we can use the patching material, or resin, to make our canoes in the first place. Marie Katerina Henrietta can design and build our canoes for us with no problem! She can weave up some of her special, light-weight, densely woven fabric, form it into a trendy canoe shape and then soak the fabric in her resin formula. When it dries the canoe will be light as a feather, sleek as an otter and as tough as the shell of a turtle. No patching required."

The Voyageurettes thought all those trade goods were too heavy, so they had a better idea. "We can just show pictures of the goods and let each *femme du pays* point to what she wants! Then we will write her choice down on a choosing form." They never carried ninety-pound packs across portages. Their multi-hued teal, black and plum colored belt-packs weighed two or three pounds when fully loaded with picture books, choosing forms and quill pens. The Voyageurettes could go 'way up North and be back home in two weeks flat.

The Voyageurettes visited each and every remote gathering place and trading post along the route. At each stop, Marie Rebecca leaped out of the lead canoe with her arms full of free samples and picture books. She whistled loud through her teeth and called out to all the ladies, "Yoo, hoo! *Venez, venez, ures belles femmes! Venez voir!* Gather around! This is what you have been waiting for, but did not know it until this very moment! Lucky for you, we are introducing Yvonne products! You can order some Yvonne perfume to attract real gentle men or get some "Epidermis So Smooth" to keep away the big mosquitos. Why don't you get some lipstick, mascara and blusher, too, and get really spruced up? These quality products will help you feel and look terrific! You can see the things you want in this handy pocket-sized picture book and write your order on the choosing form. Your orders will be filled immediately and within a few days your products will be delivered to your door by the Ladies' Instant Package Service! Maybe you would like to sign up and work with our company!"

The settlement and trading post ladies always went crazy and ordered many Yvonne products within a few minutes and signed up as company representatives and delivery people.

It was Marie Chris's turn next. She stepped to the front of the crowd and said, "Do you ever look closely at your cookware? Have you ever noticed how your woven grass baskets leak over time? Or how all the tinware is scratched and dented and has lost its shine? How much longer can you tolerate using grass baskets and eating off noisy tin plates? Lucky for you, we sell Putterware," she said as she waved free samples of stackable snack trays and colorful sets of six nesting containers with tight seals high over her head so everyone in the crowd could see. "These little beauties will never disappoint you!" she added. "You might also think about sharing these items with your friends in the future. All you have to is have a gathering, like a party. Show the products to your lady-friends and they will want to buy things. You make a little money, and it's simple for you to do. It's fun and makes everyone happy!"

The ladies always squealed and clapped their hands in delight! They loved Putterware at first sight and immediately got into a long lines to turn in their choosing forms and schedule neighborhood gatherings to sell products themselves.

When the cheering subsided, Marie Margot stepped to the middle of the crowd and, in a hushed tone, asked, "Do you ever find yourself falling into a rut when it comes to meal-time and everyone in the family wants to know what's for supper? Do you ever get bored serving dried fish and berries, or plain pemmican and cornmeal hominy cooked in grease month after month? Let's face it, ladies, you deserve a break! So does your family! How about trying some of these delicious entrees with a very long keeping life? See how cleverly they are packaged in these air-tight, waterproof bags? Simply heat them up in a kettle of boiling water, cut open the bag with your folding belt-knife and serve immediately on rice, biscuits, pasta or mashed potatoes. It's as easy as one, two, three! For your dining pleasure we offer Swiss steak, chicken breast in wine sauce, beef burgundy and cabbage rolls. How many would you like? We also offer dried fruits and vegetables from far away places— things you can't find locally. They will add spice and variety to your meal preparation!"

The ladies were so excited, they ordered the specialty food by the canoe load.

Then Marie Sue took over. "Not long ago I noticed all my clothes were a little on the gray side and not so pretty anymore. Do you ever have a similar problem? These products really work! Step right up close and compare your whites with the camp shirt I'm wearing. Why don't you check out one of these great picture books and pick out some L'Ambway clothing cleaner and bleach to freshen up your whites and other practical items for your cabin?" The ladies at every stop elbowed their way into line to place their L'Ambway orders and sign up as dealers.

Within a few days, each of the Maries had made hundreds of dollars in their spare time. They also had a network of enthusiastic sales ladies working with them. Now, the way was clear for the Voyageurettes to go adventuring in the Canoe Country and soon it would be said of them, *"Des circonstances particulières ont donné lieu à la constitution d'un groupe de femmes unique en son genre. Tous les goûts sont dans la nature.* A peculiar set of circumstances produced a unique group of women."

*Certains jours, ça peut servir
d'être bon en maths.*

Some day being good at math will really be useful.

2

Marie Chris and the Calculating Voyageurettes

Marie Chris was a *wuuunderful* Voyageurette who taught all the other Maries to say that word. She paddled hard. She shopped hard. She loved the adventure of the Canoe Country and she lied hard. She said, "I love it when it rains up here in the wilderness, and I really do love it when those little mosquitos swarm together and sing!"

Marie Chris also read hard. After a long day of voyaging, she loved to get out a book and read silently to herself while lying in her net hammock. When Marie Chris read, the other Voyageurettes dangled a big bug on a string in front of her face. Marie was not distracted one bit. They tickled the back of her neck with a pine branch. She kept on reading. They put pine needles in the hot chocolate she was drinking as she read. She did not notice. They even fastened tiny pink bows on the cowlicks in Marie Chris's hairdo.

Marie Chris finally noticed that. She said, "I know why you are so pesky. It is because your minds are working overtime and you have nothing else to do. Let's open up the Voyageurette School of Lifetime Learning and Hard Bumps. I will be the teacher and you can be the students. That will keep you busy and out of my hair."

The Maries said, "OK, that sounds like fun to us." So, Marie Chris found schoolbooks, papers, workbooks and a slate in her pack. Right away she gave the other Maries instruction and assignments to keep them occupied. Every evening before the sun went down they did their school lessons and Marie Chris read her book in peace and quiet. She told the Maries they were wuuunderful students.

They began their social studies lesson by alphabetizing the last names of all the early explorers, traders and chroniclers they could think of: Allouez, Boucherville, Bougainville, Cadillac, Clark, Dubuisson, Duluth, Frasier, Groseilliers, Harmon, Hennepin, Hudson, Iberville, Jolliet, La Salle, La Verendrye, McKenzie, Marquette, Nicollet, Pike, Pond, Raddison, Tonty, and Thompson.

Then they practiced using a sextant to determine latitude and longitude. "Yes, they are most helpful tools of the trade," said Marie Sue. "I just wish there was a way to use one in the daylight. Some day I'd like to figure out a way to push a little button and find out exactly where on earth I am without having to wait until the stars come out."

"Can we do language arts now?" said Marie Margot. "Nouns and verbs are kind of fun to think about, like *store*, "to put away in a secure spot" and *store*, "a place where you can buy things. Ha, ha, you can store things at a store!"

"How about *shop*, a small store?" said Marie Sue. "And *shop*, as in looking around for things to buy? We shop at a shop! Say, aren't those two words called homonyms, too?"

"Yes, they are," said Marie Rebecca. "Your words have set me thinking. Actually, our method of looking around for things to bring home at places like the Grand Portage trading post is more like going "mauling," because we like to touch and squeeze everything first, move it around, hold it up for a better look and turn it over to see what's underneath. I especially like to look over all the goods on the big grassy spot in front of the Great Hall — they call that place "the green" or the "mall," don't they? We can maul things at the mall!"

They zipped through their studies and always got "A's" in social studies, science, and language. There was only one problem. In math, they were not so wuuunderful. Marie Chris even told them that in math, they were skewed toward the low end of the average scale. Math made Marie Rebecca cry and it made Marie Margot and Marie Sue feel queasy in the stomach. So, they did what all true Voyageurettes would do. They cheated in math.

It must be understood that Marie Chris was wuuunderful at catching fifth-grade cheaters. However, fifth-grade cheaters had minds that were only ten years old. The Voyageurettes were much older and sneakier than ten-year-olds. Their cheating was so subtle, so sophisticated and based on so many years of experience, that Marie Chris did not even know they were doing it.

Marie Rebecca got out her pocket-sized abacus and sat all hunched over on a log with her back to Marie Chris. When Marie Chris read math problems out of her teacher's edition and asked, "What is six times four?", Marie Rebecca moved the tiny abacus beads back and forth on their wires and there was the right answer. She quickly coughed twice. Then she waited a second, and went "cough, cough, cough, cough." Marie Margot and Marie Sue knew the correct answer was 24. When Marie Chris looked up, Marie Rebecca said, "Oh, dear, I think I am catching a cold in this damp air." Marie Chris said it was wuuunderful they were doing so well. The other Maries thought it was wuuunderful that they were such good cheaters at math. They were all happy.

They were all happy, that is, until one day a wire on the abacus broke and the beads fell off into the lake and floated away. Marie Rebecca, Marie Margot and Marie Sue began to cry. Marie Chris said, "What is wrong? Why are you all crying?" They lied. They told her their backsides were sore from sitting still for so long on rough logs without a recess.

Marie Chris said, "OK, why don't you stand up and stretch while I write some work on the slate for you to do?"

Like all good teachers, Marie Chris first wrote down the date on the slate. She began to jump up and down and yell loudly. The other Maries thought she may be going crazy.

They asked her, "Marie Chris, why are you jumping up and down?"

Marie Chris said, "Look at the date on the slate. It is June 10. June 10 is the first day of summer vacation!"

The three other Maries started to jump up and down. Then they lied. They told her they were so happy because she was so happy that it was summer vacation. Really, they were happy because math class was over.

Right then, everyone went on summer vacation. In the days of hard paddling and portaging that followed, when Marie Chris got out her book and began to read, the rest of the Voyageurettes no longer pestered her. Instead, they had profound conversations about their progress in math.

"You know," said Marie Margot. "It wouldn't hurt us one teeny bit to keep up-to-date with our math, algebra, and even geometry skills. Our knowledge of such things can help us measure the length of fish and portages and how far we paddle in one day. We can even calculate interest and figure out profit margins for our business ventures."

"You're right," said Marie Sue. "We can use our knowledge to figure out the hypotenuse of a right triangle while navigating and also calculate how much money we save when shopkeepers on the green mall offer 40% discounts."

At last, when they were sure Marie Chris was really into her book and concentrating hard, they talked softly about how they were going to find someone in the Canoe Country who might like to trade something of great value for a new calculating device. They had learned important truths: Never close the book on learning throughout your life. It is good for you. It builds character. Some day, being good at math will really come in handy.

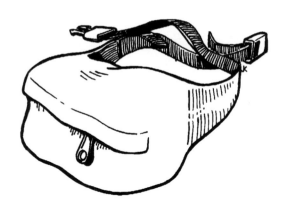

Avec un peu d'aide, on s'en sort toujours. On a tous besoin les uns des autres.

We all get along with a little help from our friends.

3

The Off-duty Nurse

When Marie Karen first joined the Voyageurettes, she announced, "On a canoe trip this nurse would like to be off duty." The other Maries did not pay much attention because they were a pretty healthy bunch.

On the first day out on the water, Marie Sue's knife slipped while she filleted a walleye and sliced her finger. Marie Sue could not even bear to look at the 1.5 cm. wound. She held out her finger and said, "Marie Karen, you are the nurse. Would you please fix up my finger?"

Marie Karen said, "Sorry, Marie, but I am not on duty."

Later that day Marie Rebecca fell down hard and stubbed her toe on a rock. She said, "Marie Karen, I hurt my toe and it is all puffed up. You are a nurse. Could you please fix it?"

Marie just said, "Sorry, but just this minute I am off duty."

Much later that day Marie Margot got a big stomach ache. She said, Marie Karen, would you please give me something to make my tummy feel better?"

Marie Karen just said, "Sorry, but I am off duty right now."

Well, the three Maries got together and made a plan to teach Marie Karen a lesson. Late that afternoon Marie Karen said, "Marie Rebecca, you better get started with supper. Today is your day to cook."

Marie Rebecca said, "Sorry, but I am not on duty."

Poor Marie Karen had to make supper all by herself.

Then she said to Marie Margot, "Marie Margot, we are all done with supper now. It is your turn to do the dishes."

Marie Margot said to her, "Sorry, I'm off duty."

Poor Marie Karen had to do the dishes all be herself.

Then she said to Marie Sue, "Marie Sue, here are the pots and pans to clean up. It is your turn to do that."

Marie Sue said, "Sorry, but I'm off duty tonight."

Poor Marie Karen had to scrub the pots and pans, too. After she completed all the camp chores, Marie Karen was very tired. She said to the Maries, "I know what you three are doing and it has worked. I have seen the errors of my ways. I am a nurse and any time you need a nurse, I will go on duty." Then she said, "In fact, I'd better get started right now." She opened up her nurse kit and started taking things out of it—things that did not look too pleasant for the rest of the Maries.

Three Maries asked, "Marie Karen, what are you doing?"

She said, "I am now on duty. Marie Sue, you need at least six stitches in your finger. Marie Margot, what you need for your stomach ache is a big dose of Castor oil, and Marie Rebecca, what I need to do is to stick this big needle into your toe and drain out all that excess fluid."

The three Maries started to laugh. They knew Marie Karen was joking and that she would not really do those things to her sister Voyageurettes. But right away, to their surprise, she did every one of those things.

Marie Karen said, "Oops, I almost forgot. According to your medical records, you are all due for tetanus booster shots. Come here and roll up your sleeves right now!"

When Marie Karen finished her nursing tasks, all the other Maries sat on a log and pouted. She said, "I knew this would happen. If you remember, I did not particularly want to go on duty, but your little trick forced me into it. Now you are angry with me, and I am sorry for what I did not do in the beginning. At first, I thought I could just be on vacation in the Canoe Country, but now I can see that does not work when I am needed."

"OK, Maries," said Marie Sue. "*Répète après moi: Nous sommes tous quelqu'un!* Repeat after me: we are all individuals. Each one of us has special skills and abilities to share with others. Marie Karen, in your case, we are glad you came on duty today. Think how it is with the voyageurs, who do not have a person like you with them on their long and strenuous journeys. If they are sick or break their bones, who can help them? Think about it. Because you are with us, we Voyageurettes are likely to have a much longer life expectancy than the voyageurs. For that we are grateful. You are needed and appreciated!"

"Let's agree that whenever anyone is hungry, we will feed them," said Marie Margot. "When someone needs a good listener, we will listen. And when someone needs a hand with a heavy load, we all will be good lifters. When there is a problem, we will think of it as an opportunity and fix it. And we can even make up a *chanson*, a new little song, to remind us what should happen on wilderness adventures: "*Avec un peu d'aide, on s'en sort toujours. On a tous besoin les uns des autres.* We all get along with a little help from our friends."

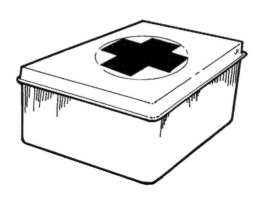

Attention à ce que tu désires; ça pourrait devenir réalité.

Be careful what you hope for. Your wish may come true.

4

Bambi and Jacques Baptiste

After the Voyageurettes counted their cash, they quickly paddled to the settlement. The Voyageurettes went straight to the beauty parlor to have their hair cut and washed, rolled and dried on twigs and combed with pine sap mousse. While they were at the parlor, they all decided to go big time and have milkweed juice facials and have their nails done, as well. That is when they met Bambi, the manicurist. All the time she worked, Bambi chomped on her spruce gum and blew big bubbles. The Maries explained to her that they were Voyageurettes and told her about some of their adventures. She was very interested—not so much in their adventures, but because they knew many voyageurs personally. It was no secret that Bambi was husband-hunting and wanted to meet a handsome and brave voyageur. She asked if the Maries knew such a voyageur who was also single and available.

It was good she asked the Voyageurettes for help rather than a voyageur, for all voyageurs would claim to be handsome, brave, single and available even if they were ugly, cowardly and married, perhaps to several women at the same time. Voyageurs all lie hard about such things.

The Voyageurettes told Bambi the absolute truth. The truth was that they did know Jacques Baptiste—a voyageur who was brave, handsome and available. In fact, the Maries told her that they knew Jacques would be at the well-known Horse Portage in about four days. Bambi got all excited and wanted to go with the Voyageurettes to Horse Portage so they could introduce her to Jacques. "It is fine with us," they told her. She was to meet the Maries at the lake at day-break for the long paddle to Horse Portage.

The very next morning they were at the landing packing up their canoes when along came Bambi with four heavy wooden trunks and three large canvas bags. All of them were full of fancy dresses, pointy-toed shoes, make-up, her hand-held, fold-up hair drying fan, snacks and last month's illustrated "Miss Goody's" newspaper. She had so many bags and trunks there was no room for them in the Voyageurettes' two light canoes. They had to put her things into a big cargo canoe and tow it behind them as they paddled.

The Maries had just settled into their canoes when Bambi made a confession. She said, "Oops, I forget to tell you I do not know how to make the paddle go, but I do know how to sit in the middle of the canoe very still." Bambi told a big lie. She did not know how to sit still at all. She sat up high on a folding lawn chair in the middle of the canoe. Then she wiggled a lot. She rummaged through her bags for her snacks. She danced around to the songs she sang to herself. She sat still only when she did her nails or gazed at herself in her tortoise shell looking-glass.

But the Voyageurettes did not complain one bit. They paddled along and listened to the stories Bambi read aloud from her "Miss Goody's" paper. The Maries learned all about a woman who thought she could soar in the air like a bird; they heard about mutant frogs, and dire predictions about hot air currents changing the climate of the Sub-Arctic. They learned quite a lot, in fact.

Later in the afternoon, they made camp. Bambi was not much of a camper. She screamed loudly whenever she saw a bug, which was often because it was black fly season. She did not like the cold damp air at night; it made her hairdo go flop. She had many complaints, but the Voyageurettes liked Bambi anyway, because she also taught them to do their nails on their own and make noises with their spruce gum. She also gave them free make-up and fashion tips and their very own tins of bear-grease rouge tinted with red raspberry juice.

After three days, the whole group arrived at Horse Portage. As the Voyageurettes were getting ready to carry their gear across, the voyageurs came paddling up. Bambi thought fast and pretended to sprain her ankle, to get the men to carry her gear across the long portage. She cried out, "Oh dear, my ankle, she is sprained!"

Jacques Baptiste came running up to offer his assistance. It was love at first sight. Bambi and Jacques Baptiste announced their engagement. It was a very short engagement. Five minutes later they were married by Jacques' *bourgeois*, who read all the right words from his book. All of the voyageurs and Voyageurettes were witnesses. After the ceremony, since Bambi's parents were not there, Jacques presented the Voyageurettes with a big roll of $100 bills as a token of his appreciation for arranging their meeting. Jacques said the contribution was not refundable, even if things did not work out.

The last anyone saw of Bambi and Jacques that day, they were paddling off in Jacques' canoe. It would be more accurate to say that Jacques was the one paddling, towing Bambi's cargo canoe behind. Bambi was sitting in the bow, blowing on her nails to help them dry faster.

The Voyageurettes did not see Bambi again until the following canoe season. They went to the beauty parlor and found Bambi working there part-time. She said she and Jacques were happily married and had a baby. They had named their baby in honor of the Voyageurettes. Her name was Marie Chris Margot Rebecca Sue Baptiste; however, they called her "Marie Petite," for short.

The very next day, Bambi asked the Maries to come to the day care cabin to meet their little namesake. They were honored to have a little baby named after them; then they saw her. Marie Petite was bald, with a pink bow stuck to the top of her head. She had no teeth at all and she was drooling. Her diaper was a little soggy and Marie Petite did not smell so good. She also made noises that were not nice. Now, the Voyageurettes did something that they do very well: they lied hard. They told Bambi that Marie Petite was, indeed, the cutest little baby they had ever seen. Then they gave Bambi a big roll of $100 bills for Marie Petite's education fund.

Je ne m'étais pas perdu; mais je peux dire que j'ai tourné en rond un sacré bout de temps!

I have never been lost, but I have been turned around a few times.

5

Why the Voyageurettes Do Not Usually Go to a Certain Place

Marie Sue was the *bourgeoise* of the Voyageurettes. That meant she was the trusted leader and boss of the outfit. All of the other Maries agreed she was the best boss they ever had. They did not tell Marie Sue, but she was the only bourgeoise they have ever had.

Marie Sue was not always a bourgeoise, but over the years, she had learned to do many things. She planned voyages because she had been almost everywhere worth going in the Canoe Country. Marie Sue was a good navigator. She studied her maps and looked for the best possible routes. She checked the compass and twisted the map to match the bearing on the compass. She squinted at the lake and at the shoreline. She checked the map and the compass again. Then she pointed in the right direction and the other Maries went that way. They did not question their bourgeoise, that is, most of the time.

Marie Sue shared her knowledge about the stars and the weather and fishing. At night around the campfire she read nature stories out loud for the other Voyageurettes. Marie Sue never complained and never lost her temper even when it was cold, windy and rainy all day; when the fish did not bite; when her back hurt; or when one of the other Maries did something dumb.

When she was a new bourgeoise, Marie Sue led a voyage from Knife Lake to the Lake One Landing. The day was foggy, humid and overcast. It was impossible to see very far in front or in back of the canoe. Marie Sue tried her best to find the way through Kiana Lake while the other Maries just paddled, paddled, paddled and thought about what they would have for lunch. Marie Sue could not find the portage. She looked and looked, but it was nowhere to be seen. She paddled along the shoreline. The other Maries noticed. They said, "Marie Sue, why are we paddling so near the shore where there are big rocks to bump into?"

Marie Sue said, "Oh, I just wanted to check to see if any ducks are still on their nests and we can see their babies." After a little bit the Voyageurettes found the portage and came to Lake Insula on the other side.

On Lake Insula, everywhere there were small islands and big islands. The shore poked out into the lake and looked like an even bigger island. The spaces between the islands looked smaller and smaller. Everyone was confused and not knowing which way to go. All the Maries looked at Marie Sue. She studied her map and compass and squinted hard at the lake and all those islands. Then she said, "Let's go that way," and she pointed to the right. The Maries went right. In two minutes Marie Sue said, "Let's go this way," and she pointed to the left. The Maries went left. Pretty soon everyone was confused even more. The only things they could see were islands and fog.

Marie Sue knew all the other Maries were relying on her to get through this lake. She did not want to shatter their confidence. And she did not want to be a wimp. Marie Sue put her head down and hoped the other Maries would think she was studying her map and compass instead of getting ready to cry.

Just then Marie Rebecca said, "I'm going to paddle to the shore. I think I heard a black bear growling over this way and I want to check it out. We will be right back, so you just wait here for a minute and do not go away, OK?"

So Marie Margot and Marie Rebecca paddled their canoe to the shore through the fog and out of sight of the other Maries. On the shore they did not find a black bear. Instead, they found a black Lab and its owners at a campsite. They asked the people how to get through the islands and out of this lake. Then they paddled back to the other Maries in the fog and said, "Too bad. That was no bear, just a big dog, ah, log rubbing on a rock."

Marie Rebecca whispered to Marie Sue, "Do not be sad. You are not lost at all, but are just turned around a little in this fog. I will help you, Marie Sue. When we get to a tricky place, just listen and watch for directions and we will get out of this maze in no time."

In the fog the Maries kept their canoes close together so they could talk about important things like lunch, supper and bedtime snacks as they paddled. As they talked, Marie Rebecca said things like, "That's right! and "Don't get left behind." Sometimes she turned her hat to the left or right or kept it straight ahead so only Marie Sue could see. Sure enough pretty soon the Voyageurettes came to the portage to Hudson Lake and got out of Lake Insula safe and sound. The Maries all said, "Marie Sue, you are, indeed, a good navigator and a good Bourgeoise to get us out of this mess!"

Ever since that trip Marie Sue never goes within two lakes of Lake Insula on purpose. And that is why there are never any navigation maps including Lake Insula in the Voyageurettes' waterproof map case. Marie Sue never, ever, says the words "Insula" or "island." If it becomes necessary, she might say, "that lake" or "that little bit of land sticking up out of the water." If any Voyageurette ever mentions Lake Insula or the word "island," Marie Sue coughs into her hand, looks the other way and changes the topic of conversation.

On the rarest of occasions Marie Sue has been heard to say, "*Je ne m'étais pas perdu; mais je peux dire que j'ai tourné en rond un sacré bout de temps!* "I have never been lost, but I have been turned around a few times."

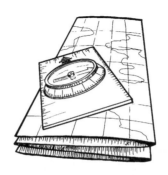

On n'a jamais vu un tel spectacle,
formidable au pays sauvage.

Never, never had anything so grand and splendid
and delightful been seen in the primitive wilderness.

6

The Ballerina
of the North

The Voyageurettes were soon becoming famous throughout the Canoe Country. In fact, people throughout the United States and most Canadian provinces had heard about them. They would not be so famous were it not for Marie Margot. Marie Margot, long before she became a Voyageurette, had been the lead ballerina for the Fort Detroit Ballet Company for three years. In the off season she was First Chair Kazooist in the Fort Detroit Symphony Orchestra. When she first considered joining the Voyageurettes, right then she sent away to B.B. Legume's catalogue for a pair of sturdy hiking boots, a warm fleecy jacket, water-proof socks and quick-drying canoe pants. Ah, yes, she looked like a true Voyageurette.

On the very first portage, Marie Margot grabbed a canoe by the gunwales and threw it onto her shoulders. She took one step and BOOM!, they both fell down. The other Voyageurettes ran to her and said, "Marie Margot, are you OK?" Like a true Voyageurette, she lied. She said, "I am just fine; however, I am more than a little worried about the condition of this brand new, twelve hundred dollar canoe."

The other Maries told her the canoe was just fine, except for one little ding. For a Voyageurette to put a ding in a canoe was a thing of honor. Now, whenever the Voyageurettes notice that ding, they smile, for it brings back fond memories of their first voyage together.

Marie Margot decided carrying a canoe was not her thing—at least for the moment. So, she grabbed the very biggest and heaviest pack by the ears and carried it five full steps until her foot got caught under a root and OOPS!, down she went again. She was very annoyed when this happened. She said, "I am a famous ballet dancer and should not be seen doing such ungraceful things."

Now, Marie Chris was a very smart person. She knew what the problem was in an instant. She said to Marie Margot, "Marie, I know what is your problem. It is those heavy hiking boots you are wearing. They are so heavy they are throwing off your delicate ballet balance."

Marie Margot said, "Yes, I think you are right, Marie Chris. It must be these heavy boots!"

Marie Margot immediately went to her pack and rummaged around inside until she found her special pink ballet slippers. She put them on, grabbed both the canoe and a pack and began to dance down the portage. She went leap, leap, leap from rock to rock. When she leaped, she twirled and spun in the air before she landed. Sometimes she leaped so high she had time to flutter her legs in the air, just like a butterfly. She pliéd, she pirouetted, and twirled her way across the portage. Sometimes Marie Margot whirled around so fast and with such force, she snapped off tall jack pines six feet from the ground, blocking the way with a tangle of splintered tree trunks and covering the trail with a thick mat of branches and pine cones. From a safe distance the rest of the Voyageurettes watched this stunning display with their mouths open wide. Never before had they seen such a graceful, beautiful sight as Marie Margot's ballet dancing across the portage with a canoe and pack on her back.

Before long other people saw her, too. Word got around about the Voyageurette who was the ballet star of the Canoe Country. Other canoeists learned of their route and paddled for miles to see the Voyageurette Ballerina with their own eyes. Each portage was lined with spectators wanting to see Marie Margot. They cheered and applauded as they saw her dance by. The applause could be heard days later, echoing back and forth among the rock cliffs.

The other three Maries did not mind the crowds that came to see Marie Margot one bit. In fact, they loved crowds. Seeing all those people gave them an idea — all of those people had something in common. They all wore underwear— plain white undershirts, to be precise. The Maries thought and thought about undershirts with a new wrinkle —

something that would make all those people want to buy new undershirts, lots of them. The Voyageurettes thought up the idea of making and selling souvenir undershirts with pictures and writing on them. They would use pictures and words and sayings to remind all those people of interesting places they had been, things they had seen in person or a statement about things they believed in. First they drew pictures of Marie Margot and the words, "I've Seen The Ballerina of the North," on their own shirts so they would have their own souvenirs to keep. Then they made a supply of other undershirts that said "Solid Rock Tavern at Grand Portage," "Prairie Chickens Unlimited," "I Dig the Iron Range," "This Is No Ordinary Housewife You Are Dealing With," "As Is," "ICANU-CANUCANU?," "Don't Mix Testosterone and White Water," and "Just Canoe It."

Then they thought some more and decided people might not like calling their souvenirs "underwear" or "undershirts." Instead, they would call their new inventions "T-shirts." T for "tourist." And they would make up the T-shirts in all sizes and pretty colors so everyone who wore them would be color-coordinated and look good.

While Marie Margot performed her dance and entertained the crowds by cutting off groves of jack pines in the middle of portages, the other Maries set up shop at the beginnings and ends and made big bucks selling their new creations.

Every night Marie Margot felt sad. She said, "I feel sad that I'm the only one receiving all this attention!" The other Maries sat quietly, counting all their money. They said to her, "Don't feel too bad for us, Marie Margot. We can handle it! We are making too much money with our little concession to be the least bit jealous."

But Marie Margot was not convinced. She wanted the others to be famous performers, just like she was. So she rummaged around in her pack and gave each of them her very own kazoo. She gave them lessons and carefully supervised their practice sessions. Before long, they could not only carry a tune, but also execute intricate and complicated harmonies and play a wide variety of musical selections from the classic fugues and chorales of Bach and the rousing marches of Souza to the best of New Orleans' jazz and the most low-down Chicago blues. Since they had their hands free while playing their kazoos, the Maries were also able to add drum parts to all their music. They used long skinny sticks on pots and pans to sound like snare drums, and thicker sticks on tree stumps for the bass drum parts. The overall result was splendid.

After their music instruction and hours of rehearsal were over, the Voyageurettes were ready to go to the water's edge for their debut in concert. As they began to play, a hush settled over the whole territory. The wolves interrupted their howling, the other canoe campers on the lake were suddenly silent, the loons ceased their wailing and the other birds stopped tweeting, squawking and chirping. After the concert was over, came the response. All around the lake people called loudly to the Voyageurettes. They thought they heard people shouting, "Brav-O! Brav-O!"

Marie Margot said the other people were not calling, but jeering. Really, they were saying "No, no!" because the Maries were so bad and noisy, they wanted the concert to end faster. But she said that with a twinkle in her eye. The other Maries knew she was just telling them a Voyageurette lie and she was really saying that they, indeed, were very good.

It is well-known in the Canoe Country that, even now, after many years, huge crowds gather on certain portages, especially those near public boat landings. It is thought by some that large numbers of canoeists are seen walking back and forth on those portages in order to catch a fleeting glimpse of Marie Margot dancing gracefully across the paths during the daytime. At night, when sun has gone down and the lake is quiet, people strain their ears, listening for the Voyageurette Evening Concert to begin. And it is even better known that visitors who come to popular tourist areas and special events all across North America still go into a wild frenzy to buy T-shirts with pictures and sayings on them, thanks to the Voyageurettes' invention.

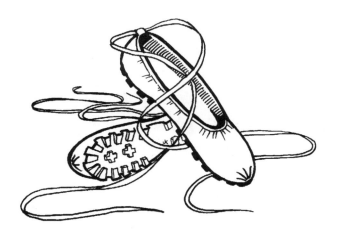

Les crapules ne sont pas les bienvenus dans la nature sauvage, et ils seront traités très durement.

Scoundrels are not welcome in the wilderness and will be harshly dealt with.

7

How the Voyageurettes Captured An International Villain

One day the Voyageurettes were paddling along, weary from the oppressive summer heat. They came to a portage, and after hauling their gear and canoes over the rocky path, they were too tired and hot to continue. They took off their boots and socks and sat on a rock by the shore to splash their feet in the cool water. They were just about cooled off when along the portage came a dark-haired man with a mustache. To them, he looked like a shifty character, but they were polite to him anyway. "Halloo," they said to him. "Isn't it hot today? We are cooling our heels and it feels very nice. We are the Voyageurettes. We are Marie, Marie, Marie and Marie. Who are you?"

The man said, "Andre Baptiste. I am one of the voyageurs. And I am lost."

The Voyageurettes could tell an imposter when they saw one. This was one. First of all, a true voyageur might very well be lost, but he would never admit it. Second, when this one spoke, his accent was not at all French. Third, he wore sandals instead of the deerskin moccasins of a true voyageur. And this one had a towel wrapped around his head.

The Voyageurettes were, indeed, very suspicious. They did not take kindly to anyone who falsely claimed to be a voyageur, especially if that person was shady and insulted the voyageurs. The voyageurs and the Voyageurettes were friends. They may have teased and poked fun at each other, but they stood united against evil and outsiders. This man was definitely an outsider.

The Voyageurettes said to him, "Why do you wear a towel instead of a red woolen *toque* on your head?

He said, "Because my head is a handy place to hang my towel. Also, it keeps my head cool in this hot weather. What do you think of that?"

Marie Rebecca wrinkled her nose, rolled her eyes and then said loudly, "Ha! I think that you are an imposter, and a shady, up- to-no-good imposter at that!"

The man got all red in the face. He said, "Yes, how did you know? I am the supreme commander of the most powerful country in the whole Middle East! I am running and hiding from your cowardly military. Now that you recognize me, I will have to take you hostage and torture you and put posters up all over my country and tell everyone you are traitors."

Now, the stranger had their attention; the Voyageurettes liked the sound of having their pictures put up all over a far away country. However, the hostage and torture part did not appeal to them the least little bit and they did not like to be called traitors by anyone. When he took out a big rifle and pointed it at them, they began to get a little nervous, but not too nervous, because they were brave and knew that this person was no match for the four of them.

Lucky for the Voyageurettes, the man was not too smart. He did not notice that minutes before, Marie Chris had gone into the woods to find a sandbox. Marie Chris soon came back to the end of the portage to see what was going on. She made a diversionary noise on the right near the water. Then she outflanked the man on the left. She moved very fast, then sneaked up behind him and FLIP! went his towel over his eyes. All the Maries together tackled him. In a flash, he was tied up with many yards of basswood cord and was hanging upside down from a limb of a tall red pine. He dangled there just like a food pack hung up high at night to keep it from the hungry bears. Too bad, the Maries forgot to gag his mouth. He hung upside down, kicked his feet, waved his hands and yelled at them. He shouted, "I am the victor. I have beaten you soundly. You Voyageurettes are my prisoners. You must surrender. The victory is mine!"

Marie Margot laughed out loud and said to him, "Too bad you are not really Andre Baptiste! You would have made a fine voyageur because you lie so good and brag so big!"

The Middle Eastern dictator said a few angry words to the Voyageurettes in Arabic. It was good for them they did not know what he said or perhaps their feelings would have been hurt.

Just then the Army came along the portage in their fast mule-drawn wagons. Sailors came paddling up in their canoes, landed and jumped on to the shore. Newspaper and magazine writers and illustrators ran down the portage with all their equipment. They all jumped for joy to see the dictator captured and doing an imitation of a food pack. All the time the supreme commander continued shouting that he was the victor and the captor.

Marie Margot quickly located her pink ballet slippers and the other Maries found their kazoos. The illustrators set up their easels and made charcoal sketches of the Middle Eastern dictator swinging upside down, yelling and cursing. The Voyageurettes got into the sketches, too. As Marie Margot danced, the other Maries played "God Bless North America" on their kazoos. The newspaper reporters were very impressed. They interviewed all of the Maries and wrote a thirty-page article, complete with illustrations, of the Voyageurettes capturing the international villain. It was a fine article, to be run in every newspaper and magazine as soon as they could get to Montreal to get it printed and distributed.

After everyone finished their assignments, the reporters and illustrators, the Army and the Navy packed up their outfits. The Army took the evil commander away. The reporters and illustrators loaded up their canoes and paddled off. But not very far. They stopped to wave good-bye and draw a parting sketch of the Voyageurettes. *Tant pis* (Too bad), their canoe capsized. The Voyageurettes quickly swam out into the water and saved their lives, but all their sketch pads and notebooks had sunk to the bottom of the lake. The crew was happy to be saved, but they were very sad to have lost their exclusive drawings of the international villain's capture by the brave and clever Voyageurettes.

Perhaps it was for the best. The arrival of many more artists and journalists and having to sit for long interviews would have kept the Voyageurettes from their work. They still had many miles to paddle and many Putterware, Yvonne and L'Ambway orders to fill before freeze-up.

There are many reasons why this story has never been released to the public. The Army and Navy were reluctant to disclose the details for national security reasons. They were also chagrined to admit that the Voyageurettes, and not the military, had caught this bad person. Reporters could not tell the story because the documentary evidence had sunk in the lake and they had missed their printing deadline. The Supreme Commander would never tell the embarrassing truth, which was that he had been caught by four ladies. Now that the whole story is told, the Voyageurettes are confident that the message gets out to all villains of the world: *Les crapules ne sont pas les bienvenus dans la nature sauvage, et ils seront traités très durement.* Scoundrels are not welcome in the wilderness and will be harshly dealt with.

La devise de la Voyageurette: Traveille dur! Rame avec force! Mens effrontement! Magasine sans retenue! Et ne marge pas du chien enrage!

Mottos of the Voyageurettes: Work hard, paddle hard, lie hard, shop hard, do not eat dogs.

8

B. B. Legume Meets the Voyageurettes

It was close to supper time. All of the Maries were sitting around the campfire, drinking coffee and watching their evening stew bubble in the cooking pot. A man paddled up in his green canvas and cedar strip New Village canoe. He was impeccably attired in his dark tan, natural fit style, double-needle stitched, seven pocket, all-cotton twill cargo pants and contrasting deep red, roomy, non-binding river driver shirt. On his feet were a pair of 12" tan and brown lace-up gum boots with padded ankle collars for added comfort. With him was a small fluffy white dog with red painted toenails and little red bows on her ears. The Voyageurettes invited the two of them into their camp for coffee and a bone.

The man introduced himself. "Hello there, girls! I am Bernie Beechwood Legume. Friends call me "B.B." This is my dog, Fifi. I own a large and successful outdoor clothing and camping supply business back East in Libertyport, Maine. Maybe you gals have heard of my company 'way out here in the Upper Midwest."

For years the Voyageurettes had known about this famous company. In fact, many times they had ordered high-quality items from the catalogue and were impressed with the great service. The Voyageurettes were pleased and proud to think they were drinking coffee and sharing their campsite with the famous B.B. Legume. They were not so pleased when they noticed Fifi's hind legs kicking frantically, first one foot and then the other, as she stirred up the forest duff into a dusty cloud five feet high. Bits and pieces of pine needles and cones flew into the air and landed in the open stew pot in front of them.

Mr. Legume said, "I am canvassing the Canoe Country searching for models for my new fall catalogue. Frankly, I am tired of trying to make city girl models look wild. I am here in the wilderness looking for the real thing."

Of course, right away the Maries gladly volunteered to be models. First, he checked Marie Margot. She had on her blue, fast-drying canoe shorts. Her shirt was plaid, with blue to match her shorts, pink to match her thongs and purple to match her sunglasses cord. She looked beautiful. To the shock of the Voyageurettes, B.B. said to her, "Look at your hat! It is GREEN! Sorry, Chickie, no B.B. Legume modeling job for you. Not until you get a hat to match your outfit!"

Marie Margot put her head down and looked away from Mr. Legume. Out of the corner of her eye she noticed Fifi busily digging herself a pit three feet wide and six feet deep in front of the open door of the Voyageurettes' tent. Inside the tent, the Maries' bedrolls were covered with five inches of dirt, roots and stones.

B.B. Legume looked at Marie Chris. She had on her blue designer jeans with matching blue socks. Her white T-shirt had blue lettering "Reading is FUNdamental" printed on the front. The lettering matched her jeans and so did her blue hat and blue sunglasses cord. The other Maries knew she would be chosen to get a job. She looked just like a perfect B.B. Legume model. To their big surprise, B.B. said, "Sorry, Toots, no modeling job for you. Look at your boots! They do not match your outfit. The laces are RED!"

Marie Chris turned around and walked toward the bushes at the far edge of the campsite. She wrinkled up her face, closed her eyes tight, tipped her head back and tried not to cry. She felt something jerking and tugging on the pant leg of her new designer jeans. Then she heard a rip and felt Fifi nip her ankle, not once, but twice. Marie Chris was brave and did not cry outloud.

It was Marie Rebecca's turn to be judged. She had on black canvas combat boots, gray pants, a dark brown T-shirt and a mouse-gray hat. "Nice try, Dearie, but you are bland, bland, bland." said B. B. Legume. "Besides, brown is definitely not right for you. You must have a professional color consultant help you before you model anything! Now, who's next?"

Marie Rebecca slowly walked over to a big, round log between the campfire and the tent and sat down. Right then, Fifi ran fast toward her, leaped in the air and crash-landed onto Marie Rebecca's chest. Over backwards they both went. The back of Marie Rebecca's head thumped hard on a rock just as Fifi's red toenails dug into her face when the dog scrambled to get away.

B.B. looked over toward Marie Sue. She had brown high-top hiking boots with matching brown laces. They were not tied, but they were brown. She also had gray socks, red pants, an orange T-shirt, a bright green sunglasses cord and a red hat to match the pants. When B.B. saw her, he choked. "You! You are an eyesore! You are one big clash. Sorry, Sweetie, no modeling job for you!"

Marie Sue moved twenty-five feet away and leaned her back up against the trunk of a jack pine. Just then Fifi came dashing out of the bushes. Around and around and around the tree she ran, barking as loud as she could. She ran around the tree so fast and barked so loud that after one minute, Marie Sue had to put her hands over her ears and sit down on a rock until her dizzy spell passed.

Finally, B.B. Legume came over to Marie Joyce, a tall, willowy blonde who was on her first trip with the other Maries. Marie Joyce was, by far, the most fashionable of all Voyageurettes. She had on her fast-drying red shorts, a powder blue T-shirt with red lettering to match her shorts, a red sunglasses cord, white socks with the red and blue trim, the blue hat and blue hiking boots trimmed in red. Everything she had on was color-coordinated, as usual. B.B. looked at her and said, "You are perfect! I want you in my catalogue! Come with me and you can start your new career right away."

Now, all the other Maries were happy for Marie Joyce. But Marie Joyce was a Voyageurette first, a true and loyal Voyageurette. She said to Mr. Legume, "I am a Voyageurette. There are five of us. We work together. We paddle together. We stick together. It is all of us or none of us. I will not leave the other Voyageurettes to go back East with you and model for your catalogue. No way!"

B.B. said to her, "Too bad, Honey Bun. You are passing up the deal of a lifetime. As my model, you could earn big bucks."

Now the voyageurs had a motto: "*La devise du Voyageur : Vis dangereusement! Ments effrontément! Dors profondément et mange du chien enragé!* Live hard, lie hard, sleep hard, and eat dogs." The Lady

Voyageurettes worked hard, paddled hard, lied hard, and shopped hard. But they never ate dogs.

There they sat around the campfire with little Fifi jumping, yapping and begging impetuously for another bone and Mr. Legume standing in front of them saying things they did not like to hear. Marie Sue looked at Marie Joyce. She looked at Marie Chris, who looked at Marie Rebecca. She, in turn, looked to Marie Margot, who looked back at Marie Sue. None of the Maries were happy with B.B. any more. He had "Chickied," "Tootsied," "Dearied", "Sweetied" and "Honey-Bunned" them too much. They wanted him and his noisy, over-stimulated, ill-mannered dog to leave their camp right that minute and never, ever to return.

B.B. Legume had been quietly watching the Maries. All of a sudden, he grimaced as if he were in great pain and put his hand to his forehead. "Oh, no! Of course! That's what this note means!" he said as he reached into his back pocket and pulled out a small, curled-up piece of birch bark.

"I am genuinely sorry for the manner in which I have been addressing you ladies and sincerely ask for your forgiveness. I should have known better, especially after having found this," said B.B. Legume as he unrolled the birch bark note and showed it to the Voyageurettes.

One side of the birch bark said:
"Ne soyez pas sexiste!
Les prostituées ont horreur de ça!"

On the other side was an English version:
"When you meet up with the Voyageurettes,
Don't be sexist;
~~Broads~~ Women hate that!"

The word "broads" had a big X scratched on top of it, and the word "Women" was neatly printed below it.

"I found this note on a rock at the end of the last portage into this lake and have no idea who wrote it because it's not signed. At first, I didn't quite understand it, but I do now, believe me! Do you suppose the voyageurs could have left this for me?" said B.B. Legume. "From now on, I shall do my utmost to be a more sensitive, new-age guy."

The Voyageurettes jumped to their feet and shook hands with B.B. Legume and said *Bon voyage!* to him and his dog. Before he shoved off, Mr. Legume handed each of them a slip of paper. "This is a coupon good for 40% off your next catalogue purchase. And if you're ever out East, please drop by my store on the seacoast and I'll personally discount your purchases. You have helped me improve my conduct and I shall be forever grateful."

Since that day long ago, it was rare for anyone in the Canoe Country to see another impeccably attired, courtly gentleman paddling a cedar strip canoe, accompanied by a fluffy, white poodle with red bows on its ears.

It has often been said that one cannot always believe the stories of the Voyageurettes. But this story is true. To this day, the Voyageurettes have remained true to their motto: *La devise de la Voyageurette: Travaille dur! Rame avec force! Mens effrontément! Magasine sans retenue! Et ne mange pas du chien enragé!* Work hard, paddle hard, lie hard, shop hard, do not eat dogs."However, if B.B. Legume had not turned out to be a real gentleman after all, the Voyageurettes certainly would have had dog stew for supper that night and enjoyed every bite.

*Les voyageurs ne peuvent
pas marcher sur l'eau.*

The voyageurs have not yet perfected
the art of running on water.

9

How the Voyageurs Learned to Portage Fast

One day the Voyageurettes were far behind schedule. They decided to make up time on the portages. Now the Voyageurettes knew a lot about human psychology, especially what motivates people. They knew people could be highly motivated by good things and bad things and decided to try out the theories on themselves.

"Let's all get our packs and other gear ready and line up together," said Marie Joyce. "We'll fix up each other with something guaranteed to get us across this portage in no time flat."

"OK, Marie Joyce, since this is your idea, you go first," said the other Maries.

They attached a stick to the front of her hat. On the stick they tied a string. At the other end of the string, they tied pieces of hard candy because Marie Joyce loved sweet things.

Then it was Marie Margot's turn. The other Voyageurettes attached a stick to the front of her hat and on the stick they tied a bag of coated chocolate bits. Marie Margot loved coated chocolate bits more than any other snack.

The Voyageurettes attached a stick to the front of Marie Rebecca's hat and to the string on the stick, they tied wild strawberries. Marie Rebecca just loved berries of all kinds.

At last, it was Marie Sue's turn. The other Maries said to her, "Close your eyes and do not peek." This Marie was good. She did not even try to peek, not even once.

"OK, let's get with it!" shouted Marie Joyce. With that, the Maries started down the portage. Marie Joyce was so excited by the hard candy, she ran after it as fast as a deer. Marie Margot was so motivated by chocolate bits, she ran down the trail like a race horse and Marie Rebecca ran toward the strawberries faster than a weasel. Marie Sue stood still and did not run at all. When she opened her eyes, there was nothing hanging in front of her, not even a string. She was disappointed.

The other Maries called back to her, "Marie Sue, look behind you!"

She thought to herself, "I bet they put a mean and ferocious wolf behind me. That would get me to run fast down the portage." She turned her head quickly around to the left to look behind herself. There was no wolf. Then she thought, "Maybe they put a mean and hungry bear in the woods behind me. That would get me to run very fast." She looked quickly to her right toward the woods, but there was no bear.

Then the other Maries shouted to her, "Turn your head around slowly and look higher, Marie Sue. Look behind your hat!"

She looked behind her hat and attached to the back of the hat was a stick with a string on it. Attached to the string was a small bowl and in that bowl was something too terrible to even imagine. That something was a cold, grayish-tan, slimy gob. It was slippery and lumpy, horrible and totally revolting. Marie Sue shrieked, "That looks exactly how my brain feels every morning!"

Marie Sue took off down the portage like a shot. Small stones and a cloud of dust kicked up into the air behind her. Her hands chopped up and down, cutting through the air in front of her. Then her arms waved around in circles like windmills. Round and round they went, propelling her faster and faster down the path. Her legs pumped like pistons. Thud, thud, thud went her feet on the hard ground. Small branches and leaves hit her in the face, but that did not stop her. She kept running at top speed and ran past all the other Maries on the path.

Finally, Marie Sue could see a patch of blue through the trees and knew the end of the portage was near. Bravely she glanced backward. "EEooow!" she screamed. The small bowl was still right behind her, wildly swinging from side-to-side. Marie Sue would not stop. When she came to the end of the portage, her momentum was so great, she skimmed over the water like a skipped stone, leaving only small circles in the water. She ran so fast on top of the water, her boots did not even get wet. Across the next portage, the next lake, the next portage, on and on she went. On the next-to-the last lake, after she had been running faster than a miler for almost six hours, out of the corner of her eye Marie Sue caught the glint of a paddle in the distance. It was a brigade of voyageurs who had rafted up their canoes to take a pipe break. She heard them shouting, but could not pause even a nano-second to listen to what they were trying to tell her. When she reached the last portage, Marie Sue began to suffer a little bit. Her heart was pounding, her lungs hurt and she could hardly breathe any more. Her legs and arms felt like petrified tree stumps. Soon the portage went down a steep hill, but she did not slow her pace. Down the hill she ran, so fast, in fact, that the wind finally blew off her hat. The stick and the string and what was attached to it all fell to the ground and rolled off the portage path out of sight under a dense growth of blueberry bushes. Finally, Marie Sue was free from the terrible thing that had followed her for sixty-one miles that day— a bowl of OATMEAL! Her ordeal was over at last. It took the rest of the Voyageurettes two hours to catch up to her.

It is often said in the Canoe Country that it was Marie Sue who first showed the voyageurs a better way to get across portages. It used to be that voyageurs took their own sweet time getting from one lake to another. They sauntered along portage paths, looking up at the treetops and down at the bushes and stopping here and there to pick berries. Now they dog-trot on every portage. This is because the brigade of voyageurs taking their pipe-break on the lake that day saw Marie Sue streak across the water and two portages like a rocket. Now they go as fast as they can, so as not to be out-done by a Voyageurette. It hurt their pride to think that a wiry little woman could move so quickly from one point to another. Even while carrying their heavily loaded *pieces*, full kegs and three hundred pound canoes, they dog-trot across portages so fast, their passengers, who carry nothing, cannot keep up the pace. However, there is still one thing the men have not been able to do. "*Les voyageurs ne peuvent pas marcher sur l'eau.* The voyageurs have not yet perfected the art of running on water."

Même le plus idiot des imbéciles sait qu'un chat court peut courir plus vite qu'un chien, quelque soit le jour de la semaine

Any fool knows that cats can outrun dogs any day of the week.

11

The Voyageurettes and the Ididarun Trail International Sled Dog Race

L ate in the fall the Voyageurettes were stuck deep in the snow far, far up North. They got going so fast in August that they could not stop until October. By then they were so far up North they could not get back to Minnesota before freeze-up. Lucky for them, they found a nice log cabin where they could spend the winter, like the "*hivernants*" (wintering partners). The place had been abandoned by an old trapper. Fortunately, there was plenty of food stored in the pantry and the ice-fishing was good. The old trapper must have been a cat lover because several hundred lived in the cabin and shed all winter. All of the cats were fat and healthy because of a generous supply of mice. By the best estimate there were 400 cats, more or less.

Month after month, the Voyageurettes were stuck in the cabin with the hundreds of cats. After awhile they were all overcome with severe cases of cabin fever. They just had to get to a settlement and do some hard shopping. They were convinced that a few days of shopping would cure their fever.

They decided to go over to Nome, where they had heard a fine new trading post had just been built. Now Nome was 1,049 miles away. It was far, but not too far for the hardy and energetic Voyageurettes to go by *racquet* or snowshoe. But they decided not to snowshoe. It was too slow and their need to shop was too intense. Going to Nome by *traineaux de glace* or dogsled would be faster than traveling on snow-shoes, but they had no dogs, only cats.

So they got busy and made up a nice cat sled. It was much like a dog sled, only lighter and more aerodynamic to cut down on drag. Next, the Voyageurettes sewed up four hundred, more or less, bright blue wool coats to keep the cat team warm on the trip. Then they decorated the cats' coats with fringes and embroidery and sewed twenty-four little bells and three feathers on each one. The Maries caught all the cats and hooked them up in tandem to the cat sled. The line of cats wearing their warm coats and buckled into their non-chafing harnesses extended as far as one could see, per-haps a mile or more. It was a stunning sight.

The Voyageurettes were anxious to get underway. They spoke to the cats, "*Mon chat, viens ici!* Come here, kitty!" *Les chats* did not respond. They just sat down and licked themselves.

The Voyageurettes called out, "*Marche! Marche, mes chats!* Start up, start up, kitties!" The cats just yawned and curled up on the snow.

Then the Maries yelled, "*Mouche! Mouche!* Go fast! Go fast!" The cats purred and went to sleep.

The ladies yelled loudly, "*Vous êtes des cochons de chat! Des grosses cochons blancs!*" ("You are a bunch of big white pigs!" That did not get the cats' attention because most of the cats were small and black. They just stretched and rolled over.

At last, Marie Margot thought of a better idea. She took a deep breath and shouted, "Woof! Woof!" That got the kitties' attention. Four hun-dred cats, more or less, all went running in the same direction at the same time, digging their sharp, curved cat-claws into the snow and ice for better traction. The Voyageurettes were not expecting such power and speed. Their bright blue *toques* or knitted hats blew off their heads. Loose gear flew off the sled in every direction. All the Maries were swept off their feet and were lucky to grab on to the sled. With the great speed, they flew out straight behind the sled, holding on for dear life. Over hills and mountains, down the trail and through the forests they went. When the cats finally slowed down, all Marie Margot had to do was say "woof" just once and they sped up again. Sometimes, to give the cats a break, the Maries jumped off the sled and ran alongside for a few hours. In one day they covered 262 miles. At night, the Maries fed the kitties a handful of dried mice each before they went to sleep. The cats were ready to be up and running fast again the next morning.

By chance, they were heading to Nome on a well-traveled path. Up the trail they blithely went with their cat sled. All along the way the Maries were surprised to come up behind many sled dogs and their mushers out having their exercise and enjoying the fresh air. They all pulled over politely by the side of the trail to wait as four hundred cats, more or less, went speeding past them. The Voyageurettes zoomed past one dog sled after another every day. The drivers just stared in disbelief and their dogs were so impressed they could not bark. Even when the Voyageurettes stopped and pulled well off to the side of the trail to rest the cats and refresh themselves with a little snack of chocolate, they were faster than any dog sled. The truth was that even a team of sixteen big, strong husky dogs was no match for four hundred cats, more or less.

After only four days out on the trail the Voyageurettes reached Nome well ahead of all the mushers and their sled dogs. They were very happy. They were happy for themselves because they had beaten everyone to the settlement and finished their shopping at the trading post before the large crowds hit and picked over all the merchandise. And they were happy for their fast cats. Marie Chris said, "I'll bet every one of our smug little cats is saying, "Ibeatadog" to itself!"

The Maries were now totally cured of their bout of cabin fever and ready to head back to Minnesota. But first, they needed to take care of one important detail. Up and down the main path through Nome they went. Three times they passed under the burled arch in front of the trading post, searching and searching. At last, they found what they were looking for—a first-rate *pension* or hotel where their cat team could spend the rest of the winter enjoying the pampered life all cats deserve.

Legend has it that the year after the Voyageurettes went to Nome with their cat sled, residents of the far North decided to organize a special event and call it the Ididarun Trail International Sled Dog Race. Its route was along the same 1,049 mile trail the famous cat team had used. However, there was one major difference; only dogs were permitted to enter this lively competition. The organizers said it was unthinkable to allow cats to participate because of the principle of unfair advantage. The Voyageurettes have long felt that the whole truth regarding this rule should be known. It is important for history to be perfectly accurate. After all, *"Même le plus idiot des imbéciles sait qu'un chat court peut courir plus vite qu'un chien, quelque soit le jour de la semaine.* Any fool knows that cats can outrun dogs any day of the week."

*De bonnes choses peuvent aussi arriver
aux mauvaises personnes!*

Good things can happen to bad people.

12

The Renegade Yvonne Lady

A s the Voyageurettes paddled off in search of adventure wherever it was to be found, large numbers of voyageurs were on their way northwest after their summer rendezvous at Grand Portage. The Voyageurettes were not far from the carrying place, "Height-of-Land Portage." As they drew near, they saw many brigades of men from different fur companies come off the portage one after another. Each group stopped and did something unusual, or so it seemed. The leader of each group said things the Voyageurettes could not hear. He swished a cedar bough in the lake and sprinkled water on some of his crew, but only the new ones. Then they shot guns into the air and the men laughed, cheered and drank a lot of something that did not look like water out of kegs. Then they were off. These ceremonies looked like fun. The Voyageurettes paddled closer to hear exactly what was going on. For one group, the ceremony was like an oath of loyalty to their fur company. The men promised to serve their bour-geois, do what he said, work really hard to make a big profit, not wreck or damage any company property or start their own little hus-tles on the side in competition with the company. Other voyageurs made other promises. They promised not to kiss another voyageur's wife without her permission. They all promised to have this ceremony for every new voyageur who joined them. At the very end, the new men were sprinkled with bog water, thrown into the lake and permitted to tuck brightly colored feathers or fluffy plumes in their caps. Then they could call one another a "Nor'wester."

Right away the Voyageurettes decided to have their own ceremony. They liked the idea of having a cedar branch represent the wilderness and water to remind them of getting washed off and ready for a clean start and something new in their lives. The loyalty part was important; the Voyageurettes would be loyal and true friends and make sure new recruits would feel welcome and important to the rest of the group. The part about asking for permission to kiss someone else's boyfriend or husband was not really necessary because the Voyageurettes were always true to their own marriage vows and would never even think of interfering with other people's relationships. They could not shoot into the air because they did not bring any firearms along, and they never drank any spirits until just before supper, so they put feathers in their caps, threw a few coated chocolate bits into the water to appease the wind and water spirits and the ceremony was over.

Two hours later, the Voyageurettes were on their second trip across a portage, returning for a few packs that had been left behind on the first crossing. As they approached their packs, something did not look right. Two of the packs were open and on their sides. Everything that had been neatly arranged inside the packs was now spread out all over the portage path in disarray. Something more unusual was down by the water. It was a bright pink, top-of-the-line solo canoe pulled up on the sand. A faint, but distinct, scent of "Epidermis-So-Smooth" lingered in the air. Atop a clump of bunchberry leaves lay a tiny black eyelash brush where it had been carelessly tossed. No one was in sight, only footprints leading straight to where the Maries stood.

Suddenly, a strange woman leaped out from behind a big tree. She was dressed in a shiny pink jumpsuit with a "Y" embroidered on the pocket; she wore matching pink shoes with skinny heels three inches high. Clenched between her teeth was a long shiny knife. As she boldly stood her ground in the middle of the path, she yanked the knife out of her mouth, waved it back and forth in front of the Maries and glared at them.

"Where are the rest of your filled out choosing forms? Hand them over!" she demanded. "I want them all for myself so I can get credit for your sales and make big, big money!" The Voyageurettes could not believe their ears. This person was not acting like any other sales representatives they had ever met at their annual training and motivation sessions. She was violating all of the rules and ethics of the company — something that would never be permitted or tolerated by management or any of the other representatives.

Marie Rebecca spoke up, "Whoa! Take it easy and put down that knife, please. Let's sit down and talk or mediate whatever the problem is here. There is plenty of room in this vast landscape for people to cooperate and flourish! Ambition is one thing; greed, avarice and robbery are completely different! Just play fair by the rules and listen..."

The woman would not listen. "NO! What's mine is mine and what's yours is mine!" Instead, she ran up close to Marie Rebecca and stomped down hard on her foot with her high-heeled shoe. Marie cried out in pain.

Marie Margot put her hands up in front of her. "Wait, wait! Please do not jump into violence! Besides, anger is a dead-end road. Before you do anything rash, try counting to ten. Do deep breathing! Think of the consequences! Violence is not the..."

The woman interrupted, "You don't fool me! With your hands up like that, I know you are going to try to karate-chop me!

Now it was well-known throughout the Canoe Country that Marie Margot was so kind and compassionate she would never think of hitting anyone else. But the Yvonne Lady picked up a big stick, rushed over and whacked Marie Margot hard on her right hand. Marie Margot bent over double, holding her hand close to her chest.

Marie Karen stepped up. "You need to think about being out here in the wilderness! Life is not just you alone against the whole world. Out here, a happy life is about working together, cooperating and being helpful to one another, like the voyageurs! It's about treating everyone as you expect to be..."

With that, the Yvonne Lady kicked Marie Karen in the knee.

Now it was Marie Sue's turn. It was one-on-one against the Yvonne Lady. Marie Sue saw Marie Rebecca hopping around on her good foot. She saw Marie Margot holding her hand and Marie Karen lying on the ground rubbing her knee. Then she noticed the Yvonne Lady looking at her, still holding her big, long sharp knife. Marie Sue was no fool. She turned around and ran the other way. Swoosh! The Yvonne Lady threw her knife right into the back of Marie Sue's head. Marie Sue cried out, "Owww! Why did you do that to me? You may have hurt me just a little, but you are the one who is in big trouble now!"

The woman turned away and ran as fast as she could toward her pink canoe pulled up on the shore. She ran so fast she could not stop in time to avoid crashing into a very big and muscular man who was standing at the end of the portage. The man had a star on the front of his shirt.

"Well, well, just look who ran into me!" he said. "I have been scouting around this territory for you for a long time, Miss Renegade. You have been on my "Most Wanted List" for many, many months because of outstanding warrants for fraud, theft by deception, criminal threatening, armed robbery and assault with a deadly weapon. And I can plainly see evidence of another one of your vicious attacks here. Now you are under arrest and in my custody."

The big man with the star on his chest turned to the Voyageurettes and said, "I am sincerely sorry for what has just happened to you and hope your injuries will not interfere with your work or pleasure in the Canoe Country. Now, if you ladies would kindly provide me with statements about what happened to you, I will be able to wrap up this case and you may continue your journey in peace and tranquility."

"Oh, thank you, Mr. Constable, for being here for us at just the right time!" said Marie Margot. "It is reassuring to know you are on duty keeping the waterways safe."

"You're all welcome," replied the Constable. "The truth is that here in the North Country we all have to rely on each other. And when people come along who break common sense rules and laws or harm others, they must be dealt with firmly and fairly. Before you shove off, here is a nice cashier's check for you as a reward for your cooperation in this matter. And by the way, the next time you visit the settlement, please look me up. Just ask for Mel."

The Voyageurettes watched as their new friend, Mel, paddled off with the renegade Yvonne Lady in custody and her pink canoe in tow. Marie Margot said, "You know, eventually some good may come out of this situation for that lady. Hopefully, she will be going to a place where she can think about what she has done and make amends for her wrongdoing. I have faith that one day she will discover that selfishness, greed and violence are not compatible with success, friendship and happiness—especially in the wilderness."

And all the other Voyageurettes agreed with Marie Margot when she said, "*De bonnes choses peuvent aussi arriver aux mauvaises personnes!* Good things can happen to bad people."

*Même les vanches peuvent rêver
et avoir leur place au soleil!*

Even cows can dream and have their moment in the sun

The Legend of Marie La Vache

O ne day the Voyageurettes were in the Canoe Country Court to testify in the criminal case against the Yvonne Lady. The Voyageurettes talked to the court reporter during recess. After she had heard a few stories of their voyages, she became more and more excited. She said, "Maybe I could come along with you, even if I never did camp or canoe before. I am strong! I grew up on a dairy farm and I know all about hard work."

Well, the Voyageurettes thought if the court reporter were indeed strong, she would be a fine Voyageurette. If she were not strong, she would still make a good Voyageurette because she could lie hard. Either way, she would be good.

The Court Reporter Sarah typed on her special machine. The message she typed no one else could read. It was her way of saying, "Bye, bye, Judge and lawyers. I'm off to paddle the canoe and make big bucks."

At first Sarah got into the canoe and began to paddle strong and hard. Zig, she went one way. Zag, she went the other way. Then she learned fast to paddle straight. She portaged hard-always carrying two packs at a time. The other Maries were very impressed and baptized her as a Voyageurette the very first day. Right away she volunteered to put up the tent, but it fell down on top of her. The Voyageurettes lied and told her she did a fine job—that was how a tent was supposed to look. She had never camped before, so she believed them.

When it got dark, the Voyageurettes crawled into the fallen down tent and went to sleep. Very soon afterward a loud thumping noise woke them. It sounded like a stampede. They peeked outside the tent and saw two huge brown eyes staring at them—the eyes of a bear, they were sure. They dived back into their sleeping bags and covered their heads. Now, Marie Sarah wanted to prove her ability to react well under duress. The rest of the Maries were happy. That is why they just pretended to be scared so Marie Sarah could demonstrate her bravery. She grabbed her Itty Bitty flashlight and her folding pocket knife and went outside. She shined the light at the creature and then she began to laugh. She said, "It is really OK! There is no bear outside this fallen down tent! It is a cow!"

When they heard it was a cow, the Voyageurettes all came out of the tent. They knew cows were usually not too vicious. Sure enough, it was a beautiful black and white Holstein. The cow batted her eyes at them as if she were in love. She had a nametag on a chain around her neck. It said, "VIRGINIA."

The Voyageurettes patted Virginia and talked nice to her and then went back to bed. In the morning they woke up to find the cow still sleeping outside the tent. Marie Sarah said, "How about waking her up? We can take her along with us!"

The other Maries said, "No, Marie Sarah. We cannot travel with a cow in the Canoe Country. We must sneak off before she wakes up."

They quickly loaded up and paddled off fast, but the cow heard them and swam after them. They reached the first portage and quickly ran across it with their gear. The cow ran even faster and caught up with them.

Marie Sarah said, "It is no use! The cow has bonded with us and will follow us anywhere we go."

So, into the cargo canoe went the cow. The Maries concluded that if this cow was to be a true Voyageurette, she must have a suitable name, better than Virginia. They decided to call her "*Marie La Vache*" (Marie the Cow). They paddled as Marie La Vache sat in the middle of the canoe. Marie La Vache was good. She sat very still, unlike Bambi, and quietly chewed her cud as they paddled along. And she did not drag her feet or splash in the water like Marie Margot and Marie Rebecca do when they sit in the middle of a canoe.

Marie La Vache gave milk for their oatmeal in the morning and for their cookies at night. She was very protective. When she saw or heard anything unusual, she made a loud "moo" noise and alerted them like a watchdog. It was not very long before all the Maries liked her very much. They liked Marie La Vache very much, that is, until the voyageurs saw the Maries towing a cow in a canoe behind them.

The voyageurs called out, "Ha! Your new Voyageurette, she is a real beauty! Can't you recruit anything better to be a Voyageurette than a black and white cow?" Then they laughed and laughed.

The Voyageurettes did not like that. Marie La Vache's big brown eyes looked so sad, the Maries knew she did not like it either. They had an idea. They dressed her up. They put mud all over her. Now she was brown. Then with woven basswood cord, they tied antlers to her horns. The Voyageurettes told everyone they met that they now had a moose mascot and that she was mean and temperamental.

The voyageurs said, "She is a funny-looking moose!"

The Maries said to them, "And you are funny-looking little bandy-legged roosters!"

The men asked, "Why does your mascot make noise like a cow?"

The Maries replied, "Why do you think they are called MOOSE? It is because they go moo!"

The Maries said these things because the voyageurs, if they believed each other's lies, they would believe theirs, too.

Before long, word got out about the Voyageurettes' mean and temperamental moose mascot. Everyone was scared by their big, new pet.

One day the Voyageurettes paddled to a large remote camp. The children were all crying because they had not had any fresh milk to drink all summer. The Maries decided to stay a few days. Marie La Vache supplied the children with all the fresh milk they could possibly drink. The counselors at the camp appreciated it so much, they paddled off to a rock ledge with an overhang and put the story in pictograph form. Then they paddled to Crooked Lake and drew their pictures with orange pigment made of iron ore dust and fish oil. Now the historians and anthropologists have long thought these were ancient pictographs of a moose and a canoe with native people in it. But the historians and anthropologists were mistaken; they did not know the real story. The truth is that the pictographs represented Marie La Vache and the Voyageurettes.

Later that summer the Voyageurettes came across a little settlement. They stopped by the convenient trading post for pizza, light beer on tap and grain. Marie La Vache stayed outside and began to paw at the ground with her hooves. She was very busy. The Maries and the locals went out to see what she had dug up. It was a pile of reddish rock. Pure iron ore. The people were delighted. They thought iron ore had great potential. This new discovery could put hundreds of people to work mining the ore. They could sell it to companies back East to make steel. After while they would get rich. Maybe the whole area around their settlement would one day be known as "The Iron Range." They wanted to name their settlement in honor of the Voyageurettes' special mascot, but the Voyageurettes questioned whether Marie La Vache was the most appropriate name for a busy, productive and prosperous mining town on this new Iron Range. The Maries asked the people to gather around and look at the chain around her neck. When they saw her real name on the nametag, they proudly named their town Virginia. And that is how Virginia, Minnesota got its name.

The Voyageurettes paddled over to Wisconsin that weekend for something different to do, and along a big river they saw a pretty red barn where there was plenty of grain in the bins and acres of corn growing in the fields. Marie La Vache was so happy she do not have to look like a moose any more and could just be herself. She mingled with the Wisconsin cows who immediately took to her and made her feel like one of the herd. The Voyageurettes were sad to realize that Marie La Vache had been lonely when she was away from her own kind for most of the summer, and they knew what had to be done.

When they got ready to leave, they promised Marie La Vache when they were in the area they would always stop by and see her. They said she could always come with them again whenever they went on voyages, but she just shook her head. She had had her one great summer of carefree meandering through the Canoe Country. As a bonus, she had a Minnesota town named in her honor and had her likeness drawn on an authentic pictograph. That was enough adventure, fame and glory for her whole lifetime and she was content to be ordinary again.

N'utilise jamais une corde pour pêcher un maskinongé.

Never use rope to catch a muskie.

How the Voyageurettes Catch A Muskie

It was an unusually calm and sunny morning out on Basswood Lake. The Voyageurettes had been paddling at their usual brisk pace for about four and a half hours without a rest when they noticed a brigade of voyageurs off to their left. As they drew closer, they heard a shout coming from the lead canoe. "*Allumez!* Light up!" With that command, all of the voyageurs stopped paddling, rafted up their canoes and took off their red hats. Inside the hats were their fine long-stemmed white clay pipes and tobacco pouches. The men filled their pipes, lit up and took a ten-to-fifteen minute pipe-break while they allowed their canoes to drift lazily in the sun. The voyageurs always took breaks after every hour or so of paddling and they mea-sured lakes by the number of pipe-breaks it took to cross. Basswood was a five-pipe lake.

The very next day the Voyageurettes went to the settlement to buy red, yellow, green, blue and purple pipes of their own. That evening after supper the Maries all sat down on a rock ledge along the shore of the lake with their new purchases.

Marie Sarah said, "This pipe is all dusty and dirty inside. Too bad this hard cake of soap will not fit inside the bowl so I can clean it easily."

"That's not a problem," said Marie Chris as she poured water in a pot. "We'll just liquefy the soap in this water, add a few drops of glycerin as a skin protection to keep our hands soft, and then we can all clean out our pipes."

The Maries dipped the bowls of their pipes in the pot and swished them around in the liquid soap and glycerin. Then they blew into the small ends of their pipes to clean the stems as well. Hundreds of pretty bubbles floated into the air. One shimmering greenish-blue bubble about 13" across drifted out into the lake and gently landed on the water.

At that very instant the water exploded. A muskie no one had ever seen before came up, grabbed the bubble in its teeth and disappeared in a swirl of water. Maybe it was 24 feet long, it was hard to tell. The Maries blew more bubbles and watched and waited for the muskie to come up again.

Then Marie Chris had an idea. She found 100 feet of stout rope in a coil at the bottom of the equipment pack. She curled one end around in a circle, tied a loop knot and got ready. When the muskie came up to bite another bubble, she twirled the rope over her head, whir, whir, whir, and let the loop shoot across the water. The lasso dropped over the muskie's head and caught on the fins behind its gills. Before Marie Chris could brace herself, the muskie took off in the opposite direction and yanked her down toward the water. Marie Sarah grabbed onto Marie Chris from the back as she was dragged by. Into the water they both went. The muskie took off about 40 miles an hour, pulling Marie Chris and Marie Sarah out into the middle of the lake. They did not let go of the rope. Instead, they were brave. They held on tight and stretched their legs out so they were scooting along on top of the water on their stomachs as they were dragged behind the muskie. They went so fast that a big "v" shaped wake followed behind them. Round and round the lake they went, shouting and screaming for help.

On the fourth pass around the lake the muskie came close to the shore and wiped out half an acre of lily pads in its path. As the muskie, Marie Chris and Marie Sarah passed in front of the campsite, their wake crashed onto the shore like a tidal wave. A wall of water fifteen feet high crested over the campsite. The big wave pushed the Marie House 75 feet back into the woods where it got hung up in the bushes. All three canoes were thrown into the air and landed in a jumble on top of one another, trapped in the branches of two uprooted jack pine trees. When the wave ran back into the lake, it had washed the campsite clean of all its top-soil, clear down to bare rock.

All the packs, hammocks, pots and pans and other gear floated in a big puddle where the Marie House used to be.

The three other Maries were lying on their backs in the same puddle, looking up at the sky, thinking they should do something. Right away they got up and ran over to the jumble of canoes and tugged and pulled one free from the pine branches. Then they launched the canoe, set chase after Marie Chris, Marie Sarah and the muskie, and caught up with them half way across the lake. Marie Rebecca reached out and snatched the two Maries by their belts and helped them safely into the canoe. Marie Margot quickly tied the thick rope to the bow with a power cinch knot. Now the muskie had five Maries plus a canoe to pull.

The mischievous, playful muskie towed the Voyageurettes and their canoe around the lake for two more hours, or so it seemed. At first, the muskie tried leaping and diving. With every muskie-leap the canoe shot twelve feet up into the air. With every dive, the canoe submerged and was pulled along underwater for five minutes. The Voyageurettes did not like having to hold their breath for so long. Then the muskie did something different. It did not leap or dive any more. Instead, it went very fast in a straight line and then stopped dead in the water. When it went fast, water shipped in over the bow of the canoe. When the muskie stopped still, water shipped in over the stern. The Voyageurettes did not like that very much, either. Too much splashing.

The muskie tried another trick. It swam fast from one end of the lake to the other, did a hairpin turn, and then came rushing back in a straight line. All the time, the Voyageurettes sat in the back half of the canoe, so the bow could plane and skim over the water more easily. The muskie was careful during the hairpin turns and did not let the canoe spin around too close to shore and hit the rocks.

Then the muskie invented another game. It swam around in tight circles, then cut across the wake and made the canoe bounce up and down hard in the choppy waves. When the muskie got bored making counter-clockwise circles, it turned around and went the other way. The Maries did not like all the bouncing.

As darkness began to fall, the muskie swam slower and slower. At last, it stopped and lay quietly in the water. It was all played out.

Marie Sue said, "Let's bring this muskie back to our camp! We can clean it and eat it up! Grab hold of this 150 lb. beauty and just flip it in the canoe."

The other Voyageurettes tried to get a grip, but it did not work. They said, "Marie Sue, this is not practical! This muskie is too, too slippery for us to hold! Besides, our canoe is only 17 feet long and this fish is eight feet longer and it will not fit inside. And it is very heavy. It is too much work, even for us. Furthermore, once we clean it, it would take ten full days of our eating nothing but fish for breakfast, lunch and dinner before it would be all gone."

Some people who catch fish brag and exaggerate so much they cannot be trusted. Their fish grow longer with each telling of their stories. To add dishonest inches to a fish was something not even the Voyageurettes would do. Also, the Maries would never stoop so low as to show off their fish in public. It might make other people feel jealous or envious. So when the muskie was all rested up, they untied the lasso and set it free.

After their day of adventure, the Voyageurettes thought long and hard about muskie fishing. Right then they decided they would use 10-20 lb. test line with a metal leader. Their lures of choice would be a spinner about 10-1/2" long, with a big hairy tail, or a shiny spoon one foot long. This, of course, was exactly what voyageurs used for catching muskies. But there was one difference. The difference was that voyageurs were fishing for muskies in the 25-30 lb. range. For them, a muskie that size was "*un maskinongé gigantesque*, a really big muskie," a proud catch, indeed. For the Voyageurettes, however, a 25-30 pound muskie was small and just the right size.

And the Voyageurettes decided to give one bit of advice to every angler they met: "*N'utilise jamais une corde pour pêcher un maskinongé*. Never use rope to catch a muskie."

*C'est dur pour une salamandre
de changer d'adresse.*

It is difficult for a salamander to change its spots.

14

The Voyageurettes and the Case of Mistaken Identity

For seven days and nights the rain came down. The Maries were muddy, wet and cold. They sat in their tent. Puddles of water were in front of the door. Their sleeping bags were wet. Black flies and mosquitos had found their way into the Marie House. The Voyageurettes decided that the very next morning they would leave the wilderness and go to the settlement for a hot shower and sauna bath. Then they would spend the rest of the day shopping indoors at the trading post where it would be warm and dry.

The next morning they arrived at the settlement still muddy, wet and cold with stringy hair and dirty nails—not the usual attractive, well-groomed Maries. In the main part of the settlement, where its two paths intersected, they saw something unusual. On a post by the inter-section was a small wooden sign with red letters. It said, "STOP." The Voyageurettes were used to their freedom. In the wilderness they could go anywhere they wished. They were not attuned to reading little signs to tell them what and what not to do. However, being compliant and law-abiding souls, they stopped at the sign and waited. They looked to the left and to the right and to the left again, but both paths were empty of horses, wagons or even people. After ten minutes, the Maries gave up waiting and boldly walked across the path. Immediately they heard a loud whistle coming from behind them. They turned around. A police wagon came down the path right toward them. The next thing they knew, their hands were bound together with cords and were they were in a wire cage in the back of the police wagon on their way to jail for disobeying a stop sign.

They said to the deputy constable, "We are the Maries! We are not big time lawbreakers! We are truly sorry if we did anything wrong, but we stopped and waited and waited at the sign. It never said, "Go." We just figured it was broken. Honestly, sir, we have never seen a sign such as that before. We are prepared, and more than willing, to pay the fine. Isn't that a more appropriate punishment than having to go to jail?"

The deputy was not convinced. He said, "I have heard of you Maries and your antics! I have seen Marie pictures on the wanted posters at the Post Office. You low-lifes don't fool me one bit! For seedy criminal-types like you, jail is exactly where you belong. You may make one call."

Marie Sue immediately called out of the window to Domingo's Pizza to order a large pizza with everything on it, except anchovies, to be delivered next door to the jail. Now the Maries all loved pizza, but they were not too happy with Marie Sue for using up their one call. Marie Sarah said they should have called to her lawyer friends who would come to represent them in court. Marie Chris said maybe she could have called out to her rich friends to put up bail money. But instead, they were in jail eating pizza. When the pizza was all gone they were still sitting in the jail cell with nothing to do.

The Maries were all heartbroken and could not even speak. They grabbed onto the bars and gazed longingly at the outside world. They were in a state of deep depression. Marie Margot started humming softly. Then she sang out loud the words, "If I had the wings of an angel, over these prison walls I'd fly..." The other Maries all joined in with their kazoos and made sweet, sorrowful music. The deputy standing on guard duty did not pay any attention. However, people walking by the jail heard the beautiful touching music and stopped outside the window to listen.

Pretty soon a big crowd had formed outside the jail. The mayor of the settlement came by and joined the crowd. He peeked into the window. He gasped, "It is the Maries, the Voyageurettes—they are in our jail!"

The people said, "Oooh! Aaah!" and pretty soon they were pushing pieces of paper and pens through the bars for autographs.

The mayor asked, "Dear ladies, how is it possible that you are stuck in this jail?"

Marie Chris said, "It is quite simple. The deputy constable arrested us for walking across the path by the strange little sign that said, "STOP," and then he told us we were seedy outlaws and low-lifes and he was going to keep us here behind these bars."

The mayor said, "That's very strange. That one sign saying "stop" is meant for fast-running horse teams, not casually-walking people. I will check with the deputy and see exactly what is going on here."

The mayor went into the jail office and talked to the deputy. The Maries could hear the Mayor say, "You fool! You have arrested the famous Maries on trumped-up charges of disobeying a stop sign, no less."

The deputy said, "But, Your Honor, I needed probable cause to arrest this whole evil gang of Maries, who are on the government's Most Wanted List."

The mayor said, "You are a double fool! These Maries are all Marie Baptistes! They are the Voyageurettes, *les femmes du nord*! I know them well! They would never, ever, do anything bad on purpose. These ladies are real straight-arrows! The gang you are thinking of are the Marias, with an A. They are Maria Carbones from Chicago. You know. The Mafiaettes. They all work with Al Carbone."

The deputy said, "Oops, I got the wrong girls."

The mayor said, "You bet you do! You really jumped to the wrong conclusion, this time! Next time you see a group of adventurous women, check out their faces. How could you mistake the winsome smiles of the Voyageurettes for those of women of easy virtue or mean-spirited, hardened criminals? OK. Write them out a ticket for disobeying that sign, if you must, but get in there and release the Maries immediately!"

The deputy put his head down and closed his eyes. Then he went to unlock the cell right away, but he could not find the key anywhere. Only the Constable had a spare set of keys and he was out at his cabin and would not be back until morning. So the Maries, who were mixed up for the Marias, were stuck in jail for the whole night.

The people out on the street felt terrible. They were sad to think of the wet, cold, muddy and hungry Maries cooped up behind bars. Immediately, the people decided to cheer up the Maries by staging a parade right past the jail window. They called out the veterans honor guard, six men to pull the hand pump fire wagon, the retired Voyageurs "Passe Packers and Paddlers" group, the newly formed Tuba Band, the Farmers of the Future and their green and yellow plow pulled by a team of oxen, a troupe of leaping Morris dancers waving their hankies, the Festival of Blueberries Prince and Princess, axe twirlers from the lumber camp, cats and dogs all dressed in frilly costumes, the ladies' quilting circle, and the young scholars' marching band. It was a marvelous parade. The Maries said, "Oooh! Aah!" and clapped their hands and shouted compliments and encouragement to every unit as it passed by. After the parade was over there were fireworks and free ice cream for everyone.

When the festivities were over, the Maries got ready to go lie down on their rough plank bunks. As darkness fell over the settlement, the Sons of Scandinavia Barber Shop Quartet stopped by and sang lullabies for them. The Maries fell asleep with lovely visions of the evening still in their heads. It had been a wuuunderful night, even if they were behind bars.

The next morning the Constable came back to the office with his set of keys and unlocked the door of the cell. Right away he took the Voyageurettes to the sauna out back of the Constable's Office and brought them pecan rolls and hot coffee for breakfast. He felt so bad he drove them in his patrol wagon from shop to shop. The merchants felt so bad they offered the Maries a 25% discount on all their purchases. When they were ready to leave to go back to the boat landing, the Constable drove them through the settlement one last time as the Voyageurettes waved good-bye to the people lining the street to wish them well.

Before long the Maries were back in their canoes paddling the wilderness lakes. Several days passed and they came across the Constable in his patrol canoe. They were happy to see him again and told him how kind and thoughtful the people in the settlement had been. He told them his former deputy had a new job. "He asked for a temporary leave of absence to learn more about human nature. I didn't quite understand it, but he said it was because of something the Mayor told him about needing to be a better judge of character. Now he's managing a fishing lodge for the summer."

The Maries did not say anything. To themselves they were hoping that he would, indeed, be a smarter, gentler and kinder manager of the fishing lodge than he was a deputy. And they hoped he would not be quite so quick to jump to conclusions about groups of people he met out in the woods and waterways in the future. They were also thinking it was not likely. It is hard for a salamander to change its spots.

Un serpent sur le gazon peut avoir soif.

A snake in the grass may be thirsty.

15

The Voyageurettes and the Striped Snake

D*ebout, mes filles! Réveillez-vous!* Hey! Get up, ladies!" called Marie Margot before the sun came up. "Maybe we Voyageurettes, who are brave and strong and as tough as grindstone grit and bumble-bee stingers, could just stay at our camp today and putter around and relax. The wind, she is blowing out here just a little bit. And the waves on this lake, they are making small ripples only about nine feet high. Come out here and see for yourselves."

All the other Maries came outside. "Hmmm," said Marie Chris. "This looks like a perfect day to spend *en degrade*, waiting for this breezy spell to pass."

After breakfast the Maries got busy. They quickly did all their laundry and hung it out on bushes to dry. They cut and stacked four cords of wood for the campfire, sealed the seams of the Marie House floor, reorganized all their gear, picked sixteen quarts of blueberries, and polished all the pots and pans and silver in their camp. By 6:00 a.m. they had finished their chores. Then they each got out their net hammocks and tied them to the trees around the campsite. For five minutes the Maries rested. As they swung back-and-forth, they did not say anything. They were thinking. Thinking about being *degradé* and bored.

"What do you say?" said Marie Sue. "Let's hike along the shore to that sheltered bay over there and go fishing! We can catch ourselves some fine bass and have an early lunch!"

The Maries knew about fish. They knew some fish have a keen sense of smell. First, they baited their hooks with bite-size chunks of a dead crayfish they found along the water's edge. Not one bass nibbled on the stinky bait.

They knew some fish had especially good eye-sight. Next, they used a shiny silver spinner. The bass did not pay any attention to the flashy lure.

The Maries knew some fish are attracted by certain colors. They tried a red-and-white wobbly lure. That did not work. Then, they tried small white marshmallows and a flesh-colored bandage that looked like a worm. That did not catch fish, either.

The Maries remembered that some fish like noisy lures and tried one that made popping sounds as it flopped on top of the water. No bass came to bite the popper.

Now the Maries were running out of ideas. Finally Marie Rebecca said, "I remember a fisherman who told about using a lively white mouse to catch a nice bass. Maybe we should try live bait." But no one knew where to find live white mice in the wilderness.

Suddenly Marie Margot screamed, "Eeek! A snake!"

All the other Maries ran over to see the snake while Marie Margot ran the other way. The striped snake was not large itself, but in its mouth was a big green frog. Marie Sue picked up a long, skinny beaver twig and rapped the snake's head hard. The snake's eyes shut tight. The rest of it did not move any more. Then its mouth opened ever so slightly and out came the frog which Marie Sue quickly grabbed and put into her frog bag.

Now Marie Chris was a kind-hearted person who never liked seeing anyone or anything get hurt or suffer. She felt bad about what Marie Sue had done to the snake. Right away, Marie Chris turned and ran back along the shore path toward the campsite. In two minutes she came running back and knelt down by the snake. Gently, she pried open its mouth and poured in a capful of peppermint schnapps from her 4" bottle. The snake's eyes snapped open. It licked its lips, grinned a big grin, hiccupped once and started to move. It went to the left and to the right. Then it went in big circles and bumped into rocks and tree trunks. The snake was feeling no pain. It seemed very happy. The Maries watched that snake until it finally reached a patch of grass and disappeared from sight.

Using the snake's present for bait, the Maries caught four fine bass in nine minutes. The tiniest one weighed 8-3/4 lbs. They hiked back to camp and sat around the fire while they cooked the bass for lunch. Marie Chris was ready to take the tiniest little taste of peppermint schnapps from her small bottle when she felt a tap, tap, tapping on her ankle. She looked down to see what was tapping at her. There was the striped snake dreamily gazing up at her with its eyes half-closed. In its mouth was another frog.

And to this very day, the Voyageurettes are well-known for carrying one small bottle of peppermint schnapps on each of their adventures.

Un oiseau est un oiseau, quelque soit le nom qu'on lui donne.

A bird by any other name is still a bird.

16

The Voyageurettes Become Bird Nerds

Marie Sue carried the biggest pack and the heaviest canoe across the long portage. She walked alone, day-dreaming to keep her mind off the big load on her shoulders and the clouds of mosquitos swarming around her head. She was softly humming Christmas carols to herself and minding her own business when she noticed a bird in the middle of the portage path about 50 feet away. When the bird spotted her, it lowered its head, fanned out its tail feathers and took a few steps forward. Then it flapped its wings, hissed like a snake and ran at top speed toward her.

Marie Sue had never admitted to being scared, but this time, she was all white in the face. Her heart pounded, and her knees banged together. The bird came closer and closer. Marie Sue did not know what to do. The portage path was too narrow for her to turn around with the canoe on her shoulders. The bird kept right on charging, flapping its wings and hissing at her.

For half a mile Marie Sue ran backwards, trying to escape her feathered attacker, but she could not see where she was going. Eleven times she backed into trees along the portage path and bumped her head on the inside of the upside-down canoe. Finally, she bumped into a tree so hard that the canoe came off her shoulders and fell to the ground sideways and blocked the portage path. Marie Sue ran behind a jack pine and hid so the killer bird would not see her. Sure enough, the bird ran up to the canoe, but it was not tall enough to peek over the top and see where Marie Sue had gone. Soon the bird gave up its chase, turned around and went back down the portage path, leaving Marie Sue all alone in the woods by herself.

Just then the other Maries came running along the path. "Marie Sue, where are you?" they said as Marie Sue stumbled out from behind the tree. "Are you OK?"

Marie Sue could hardly wait to tell the other Voyageurettes about her close encounter with death; she breathlessly told how a ferocious wild turkey had just tried to kill her. The Maries all listened intently to the tale. Marie Sue said, "The bird, he is big and brown, much bigger than a sparrow and maybe a little smaller than a chicken. His tail, it looks like a fan all spread out."

Marie Rebecca smiled and then laughed out loud. She said, "Marie Sue, you have just described a ruffed grouse, that is, Bonasa umbellus. It was no wild turkey at all. This is the boreal forest—not what is usually considered to be suitable wild turkey habitat. What you saw was a grouse, also called a partridge. And it was a mamma. She was just trying to protect her babies." All the other Maries nodded their heads.

Marie Rebecca was still laughing, "You mean to tell us you don't know a wild turkey from a ruffed grouse? "

Marie Chris looked at Marie Sue over the top of her glasses. Then she held her sides and laughed out loud.

Marie Sarah said, "Marie Sue, is your brain made of oatmeal?"

Marie Margot just danced all around saying, "Wild turkey! Wild turkey!"

Marie Sue knew what she had seen on the portage path and she knew it was a wild turkey. She just kept quiet. Deep down, she was not ashamed because she knew what she had seen.

That afternoon the Voyageurettes paddled into a bay of the South Kawishiwi River looking for a special campsite. On the shore they saw very large bird standing on a flat rock on the water's edge. The bird's wings were dark brown on top and white underneath. Its legs were white and its head was white and brown. It was busy eating a Northern pike. Marie Rebecca studied the bird for a second. Then she announced, "That definitely is an immature eagle, Haliaeetus leucocephalus. In birding circles it is well-known that bald eagles' heads do not turn all white until they are about four years old." All the other Maries nodded their heads.

Five minutes later the Maries had set up their camp. When the other Maries were not looking, Marie Rebecca sneaked a peek in her bird book.

"Uh, oh," she said to herself. "Eagles have brown legs and no white at all under their wings. This bird we have seen is not an immature eagle. It is a full-grown osprey (Pandion haliaetus) instead.

Later that evening the Voyageurettes sat around the campfire. As they waited for the northern lights to come out, they talked over the events of the day. "Remember that handsome, young, mostly-white bird we saw eating the Northern this afternoon? " said Marie Rebecca. "I think when it grows up some more, it will look just like an osprey. What do you think?" The other Maries nodded their heads.

Then Marie Sue said, "About the bird that chased me for half a mile backwards down the portage today, I have been thinking. To answer the questions why the bird was little, and why it did not gobble and why it had a short, fat neck instead of a long skinny one, it is easy. The bird was a baby. It was an immature wild turkey, that is why. And that is the truth."

Marie Chris, Marie Margot and Marie Sarah looked at one another and then smiled at Marie Sue and Marie Rebecca. "We have learned today many things about the wild birds from the two of you," said Marie Chris.

"That's right," said Marie Margot. "And maybe we also can share some wisdom with you tonight!"

"And what might that be?" said Marie Sue and Marie Rebecca together.

"It is a truth known far beyond our small circle here around this campfire," said Marie Sarah. "*Un oiseau est un oiseau, quelque soit le nom qu'on lui donne.* A bird by any other name is still a bird."

*Même un ours connaît la différence
entre la dignité et l'humiliation.*

Even a bear knows the difference between
dignity and humiliation.

17

How the Bear Listened to Reason

The Maries were waiting for it to get dark so they could have their usual evening campfire before turning in for the night. Marie Sue looked in her book to see what stories she would read out loud for everyone else a little later. Marie Margot was fooling around, playing a little game by herself. She leaped from rock to rock and tried not to step on the ground, only on rocks that were sticking up from the dirt. Marie Sarah and Marie Chris were down by the water watching the sunset and day-dreaming.

Marie Rebecca sat all alone on a big log by the firepit. She was thinking about night-time. She was also thinking about bears. Bears that have big strong paws, long sharp claws, very big teeth and even bigger appetites. And bears that get mad and growl loud and try to eat people's food. Marie Rebecca wished it would get dark quickly so she could go in the Marie House, get into her sleeping bag, close her eyes and go to sleep. Then she would not see or hear when the bear came to sniff around, climb the tree and get the Maries' food pack. Marie Rebecca had a bad feeling, but she did not tell the other Maries because she did not want to scare them.

In her quiet way, Marie Rebecca got busy. On the ground she found many little stones and put them in a big pile four feet high under the place where the food pack hung on a rope. She rummaged through the food pack and found a big can of black pepper. She sprinkled all the pepper on the stone pile under the food pack and around the tree where the food pack was tied. Marie Rebecca was not taking any chances. She located her whistle. Then she found dependable wooden matches, a small candle, nine pounds of birch bark and five big piles of dry sticks. Finally she found a handful of some black grains of powder and put them in a small see-through bag.

When it started to get dark, all the Maries came to the campfire to hear Marie Sue read stories out of her book. It got darker. The Maries talked about important things. They laughed and sang a little. They popped some popcorn and heated up some water for hot chocolate and had a little schnapps.

Marie Rebecca was all the time listening for crunching sounds in the woods. She watched for animals in the bushes. The other Maries noticed.

Marie Margot said, "Ha, ha, Marie Rebecca is afraid of the dark. She is watching for eye glints and listening for noises!"

Marie Sue said, "You 'fraidy cat! Here you are supposed to be the Voyageurette nature expert and you are afraid a bear will come in the night. What good is a scared nature expert when there are bears around?"

Marie Sarah and Marie Chris said, "Marie Sue always has firecrackers and a Flic lighter in her little bag by the door of the Marie House. It is silly for you to worry. Marie Sue, she will protect us."

Marie Rebecca said nothing. After a while she said, "Is it dark yet?" Then she went to the Marie House, got into her blue sleeping bag and shut her eyes tight until the dark spell passed. The other Maries stayed around the campfire and whooped it up a little longer.

About three o'clock in the morning all the Maries were sound asleep, except for Marie Margot. She heard a far away noise outside the Marie House. "Shuffle, shuffle, crunch, crunch," it went. Marie Margot's eyes get big and she sat up straight. She said, "Psst! Psst! Marie Sue! What is that noise?"

Marie Sue was sound asleep and did not hear anything. Then she woke up a little and fumbled around for her firecrackers and Flic lighter in her special bag by the door of the Marie House. "Flick, flick, flick," went the Flic.

The crunching noise in the bushes got louder and closer. "Flick,

flick, flick," no flame came out. Marie Sue said one little bad word to herself, "Rats!"

"Flick, flick, flick," and still no flame. Marie Sarah gave Marie Sue another lighter. This one worked.

"CRUNCH, CRUNCH, SNUFFLE, SNUFFLE, SNUFFLE," the noise outside got very close and very loud. Marie Sue lit the fuse on a big wad of firecrackers and threw it outside the Marie House. "Pffft!" went the fuse.

Marie Chris whispered loud to Marie Sue, "Try it again!"

Two more times she tried. "Pffft! Pffft!" Nothing happened. Now Marie Margot, Marie Sarah, Marie Chris and Marie Sue were very scared and very quiet. They did not know what to do next.

They heard "rattle, rattle, tink, tink." Then they heard, "A-choo! AH-CHOOO! AHHH-CHOOOO!" With that, Marie Rebecca woke up, scrambled over all the other Maries in their sleeping bags and ran outside with her see-through bag and her Little Bitty flashlight. Top speed she ran to the firepit and threw in the candle, birch bark and all five piles of sticks. "Tweeeet! Tweeeet! TWEEET!" went the whistle. All the other Maries peeked out of the Marie House. Marie Rebecca stood there shaking her pointing finger and talking to the bear.

"Now that I have your attention, Ursus americanus, listen up! Yours is a fine and noble heritage. You prowl these woods in search of perfectly natural foods which are just right for you. Think about delicious white, juicy and wiggly grubs. Think about tasty red and black ants under rotted logs. And berries! You love berries, nuts and acorns! And fish! Oh, those nice dead fish along the shore and the live ones you so cleverly catch. Yum!"

"But, Mr. Bear, instead of being a good bear, here you are trying to free-load off of a bunch of humans. Our food is full of sugar and fat. It is high in cholesterol and loaded with additives and preservatives. All those plastic containers and sugars will disrupt your digestion and rot your teeth. Besides, we humans are cunning, wild and totally unpredictable. We may look cute, but we can never be trusted. One false step on your part and watch out! We turn ugly. We will make loud noises, yell bad words and throw rocks at you!

Think about it! What do you want? Dignity or humiliation? Grubs, ants, fish, and self-respect sound pretty good, don't they? The choice is yours!"

Marie Rebecca quickly scratched a trusty wooden match on her thumbnail and lit the candle underneath the birch bark and sticks in the firepit. Quick as a flash there was a fire blazing twenty feet high. It illuminated a circle forty feet across. For good measure, she stepped way back and tossed the little see-through bag of black grains of powder into the raging fire. "Ka-BOOM!" went the black powder so loud that the bear shook its head to make the ringing in its ears go away.

"Thumpety, thumpety, splash, splash, SPLASH!" Marie Sarah, Marie Chris, Marie Sue and Marie Margot watched as the bear turned tail, scampered to the water and swam fast across the lake.

Then they said, "We cannot believe this! How did you convince that bear to leave so quick?

Marie Rebecca just smiled a big smile and said, "Oh, really, there was nothing to it once I got his attention. That is when he showed us his better side."

*L'héroïne de chaque épisode des
Voyageurettes est elle-même.*

The heroine of every Voyageurette's tale is herself.

18

A Legend Joins the Maries

For many years the Voyageurettes had heard of another famous lady canoeist called Marie Ramona. The Maries of the North wanted very much to meet this person. They were thinking in their mind that she would be a wuuunderful addition to their group. Though they did not know her, they often spoke about her.

Marie Margot often said when she was slightly irritated that the other Maries did not get up at 5:00 a.m., "I bet Marie Ramona, she gets up early, not at 10:00 a.m. like some other people I know."

The other Maries said, "Yes, Marie Margot. We bet Marie Ramona, when she gets up early, she is knowing how to start the multi-fuel stove and make coffee and not stare five hours at a cold stove."

When Marie Sue and Marie Joyce went fishing and came back fishless, Marie Chris said, "Too bad Marie Ramona is not here. She would be knowing how to catch fish and not branches, hats and boots like you two."

When Marie Sarah put up the tent and it fell down, she said, "I am wishing Marie Ramona was with us right now. She would be knowing how to pitch a tent."

When Marie Candace looked at an anemic bowl of oatmeal, she said, "I wish Marie Ramona were here. She would be knowing how to bake and we would be eating delicious blueberry and apple muffins instead of mush."

One day it happened. The Voyageurettes were sitting around the campfire drinking coffee, wondering what to fix for seven hungry people, when they heard someone singing. They ran to the shore and there was Marie Ramona fishing in the bay next to their campsite. She had a big stringer full of walleyes in her solo canoe. They recognized the walleyes by their eyes and Marie Ramona from her picture in Who's Who in American Voyageuring. They invited her in for coffee. They said, "Why don't you join us for coffee and, if you want, we would eat up some of those fish for you.

Marie joined them for coffee and a fish fry. Now the Maries, including Marie Ramona, were all of one mind. They did not have to ask Marie Ramona to join them. She did not ask them to join her. They just knew immediately that all of them belonged together in the same circle.

All their expectations of Marie Ramona were true. She got up early, knew how to light the stove, build a fire, fish, bake delicious coffee cakes and put up tents—and *Bon Dieu* how she could lie! She was a true inspiration. Also, she knew how to make a paddle work. This was the truth.

Well, the next day as they paddled along the Maries came across a Voyageur Play Day. All the voyageurs were involved in high-energy canoe competitions. They asked the Voyageurettes to compete, which they declined, except for Marie Ramona. She joined right in. The first race was a fast paddle across the lake and back. Marie Ramona paddled so fast the wake of her canoe swamped all the voyageurs' canoes. By the time the men bailed out their canoes with sponges and begin to paddle again, Marie had been across the lake and back three times. She came in first, second and third.

The next race was the slalom race, paddling around a course of buoys. Marie Ramona paddled so fast, she won in record time with a score of twenty-seven seconds, beating previous best score of 5:02 minutes.

The men were amazed. They asked, "How did you ever learn to paddle so well?"

Marie said, "Well, I exercise, practice a lot and have a few technique secrets."

The men, of course, wanted to hear all about her technique secrets. She was coy, demure and mysterious at first, but finally she told them.

"Well, every day you must exercise the lateral sternocleidomastoideus muscles of your arms to make them strong." Then she said, "Also, you need to reduce the angle of the power side of your paddle blade by three to four degrees on your offside stroke. On the slalom course, you must always remember to overpower the keel side of the reverse sweep and decrease the recovery phase of the inverted S-sweep."

The Maries scratched their heads and wondered what Marie Ramona was talking about. The men all nodded their heads up and down and acted as if they understood every single word.

The men paddled off, happy to hear Marie Ramona's advice, while the rest of the Maries were trying to puzzle out what she had said. So they asked her, "Marie Ramona, whatever were you taking about?"

She said, "I have absolutely no idea. I just made it all up. Did it sound OK?"

They told her it, indeed, sounded good.

Now Maries lie hard and they lie big. They did not know for sure if Marie Ramona told them the truth when she said she made it all up or if her advice was all factual and true and she was now telling them a lie.

They took no chances. They quickly exercised the sternocleidomastoideus muscles in their arms, reduced the angle of the power side of their blades by three to four degrees and overpowered the keel side of their reverse sweeps and decreased the recovery phase of their inverted S-sweeps and then paddled like crazy to the settlement to help Marie Ramona spend the $500 she won at the Voyageur Play Day races.

They did get to the settlement in record time and shopped hard. Some people say the Voyageurettes went into a shopping frenzy that day. That was not true. The truth was the Maries were patriotic, compassionate and civic-minded. They were just especially eager and inspired that day to help stimulate Northern Minnesota's economy.

Cueille-toi un bouquet de vertus!

Associate with virtue.

19

How the Voyageurettes Saved Forty-six Little Girls

It was a rainy day in the Canoe Country. The Maries were paddling along in a heavy downpour. Marie Joyce was sad that her pretty hairdo had gone flop in the rain. Marie Ramona was hoping to herself that the rain would soon stop so she could do some baking. The rain was coming down so hard, no birds were out and about for Marie Rebecca to misidentify, so she was feeling *la misère* about that. Marie Chris was wondering what would happen next in the book that she could not read because of the rain. Marie Candace was wondering how Noah and his wife managed to stay warm and dry for forty days and forty nights in a row. Marie Margot was paddling along feeling sad that the next portage would be too muddy and slippery for her to dance across.

Marie Sue and Marie Sarah were busy in a deep scientific discussion. Marie Sue said, "I am wondering if we should slow down our paddle speed. By paddling so fast, we are just getting wetter because we are exposing ourselves to even more rain drops per second."

Marie Sarah thought about that. Then she said, "No, I think we should paddle even faster. The faster we go, the faster we get by the raindrops before they have a chance to hit us."

All the other Maries contemplated the mind-boggling dilemma

that Marie Sue and Marie Sarah had raised. Eight Marie minds became one—thinking, thinking, thinking, thinking, thinking, thinking, thinking, thinking. No one spoke. The one Marie mind became tired after a few minutes of so much thinking. Luckily, the rain stopped and the sun came out so all the Maries could stop thinking about whether they should paddle faster or slower. At that very moment they approached a big waterfall where they heard cries of "Help! Help! Help!"

Marie Ramona recognized the cries as distress calls. She could not see who was making these calls, but for years, Marie Ramona had known little girls and knew very well what they sounded like when they needed help. "Oh, dear, " she said. "Those are girls in trouble! Quick! The Maries are needed!"

First, all the women put on their Marie hats so they looked official. Then they beached their canoes and ran fast toward the source of the cries at the base of the falls. Forty-six girls were bobbing up and down in the swirling waters, all shrieking for help. Between the forty-six cries for help and the roar of the falls, the noise was deafening.

Each Marie knew what the others are thinking. No instructions were needed. Marie Margot shouted, "One, two, three!" All the Maries immediately held onto their hats and quickly waded into the water all at the same time in formation. One might expect the Voyageurettes to have dived into the water, but the Maries never dive into the water wearing their hats. They waded in and swam with their heads held high so as not to lose their royal blue Marie hats; it was important for rescuees to see their hats and to know it was the Maries rescuing them. Not that the Maries were vain and wanted credit for being heroines. It instilled feelings of confidence in the rescuees to know it was the Maries who were there and were helping them.

Eight Maries made a dramatic rescue that day. Lucky for them, one little girl waded to safety on her own and the other girls were small enough to be rescued several at a time. Within thirty seconds, all the little girls were safe on the shore. They were so happy to be rescued. They wanted to reward the eight heroines for saving them, but the Maries said, "No, just seeing you *chéries* all safe and sound is reward enough." Had they been rich fur company shareholders, only then might the Maries have said "yes" to a reward.

Once they were safe on the shore, the forty-six girls told their story. It seems they had a habit of awakening early every morning before their two adult guides did. That day they decided to go off exploring in the pre-dawn hours. They got lost and then, swoosh, over a waterfalls they went, canoes and all. They said, "Now we have learned our lesson and will never wander away from our guides ever again."

The Maries were glad the girls had learned their lesson, but there was still work to be done. The Maries fished all twenty-three of their canoes and paddles from the water and headed out with the girls in search of their guides.

"What direction did you come from?" asked Marie Ramona. The girls were not sure.

Marie Margot inquired, "What does your campsite look like?"

They said it was on a lake surrounded by trees and rocks.

So the Maries asked, "Are there any islands by your campsite?"

The girls thought for a moment and said, "Yes, there is a big island off to the right and two little islands off to the left of our campsite."

Marie Sue knew the area pretty well. She said, "Oh, yes, I think I know exactly where that campsite is. It is about two hours from here."

Two hours in the company of forty-six girls was a delightful experience for the Maries. However, they heard, "How much farther it is?" a little too often. The first two hundred times was OK, but the next 1,417 times were a little too much. Finally, the Maries quietly asked the girls to please not ask anymore. Then the girls did other things. They taught the Maries modern girl songs like "Fred, the Frog", "Tom, the Toad", and "The Lost Girl Blues." In turn, the Maries sang some old time songs like, "Tell Me Why" and My Paddle's Keen and Bright". The girls then demonstrated several knots which the Maries, of course, already knew but pretended that they did not. They stopped every fifteen minutes for a break.

During the breaks, Marie Margot demonstrated her fancy ballet steps. The girls, in turn, blew bubbles with their spruce gum and the Maries taught them how to make their gum pop and snap. As they paddled along, Marie Rebecca talked to the girls about the birds they were seeing. She said, "See that bird flying overhead? That is an eagle." Then she said, "See that bird over there on the shore? It is a ruffed grouse." The girls, not knowing any differently, were very impressed.

All the girls were interested in the Maries and their stories and adventures. In fact, they all begged to become Voyageurettes. "How can we qualify to be real Maries like you?" the girls asked.

Marie Ramona said, "First, you must know how to work hard, paddle hard, portage hard, shop hard and lie hard. Then you can move up through the ranks and learn to do more complicated and interesting things."

"How can we learn to do all those things, Marie Ramona?" asked the little girls.

"You need experience." said Marie Ramona.

"And how are we to get experience? they said.

One little girl said, "My brothers and the other boys I know are always doing things that our father and other men do. They go off into the forest and chop wood together, train their sled dogs, run trap lines and go fishing together on weekends. When they come home, they say they have been "bonding." Is that what you mean by experience? Is that what we are doing now?"

Just then, Marie Ramona heard frantic calling off in the distance. She had heard this particular type of calling many times in the past and immediately recognized it. She and Marie Candace paddled off toward the source of the distress calls. They found the two guides in a flash and said, "Why are you crying?"

The ladies said, "We woke up this morning and all forty-six girls were gone without even a note or a trace."

Marie Ramona said, "Sob no more. We have all forty-six girls with us. They should be paddling around the corner in just a minute."

Exactly thirty seconds later, all twenty-three canoes plus three Marie canoes came around the corner. The huge flotilla was a breathtaking sight. The guides were delighted to have all their girls back. The girls were ecstatic to be back under watchful eyes and tender care again. The reunion was, indeed, touching for the Maries to see.

The girls and their guides invited the Voyageurettes to their campsite for a celebration. They had fresh strawberry juice, pigs-in-a-blanket, eggs-in-a-nest and crispy black marshmallows for dessert, followed by an awards assembly. The guides insisted upon presenting the Voyageurettes with the prestigious "*Sauveurs des Petites Filles*" ("Rescuer of Little Girls Award") plus the meritorious and rarely-given "Little Girls Medal of Honor Award." Pretty pins came with each award and since the leaders did not have enough pins for each of the eight Maries, it was decided the two pins they did have should be given to Marie Ramona, since she was once a little girl herself. She proudly put the two pins on her Marie hat.

All too soon it was time to part company. As the little girls were busy tidying up their campsite and packing to leave, Marie Ramona spoke to one of the guides.

"You two ladies deserve a lot of credit," she said. "What you are doing with these forty-six little girls is truly admirable. You have many good ideas to help little girls learn new things and stand on their own two feet."

"I know a super woman who has been looking for something important to do with her life. Her name is Julietta. She's a whiz at organizing and getting people to volunteer their time. Maybe she could figure out ways to make your guide job easier, like dividing your forty-six girls into very small groups so they won't all get lost at the same time. I know Julietta would really like to talk with you when you get back home!"

A few minutes after their fond farewells were said, the Voyageurettes heard the forty-six girls and their guides off in the distance. They were paddling vigorously and singing the Marie theme song, "Let's Go Shopping", sung to the tune of "Frère Jacques".

"Let's go shopping, let's go shopping,
To the mall, To the mall,
There's so much to buy there,
there's so much to buy there,
Let's go, all! Let's go, all!"

Then they heard the guides cheer, " We're off to the green mall at the trading post to shop hard!" All forty-six girls yelled, "Yes! Yes!"

Some people might think that song and cheer would make the Maries smile big smiles, but that was not the case at all. The Maries were horror-stricken. Thoughts of forty-six girls plus two guides beating them to the green grassy mall in front of the trading post and picking up all the good bargains first, put the Voyageurettes into a panic. Immediately they scrapped their plans for a little snack, hopped into their own canoes and took a shortcut to the trading post. Fortunately, the Voyageurettes made it to the little grassy mall long before the girls did. Unfortunately, they paddled so hard they were too tired to shop in their best form. However, everything turned out just fine because there were no good sales going on that day anyway.

Une vérité décorée n'est pas la même chose qu'un mensonge.

Truth-decorating is not the same as lying.

20

Father Jean Pierre Baptiste

The Voyageurettes were paddling on Hope Lake, far from any of the busy, well-traveled waterways of the Canoe Country. On the eastern shore was a small, neatly constructed building. On the roof was a vertical pole with a short horizontal bar on it. Outside the building was a man wildly waving his arms. The Maries were alarmed and concerned. They figured the man needed their help, so they paddled fast over to him. They landed on the shore and quickly ran to the man, who was dressed all in black with a white collar turned around backwards.

The man clapped his hands two times, folded his hands under his chin, looked at the Maries over the top of his glasses and smiled a big smile. He said, *"Bonjour, mes filles! Bienvenues!* Welcome! Welcome to the Little Chapel of Ste. Anne! I am Father Jean Pierre Baptiste, the mission priest. Am I glad to see you here! I am stuck at this mission station which is so remote, no one ever comes this way on purpose. Even on Sundays. It has been seven and a half months since I have said Mass and that was when I passed through Grand Portage on my way out here. Very few people ever come to the three campsites on the other side of this lake. And there are no settlements anywhere within miles of here, so I cannot set up a school for children or even go calling on sick or elderly parishioners. In fact, my parish register is full of blank pages. And no one ever comes to, comes to see or visit with me, either." With that, Father Jean Pierre put his arms by his sides and his chin down on his chest.

"Oh, dear Father," said Marie Margot. "Do not be sad! There is a solution for your dilemma. Look on the bright side! Hope Lake is a perfect place for having a retreat! The rest of the time you can try something else. You can leave Hope behind and relocate for awhile. You can go where there are more people or where they pass by frequently. You can meet people at the point of their need! This works for circuit-riders out on the frontier, and it can work for you, too, trust me."

Father Jean Pierre Baptiste looked up. "*Merci, merci mille fois!* What a perfectly sensible solution! I will certainly take that idea up with the hierarchy as soon as possible!" he said.

"Well, Father, if there is no emergency here and everything is all set, we'll be shoving off now," said Marie Sue.

"*Ah, non, mes filles*, please do not leave right away! Can you stay a little longer and come into the Chapel so I can say Mass, offer communion, hear confession and give a short homily?" said Father.

He was so happy at the prospect of having priestly duties to perform for real people, the Voyageurettes did have the heart to tell him that, except for Marie Sarah, none of them were Catholic.

In a minute they were sitting inside the Little Chapel of Ste. Anne pretending to be Catholic and trying hard to do the right thing. Lucky for them, Marie Sarah knew just when to do everything. She knew when to be quiet and when read out of the prayer book. She knew when to sit and when to stand and when to kneel and make the sign of the cross. The rest of the Maries copied Marie Sarah. They watched everything. They saw Father Jean Pierre light a fire in a little metal box and watched when he walked around the Chapel waving it back and forth. They saw and smelled the smoke that came from the box and wondered what was cooking. The Maries watched Father sprinkle drops of water out of a little shaker. They heard Jean Pierre ring a small bell. Then it was time for communion which made them very happy. Kneeling and standing so much had made them hungry and thirsty. They were a little disappointed to see the small portions served by Father Jean Pierre, so they asked for seconds. Father gave them a strange look, but they looked so angelic and innocent he give it to them. When they asked, "How about just a little bit more?" he said, "You ladies are not that bad that you need a third serving of communion!"

Next was confession. Father Jean Pierre said, "Oh, I am so embarrassed! I have not conducted Mass for so long I have slipped up and forgotten the right order of service! I really know confession always comes before anything else! Please forgive me!"

The Maries nodded as if they knew that all along, but they were relieved to make confession last instead of first. Father Jean Pierre said they must do their confessions individually. That would mean they would not have Marie Sarah to copy, so they told Father, "We are the Voyageurettes. There are five of us, but we are of one mind."

Father Jean Pierre said since they were of one mind, group confession would be acceptable. Then he said, "So, you are the Voyageurettes! I have heard of you and know of your reputation. And I have heard it is possible that you do not always tell the truth. Are you prepared to confess to that?"

Even though they were Protestants, they knew better than to lie to a priest. They said, "No, Father. We used to lie hard, but not any more." That was the truth. For them, lying used to be hard. Now it was very easy because of so much practice.

Father said, "Well, if you do not lie hard, then what do you call it?"

They said, "Lying means to be less than truthful. We Maries, we do tell the truth, only we add a little to it. We inflate the truth. That is what we do. There is nothing very bad about inflating the truth since the truth is present- somewhere."

Father Jean Pierre rubbed the top of his head. He said, "Truth-inflators? Well, I guess that is not really bad. But since it is the closest thing to bad that you do, would you please confess to it? Otherwise, I will have nothing for which to forgive you."

Poor Father wanted so badly for them to confess to something so he could finish up his priestly duties. They did admit to truth-inflating and humbly asked forgiveness just to make him happy.

Father Jean Pierre said they must recite ten "Hail Marys" to themselves for penance. They bowed their heads and folded their hands. They quickly said "Hail Mary" to themselves ten times. Then they looked to see what Marie Sarah was doing. It was taking Marie Sarah longer because she seemed to say a lot more words to herself than just "Hail Mary" ten times. Then Father said, "Now you must publicly deflate your stories and tell just the truth."

Marie Sarah volunteered, "OK, Father. It is widely known that we traveled the Ididarun Trail with a team of 400 cats. Actually, it might have been only 398 because it was difficult to count so many cats accurately. When we tell of saving 46 little girls from the swirling rapids, well, the truth is we probably saved 45 because one swam to shore by herself. Finally, we really were going to eat B.B. Legume's dog for supper. These are uninflated truths."

At last, confession was over. Penance was over. The Voyageurettes could tell Father Jean Pierre Baptiste was happy. So were they. They were getting ready to shove off in their canoes when Father said, "Before I can give you my final blessing and benediction, you must promise never to inflate the truth again."

They said, "OK, Father, we promise never to inflate the truth ever again."

One may wonder how the Maries could ever make such a promise to a man of the cloth. It was simple and easily explained. Some truths are small and can stand a little inflating. This, of course, they could not do any more. Other truths are like cake. They are fine and good all by themselves, but frosting makes them even better. The Voyageurettes promised never to inflate the truth. Truth-decorating, however, was another matter.

Maintenant, nous allons savoir
qui est le dindon de la farce!

Now we will see who gets 'soaked.' (taken advantage of)

21

Hegman Lake Revenge

When Marie Candace joined up with the Voyageurettes, she fit in immediately. She paddled hard, she portaged hard, she lied hard and she shopped hard. They all liked her very much in spite of her speech patterns. That was because she sometimes spoke in the accent of a person from one of the northeastern colonies or like someone from the inland hill country far to the south. But Marie Candace was a fast learner. Very quickly she learned to say "hot dish," instead of "casserole" or "warmed over vittles." She caught on fast to say "you bet", "that's different" and "whatever," instead of saying, "that's plum wonderful" or "whatev-ah".

It was well-known that the voyageurs delighted in poking fun at one another's mistakes and weaknesses. They often said that being able to tease a fellow voyageur was to relish life. The Maries delighted in teasing each other as well. On this particular journey, Marie Sue had turned over a new leaf. She decided to modify her mischievous behavior just a little. Almost every evening she went to sleep right away instead of keeping the other Maries awake by talking and humming loudly all night. She got up early in the morning without complaining most of the time. She even ate oatmeal without making faces and without using her spoon to flip oatmeal at Marie Rebecca. She hardly teased anyone. She only tickled Marie Chris' neck once with fir balsam branches while Marie tried to read a book. She did not put pine needles in Marie Ramona's sleeping bag. Also, she did not pester Marie Candace. She did not tease her about her northeastern and southern accents. She even tried being helpful to Marie Candace by giving her the name of a good speech rehabilitator. Also, when Marie Candace fell asleep paddling, nice Marie Sue was extra careful not to splash her more than once or twice to awaken her.

One day right after a long journey, the Voyageurettes arrived at the settlement and immediately headed out on an afternoon excursion to see the newly discovered pictograph attraction on Hegman Lake.

Marie Candace, in her northeastern voice, said, "Marie Sue, you paddle in the bow. That way I can keep an eye on you to make shuah you are keepin' the paddle goin' in the wa-tah."

Marie Candace had an especially mischievous twinkle in her eyes. Had Marie Sue been a little smarter, she might have suspected something right then. But she didn't. She just said, "Whatever" and hopped in the bow and began to paddle. They found the cliff where the pictographs were. Marie Candace decided she wanted a picture of a tree that has fallen atop a cliff right next to a rushing, 40 foot high waterfall. She said, "Hey, Marie in the bow, paddle us closer so I can get a perfect picture."

Marie Sue paddled slowly toward the falls, praying that Marie Candace would soon tell her to stop. The closer and closer she got to the falls the worrieder and worrieder Marie Sue became. She did not say anything because of her bravery. Finally, poor Marie Sue sat directly under the raging falls when Marie Candace, who was high and dry said, "Stop right here. This is the perfect angle for the picture I want to make."

Poor Marie Sue was getting drenched while Marie Candace took much more time than necessary for picture-making. When Marie Candace said, "Hang on, I must change pastels," Marie Sue got the definite idea that she was being set up. Marie Candace was expecting Marie Sue to get upset, yell and scream. But Marie Sue was too busy thinking. She was thinking about her impending doom. Thinking how sad it was that her last meal on earth had been a bowl of oatmeal. Marie Sue tried to paddle away from the falls, but the cold water had frozen her muscles and she could not make the paddle go.

In a most pitiful, humble voice she attempted to say to Marie

Candace, "Please, let's back up a few feet." But the rushing water got into her mouth and she began to choke. "Cough, cough," she went. On top of choking, she had caught pneumonia, hypothermia and frostbite from the cold water. Her second to the last thought was, "What have I ever done to deserve this?" Her very last thought was, "How can I get revenge?"

Right then Marie Candace noticed the canoe was filling with water and decided Marie Sue had been drenched enough. She said, "Well, I have finished making the picture. We can paddle back now."

So they paddled to the settlement and Marie Candace had to clean up before she could go shopping. It took her an hour to shower, do her hair, do laundry and put on clean clothes. Marie Sue was already clean from her shower on Hegman Lake and had an hour head start. Poor Marie Candace. By the time she got to the trading post, Marie Sue had snatched up all the bargains and cleaned out the stock room. Marie Sue came back with 160 T-shirts, 27 pairs of moccasins, 81 books, one light canoe, seven signed and framed Terrance Redline prints, four bronze loon statues, one real stuffed bear, plus items too numerous to mention.

Marie Candace came back with only one purchase which was the only item Marie Sue left in the store because she didn't want it — a black sleeveless Harvey Danielson T-shirt.

The rest of the Maries said to Marie Candace, "We just knew Marie Sue would pay you back for that incident on Hegman Lake and sure enough, she did. She bought out the stock and kept you from shopping hard."

Marie Candace said, "Revenge! Ha! It was worth it seeing her getting drenched. I am thinking of all the coins I just saved by not shopping hard. Ha, ha! Anyway, Marie Sue did leave behind the one item I really wanted, this lovely T-shirt I am wearing!"

Now just seeing Marie Candace in a black sleeveless Harvey Danielson T-shirt might be revenge enough for some people, but not Marie Sue. She just smiled and said to herself, "Now we will see who gets soaked!" The best revenge was yet to come.

What Marie Candace would not know until the next month's trading statement came was that when Marie Sue went on her shopping spree, she put all $12,970.54 worth of goods on Marie Candace's trade debt account.

L'imitation est la meilleure forme de flatterie.

Imitation is the greatest form of flattery.

22

The Voyageurettes Invent the Bent-shaft Paddle

Very early one morning the Voyageurettes sat in their camp with nothing much to do. The wind was not blowing. No rain or storms were in sight. Marie Candace said, "Paddle off in the rain and damp; spend sunny days around the camp." The Maries decided it would be a good day to paddle down to the far end of the lake and poke around in the swamp. On their way they saw something moving across the water. It came closer and closer. Finally, they could see a solitary *canot du nord* with a full crew of eight voyageurs. The Maries stopped paddling and quietly watched the men from a distance. The *avant* (bowman) stood in the bow and the *gouvernail* (sternsman) stood in the stern with their long, skinny paddles while the other eight voyageurs sat in between paddling like crazy with shorter, thin paddles. Marie Margot said, "Gol-ly! Those little banty roosters in the middle, the *milieux*, really do work hard when they paddle, don't they?

"Yes, they do," said Marie Candace. "And from here their paddles look so short and skinny, it's amazing they can make any headway whatsoever. Why, it looks as if they are taking a paddle-stroke just about once every second. I never really noticed that before."

"Marie Candace, maybe you are having a spell of the short-term memory loss," said Marie Rebecca. "We do the very same thing when we paddle!"

Marie Sue said, "Yes, but we can still go faster than the men. With only six of you paddling together side-by-side, our light-weight, straight-tracking 18' canoe can go so fast I can hold on to a rope and stand straight up on two barrel staves while you drag me around the lake."

All this time Marie Chris had been carefully studying Marie Ramona's paddle. "Marie Ramona," she said. "Ever since you joined up with us, I am wondering why your paddle, it is almost five feet long and its blade is five inches wider than ours. Is that the reason you are the best paddler of all the Maries?"

Marie Ramona rubbed the top of her head. "Well, exactly why, I do not know. The paddle, it is long enough to reach the ground from my chin. The blade I made eight inches from side to side because I am thinking it pushes more water, making more power for every stroke than the paddles you use. Besides, I thought it would be nice to have a blade that looked like the wide and flat tail of a beaver instead of the skinny tail of a muskrat."

Now the Voyageurettes, like most paddlers, at first were reluctant to discard their traditionally shaped paddles and replace them with something newfangled. Then they changed their mind. They all decided to join Marie Ramona and use weird shaped paddles too, just so she would not feel out of place. They took an axe into the woods, chopped down a big spruce tree, and split the trunk into slabs two inches thick, eight inches wide and five feet long. Each Marie took her knife and began to fashion herself a new paddle.

By the next morning, all the Maries had paddles just like Marie Ramona's. Off they paddled. They were amazed how much faster their canoes skimmed across the water. No longer did they have to paddle one stroke each second to keep their canoes going fast. They could make one stroke, stop, take a bite of candy, comb their hair and even swat a few mosquitoes before they had to take another stroke.

They were, indeed, very satisfied with their stylish new paddles with blades that looked like beaver tails. The Maries, in their tandem canoes, proudly zoomed past ten voyageurs paddling in one *canot du nord*. If the voyageurs called out or teased them about using weird shaped paddles, the Maries were traveling too fast to hear them.

The very next day the Voyageurettes paddled across Saganaga Lake during a high wind. Even though they were strong paddlers and had fine new paddles, the going was difficult. With every stroke, each Marie had to paddle her hardest. There was no time between strokes for any Marie to have a snack, fluff her hair or mash mosquitoes. Paddling was just one muscle-wrenching pull after another. After sixteen hours of paddling they finally reached a campsite at the end of the lake. The Voyageurettes were all too exhausted to tell even one little lie. All they had strength to do was collapse on the shore and whimper, "I'm exhausted."

After a ten-minute break they recovered sufficiently to unpack their canoes and set up camp. Marie Candace gathered up all the paddles and put them safely on shore under the dense brush near the Marie House. "Oh, my goodness!" she squealed. "Look at our paddles, would you? We paddled with so much force, the shafts on these new paddles, they are crooked! They are all bent forward about 15 degrees!"

All the Maries ran over to look at the paddles. Some Maries laughed out loud, two cried and one wise Marie just shook her head and said, "We should have known better than to have done that."

That night they sat around the campfire popping corn, resting and thinking about important things. All the Maries were quiet. Marie Ramona began to calculate softly to herself. "Sixty times sixty equals three thousand, six hundred. Three thousand, six hundred times six, that would be..."

Suddenly Marie Sue blurted out, "I wonder where the white goes when snow melts." All the Maries looked at Marie Sue.

"Marie Sue! Try not to interrupt Marie Ramona's thought process! She's on to something! At least she is contemplating something on a little higher level than the rest of us. Please let her finish! said Marie Rebecca.

"...twenty-one thousand, six hundred strokes in six hours, that's it! said Marie Ramona. "Maries, I've been thinking about our new paddles with their shafts warped by stress. We should keep using them. It occurs to me that by using a paddle with a bent shaft, the blade will stay closer to vertical in the water than does a paddle with a straight blade. That means it won't pull the canoe hull down into the water so far. Do you realize the implications of that? There will be less friction due to less wetted surface area of the hull and that translates to reduced hydrodynamic drag. Why, according to my calculations, the number of strokes we would need to take using a bent shaft paddle, compared to using a straight shaft paddle, would be reduced by a whopping 1/5! That means as we paddle with bent shaft paddles, we would be taking about eight strokes for every ten strokes with a straight shaft paddle. With a bent shaft paddle, we would paddle at a rate of 50 strokes per minute, or 3,000 strokes per hour, or 18,000 strokes in 6 hours of paddling. If we use a straight paddle, we would have to make 60 strokes per minute or 3,6000 strokes per hour which adds up to 21,6000 strokes per 6 hours. That's a difference of 3,600 strokes! Imagine that, will you?"

"That sounds neat—3,600 strokes. But I still don't get it," said Marie Rebecca.

"OK," continued Marie Ramona. "What I'm saying, in simple unscientific terms, is this. Using bent shaft paddles means more time for napping, fooling around, eating, fishing, and shopping — to the tune of at least an extra hour every day!" That, the Maries understood.

Right away the Maries agreed with Marie Ramona's scientific explanation and did not throw away their warped paddles. They used them for the rest of that season. During the winter, they used properly seasoned red cedar wood to make new paddles with shafts bent on purpose to use on their next canoe adventure.

Using paddles two-feet long, with blades three inches wide at the rate of 60 strokes a minute is now almost unheard of in the Canoe Country. Legend has it that the extinction of this practice first began when Marie Ramona introduced the longer, wider paddle that looked a little like the tail of a beaver. Legend also has it that it was the Voyageurettes who invented the bent shaft paddle. No Marie would ever acknowledge this was true, however, because to do so would be to admit that, in their haste, they used green wood instead of seasoned wood to make a paddle. No self-respecting paddle maker and, for sure, no Marie would admit to making such a gross mistake. All the Maries would ever say was: "Imitation is the greatest form of flattery and we are, indeed, watching the growing use of bent shaft paddles in the Canoe Country with great interest."

Si une chose t'embarrasse, ignore-la.

If something is embarrassing, deny it.

23

How the Voyageurettes Got Lucky

The Maries always used to shoot wild rapids. In fact, there were no better wild rapid-shooters than the Maries. But the Maries stopped doing that after one particular spring. It was not that they were afraid of fast white water. The reason was religion. The Maries were all very religious, except for Marie Sarah, who was much more than very religious. She was Catholic. She always gave up something for Lent. The rest of the Maries gave up things for Lent, too, but they gave up meaningful things like chocolate-covered ants and pickled pig's feet. Marie Sarah was a dedicated Lenten giver-upper. She made the big sacrifice. During one Lenten season she gave up shooting rapids which was, indeed, an important sacrifice because she absolutely loved rapid shooting and was very good at it. So when she gave it up, of course, the rest of the Maries gave it up, too, because the Voyageurettes stuck together.

That particular spring, all during Lent, the Maries portaged around every single rapids. The voyageurs watched them carry their gear. They teased the Voyageurettes for being wimps and 'fraidy cats, but the Maries told the truth. They said, "We are giving up shooting the rapids for Lent." And the voyageurs said no more. Even the rowdy voyageurs respected religious convictions.

Now that summer, the main topic of conversation in the Canoe Country was the comings and goings of seven tickets to the Black Bears and Scandinavian Vikings pick-up football game. It seemed the Hudson Bay Voyageurs had bought seven tickets to the big game, which was to be the first of its kind. Rumor had it that the Yvonne Lady stole the tickets, but the Hudson Bay Voyageurs denied it. The Yvonne Lady supposedly lost the same tickets in a poker game with the voyageurs from the American Fur Company. These voyageurs, the gossips said, promptly lost the tickets betting on a canoe race with the Northwest Fur Company voyageurs.

Well, one day the Maries were paddling along the Kawishiwi River and portaged around some rapids which they would easily and without incident have shot had they not given it up for Lent. They were nearing the end of the portage when they heard mens' voices shouting excitedly, *"Depechez-vous! Vite, vite à la cache! C'est les Manes qui arrivent!* Hurry and hide! The Maries are coming!"

The Voyageurettes reached the end of the portage and saw why the voyageurs were hiding. Their three smashed birchbark canoes were pulled up on the shore being patched. Everything in their outfit was soaking wet. Shirts, pants, sashes, hats, ostrich plumes, food baskets and bales of fur were hanging out to dry on all the available bushes and tree limbs.

Marie Rebecca made pictures of the pitiful scene. Marie Joyce spoke loudly so the hiding voyageurs could hear. She said, "Ha, ha! No wonder the men they are hiding. We would hide, too, if we smashed up on these easy Class I rapids!"

Marie Sue said, "Looks like someone we know forgot to ask the Virgin Mary for help before they started through this little chute! Thank goodness, no one lost his life here. At least there are no new white crosses set up on the shore!"

Marie Margot called out, "Oh, my! Look here! On this tree stump are seven football game tickets sitting out to dry."

"We'd better take them before someone else comes along and steals them." said Marie Chris.

Marie Ramona wrote a note on a piece of birch bark and put it where the tickets had been left. The note said,

"Dear Unknown Voyageurs Who Are Not Knowing How To Shoot The Rapids:

We have your tickets for safe-keeping. Be at the Trading Post Bar at 11:00 on Saturday night and you can claim them.

Yours truly,
Marie, Marie, Marie,
Marie, Marie and Marie"

Saturday night the Voyageurettes were at the bar at 11:00 p.m. sharp. At least one hundred and fifty voyageurs were all crowded inside. Marie Sarah stood up on a bar stool, waved her arms high above her head and spoke right up in a loud voice, "Attention, please! We Maries, we have seven football game tickets found at the Kawishiwi Rapids. The group that lost them, they smashed three fine-doing canoes all to pieces on those rapids. If you are that group, you may claim these tickets now. By the way, here are some pictures of the accident scene."

She passed the pictures among the voyageurs. They all looked at the pictures, laughing and wondering out loud what fools were the ones who got dumped in those easy rapids.

Then Marie Sarah said, "OK, who lost these tickets? Step right up here and claim them!"

With one voice, all 150 voyageurs at the bar said, "No, no, these tickets, they cannot be ours."

And that is the true account of how the Voyageurettes ended up with seven free tickets to the Black Bears and Scandinavian Vikings football game.

Un peu de compétition ajoute du piquant dans la vie.

A little competition adds to the joy of life.

24

The Voyageurettes and the Football Game

One crisp clear fall day the Voyageurettes paddled up the creek to the meadow for the big pickup football game between the Bears and the Vikings. They did not know much about this new game, but they did know a lot about bears and vikings. They knew bears were crafty strong creatures. They also knew that vikings were mighty adventurers of old. The Voyageurettes thought that vikings, indeed, must be very old men by now and being so old and playing against a bunch of bears, they must be hardy, strong and rugged. All the way as they paddled along, the Voyageurettes were wondering just who would win the contest between the fierce bears and the tough Scandinavian vikings.

When the Maries got to the meadow they discovered a nice winding ridge of sand, called an esker, which had been left behind by a glacier. The esker was in the shape of a "C" and it went almost all the way around the meadow. They had brought along their sit-upons, which were two square rush mats held together with straps. One part was for sitting and the other part was a backrest. The Maries sat down and made themselves comfortable. Other people were sitting on the inside slope of the esker and on the very top, too, so they could see what the bears and vikings were going to do to each other.

Someone had made long white stripes evenly spaced all up and down the meadow and there were shorter stripes going the other way at both ends.

It was not long before a man blew into a buffalo horn to get everyone's attention. Then he yelled, "Here come the Black Bears!" On to the meadow ran a bunch of young men wearing tight pants and furry black bubble hats. They were not bears at all.

The deception continued when the man lied again, "Now here come the Scandinavian Vikings!" More young men ran out in tight pants and bubble hats with horns painted on them. They were not vikings at all.

Then out ran five or six more men wearing black and white striped shirts. The Maries thought they must be pretending to be skunks just like the players were pretending to be bears and vikings.

The game began when one of the skunks ran out in the middle of the meadow and put a funny shaped ball made out of an air-filled buffalo skin on the ground. The Bears who were not bears kicked the ball to the Vikings who were not vikings. They all began to run after the ball. Then they all fell down on the ground or on top of each other. The skunks were still standing up.

Then the fallen-down Bears and Vikings all got up and ran to make a circle with their teammates. They bent over and whispered secrets to each other. After that, both teams all lined up and one, two, three, they ran toward each other. Then they all fell down again. Once in a while one of the players was able to catch the ball when someone else threw it to him and he would not fall down. Instead, he ran fast carrying the ball and everyone else chased after him. When he got to the end of the meadow where the white stripes went the other way, he threw the ball down on the ground and danced by himself. Then all his teammates ran to him and they all jumped up and down and danced together, and the people sitting on the esker jumped up, too, and yelled very loud. A few times during the game, all the players lined up and one of them tried to kick the ball over a long pole that was fastened up high on two tall posts. Then everyone sitting on the esker stood up and yelled some more.

The head of the Bears was not a bear either, although his manners were like a bear's. He stood by the side of the meadow, looking mean and spitting on the ground.

The head of the Vikings was not much to brag about either. He folded his arms across his chest, walked up and down the edge of the meadow and sometimes pointed his finger, waved his arms and shouted at his Vikings.

For more than half an hour the players got up and fell down, chased each other, threw and kicked the ball, danced a little and whispered secrets in their circle. Then all of the people sitting on the esker yelled extra loud and the players all ran away in two bunches. The meadow was suddenly empty.

"Now, just what do they call this game?" asked Marie Margot.

"It's called "football," Marie Margot." said Marie Sarah. "But for the life of me, I do not know why, since the players spend more time throwing and carrying the ball than they do kicking it."

"Oh, of course," said Marie Margot. "After what I have seen here, I have been thinking this game should be called "footbrawl." Now I understand why our voyageur friends would really like to have been here. The young men who play this game are big, strong and rough. In fact, they are all much bigger and stronger and rougher than any of the voyageurs are. They run fast and bump each other hard. They yell and fight and do lots of things the voyageurs would like to be able to do, I am sure of that."

The Maries stood up and started to fold up their sit-upons and got ready to leave when suddenly a band marched on to the meadow. Now that was something the Maries enjoyed—fine marching music! Right away they sat down again. After they finished playing eight lively tunes, the band members marched away and the Maries got ready to leave again.

All of a sudden the players and skunks ran back out on to the meadow for more football. So the Maries stayed put and watched the young men fall down, get up and run and kick the ball for thirty more minutes. They also watched the skunks run around the meadow blowing whistles, throwing their hankies on the ground and waving their arms in the air. After a long time, someone blew hard into a buffalo horn again and most of the people sitting on the esker jumped up and down, smiled and made lots of noise. The rest of the people looked sad.

When that happened, the players and skunks all ran away and everyone else who had been sitting up on the esker walked across the meadow and left, too. The Maries sat patiently on their sit-upons waiting for the band to reappear.

There they were all alone in the meadow feeling tricked and deceived. They had traveled several hundred miles by canoe to see a game between bears and vikings and had seen nothing but impostors who were not even good impostors at that.

Now the Maries were all of one mind. Without saying a word, they knew what the others are thinking. They all stood up exactly at the same time. They walked away single file, out of that meadow, down the path and straight to the nearest trading post.

The next Saturday night they were back at the Trading Post Bar up North. One hundred and fifty voyageurs crowded around them and asked, "How was your trip to the meadow for the big game?" The Voyageurettes told the truth. They said, "We had a wuuunderful time." And, indeed, they did. At the trading post.

*On boit rarement, mais on
mange souvent.*

Seldom eat, but often drink.

25

Seldom Drink, but Often Eat

Early one morning well before the sun rose, the Voyageurettes were preparing their breakfast of coffee, bacon and eggs, apple-sauce and pancakes with butter and maple syrup. Just then a brigade of forty voyageurs passed by in their fully loaded canoes. "Halloo!" called Marie Candace. "Would you fellows like to stop and have breakfast with us? We are making enough to share with you!"

"Thanks, but we have already stopped for our usual breakfast a couple of hours ago, and we're all set," said the *gouvernail* paddling in the stern of the lead canoe.

"So, what do you fellows usually have to eat that early in the morning?" asked Marie Candace. "We're always open to new menu ideas!"

"Pemmican! For breakfast, we boil it." he replied.

"And what recipe do you use for making your pemmican?" asked Marie Sarah.

"It's easy enough!" he said. "We first dry buffalo meat and then pound it for a long time. After it is pulverized in good shape, we mix in rendered buffalo fat. Then we put 90 lbs. of it at a time in sacks made of buffalo hide, that's about it."

"Well, that's certainly high energy food! Thanks for the recipe!

We'll probably see you out on the water again some time. Have a safe trip!" said Marie Candace as the voyageurs quickly disappeared from view.

The Maries leisurely finished their breakfast, tidied up the campsite, packed up their outfit and off they paddled.

About mid-day, the Voyageurettes spotted a portage at the end of the lake. As they paddled closer, they discovered they had caught up with the same brigade of voyageurs who had passed by their breakfast site earlier. The men were unloading their four canoes.

Maries paddled nearer and rafted up just offshore, allowing the first arrivals at the portage to cross without being overtaken. This not only saved mixing up packs and gear along the pathway, but it was also considered to be good manners.

While the Maries were courteously waiting out on the water, they carefully scrutinized the voyageurs' outfit. The men carried their 90 lb. *pieces* of trade goods bound for the Far North and all the necessary items for themselves on their long and arduous journey to the next outpost 500 miles away. They spotted small bags of what appeared to be flour as well as dozens of wooden barrels of various sizes.

"Look at all those kegs!" said Marie Joyce. "I didn't realize the voyageurs carried so many of them! What's inside, do you suppose, molasses from the West Indies? Maybe it's cane syrup for trading. What else can be in all those barrels, casks and kegs?"

Just then one of the voyageurs went over to a two-gallon keg when no one else was watching. The bung-hole had a spigot driven into it. He took a cup, turned the spigot and drew off an amber liquid and took a long quaff. Then he smiled a big smile and his eyes got bright.

Marie Chris was not bashful. She called out, "Halloo, Jean Baptiste! What is in that keg of yours and what is it that you are drinking that makes you smile so big?"

"Oh, nothing much," he said. "Just a small treat!"

"You stopping for lunch?" she asked.

"No, we don't do lunch," said Jean Baptiste. "Only the breakfast and the evening meal do we voyageurs eat."

The Voyageurettes did lunch when they reached the other end of the portage. There was nothing else quite like a Voyageurette lunch — nice hard salami sliced thin, an assortment of the finest cheese available, homemade jams and jellies, their special skinless, pulverized peanuts which were ground to the consistency of butter, freshly baked bread, trail snacks, sweet drinks or tea.

A little later that afternoon, after paddling through eight lakes and portaging seven times, the Voyageurettes found a campsite on a promontory overlooking a beautiful bay. During supper Marie Joyce said, "Tonight, when it gets dark, let's go see if we can find some flying squirrels in those woods across the bay. It will be a full moon and we can see our way over and back with no problem."

Three hours later, as the Maries were almost ready go look for flying squirrels, they noticed activity across the bay. It was the same brigade of voyageurs they had already seen twice that day. The men were busy setting up their camp for the night after their eighteen-hour work day. The canoes had been carried ashore and had been emptied and overturned. The Bourgeois' tent was set up and someone had a big fire going. In the bright light, it was easy to see what the voyageurs were doing. Some were bent over their birchbark canoes, mending leaks with pine pitch. Others were standing around, waiting for supper. The Voyageurettes decided they would paddle over and visit for a few minutes.

As they approached the voyageurs' campsite, the Maries could see all the men gathered near the fire. Some of them had spoons and were dipping their supper right out of the steaming kettle and eating whatever it was without using a plate or a bowl or even a cup. Other voyageurs were down on all fours on the ground in little circles of four or five. It looked as if they were pressing their noses on the bare rock and it was difficult to tell just exactly what they were doing.

"Halloo, there!" called Marie Ramona from out on the water. "What's on for supper tonight?"

"It's pemmican! But tonight we're having it fixed special. We are calling it 'rubbaboo.' It is made first with flour and water all mixed together and cooked until it is nice and thick. We hope it is not burning on the bottom. Then we are throwing in cut up chunks of the pemmican, but maybe some sticks or pine needles also get in, by mistake! Some of the men like it very hot, right out of the pot. The others over there are cooling it in hallows in the rocks, and they are really lapping it up."

"Oh, Marie Ramona, aren't you glad you asked?" whispered Marie Chris.

The Voyageurettes paddled along the shore past the voyageur's camp. In the bay they saw three flying squirrels gliding from tree-to-tree in the moonlight. They also watched two 75 lb. beavers swimming toward their lodge with freshly cut branches of birch in their mouths. After awhile, the Maries passed by the voyageurs again on their way back to their own campsite. This time, something else was happening. Three or four men were still hard at work patching a canoe, while the rest them were lounging on logs or on the ground. Frequently the men got up and went over toward a long row of kegs and then returned to their places with cups in their hands.

As the Maries quietly approached their camp, Marie Ramona could not hold back. "What is it that you fellows are drinking this time of night?"

"High wine, rum, brandy, whatever!" said the voyageur sitting at the water's edge. "Have you ladies not heard of our grand and famous saying? *On mange rarement, mais on boit souvent!* Seldom eat, but often drink!"

"These fellows must be opportunistic drinkers! They do not need a reason or an excuse, they just drink at every opportunity," whispered Marie Sue as the Maries turned and paddled back to their campsite across the bay.

The very next afternoon, the Maries found themselves in a confusing situation in a lake of the same name—Lake Confusion. For two full minutes they could not find the portage, but it was there, hiding beside a waterfall. Marie Joyce was the first to carry a canoe over the wet rocks, up a steep bank and into the woods. Just then, without any warning, a wind came out of the southwest, a very big wind. When the wind hit the treetops, they snapped like match sticks. Five treetops fell into the waterfall and two crashed into the woods. One fell down right on Marie Joyce. The canoe was not damaged, but Marie Joyce did not fare so well.

Until the tree fell on Marie Joyce, she was 5'8" tall and had size eight feet with high arches. Her head was the normal shape, only slightly rounded on the top. After the tree fell upon her, Marie Joyce was only 5'1" tall, she was flat-footed, her shoe size was twelve and her head had a six-and-a-half inch pointed lump on top.

All the Maries ran to Marie Joyce and said, "Marie, are you OK?"

She answered in a whisper, which was all she could manage. Her first words were, "Does my hair look OK?"

They told her the truth which was that her hair looked fine. They did not tell her about the big lump sticking out from underneath her hairdo.

Marie Chris said, "Is there anything we can do for you?"

Marie Joyce whispered again, "Well, I am a little hungry. Something sweet sounds good."

The Maries all worked together to help Marie Joyce. Marie Candace took charge because she knew just what to do in such situations. She gave Marie Joyce a box of cookies and a large jug of fruit-flavored water. Marie Joyce was so busy eating and drinking, she did not notice three Maries at her head and four at her feet pulling her in opposite directions. Marie Joyce was still busy eating by the time they finished stretching her back to 5'8". For the head lump, Marie Candace had a perfect cure. She put a forty-pound flat rock on Marie Joyce's head. The weight of the rock pressed the lump down to a more normal size. For Marie Joyce's size 12 flat feet, Marie Candace could do nothing. She said, "I am just a nurse, not a miracle worker. For miracles, you will have to see a podiatrist."

With Marie Joyce on the mend, Marie Ramona got all excited and slipped on a rock and ended up with a big black and blue mark on her leg. Marie Candace took one look at it and said, "Oh, dear, Marie! You have a hematoma with massive internal bleeding. You could get anemia, low blood pressure and go into shock. Even worse, you could get a blood clot and gangrene and end up with no blood pressure at all. Of course, I could always amputate your leg, but then..."

That is when Marie Sarah stuffed a left-over blueberry muffin into Marie Candace's mouth. With Marie Candace busy eating the muffin, Marie Rebecca consoled Marie Ramona by saying, "It's just a bruise. Soak it in cold lake water a few minutes and keep it elevated."

After a few minutes of soaking, most of the black washed off. It was simply dirt and the bruise did not look so bad after all. It was just sore. Amputation was not necessary.

Marie Ramona's leg was feeling so much better she grabbed the post bug-bite medicine and proceeded to make the rounds, dabbing medicine on all the Maries' sore, swollen no-see-um bitten ears.

Now the medicine stung so much that the Maries all jumped around trying to make the sting go away faster. Marie Margot saw this as a teachable moment and began to demonstrate ballet leaps and jumps for the Maries so when they jumped around because of the stinging medicine, they could do it with dignity, beauty and grace.

During her instruction, Marie Margot landed on a loose rock, slipped and gracefully fell down on her thumb. It immediately puffed up. The Maries stuck together. By the end of the day, most of them were sore, battered and bruised. They needed a cure.

Fortunately, they found a bag of dried apricots, peaches, bananas, papaya, pineapple, figs, dates, raisins, flaked coconut, and three kinds of nuts in their food pack. They had several handfuls of Marie Joyce's cookies, ate up all of Marie Ramona's lemon bars and sampled Marie Margot's coated chocolate pieces before supper. An hour later they had supper.

"I am thinking about what the voyageurs would do in a situation like this," said Marie Rebecca. "Undoubtedly, they would just drink, drink, drink and wake up with splitting headaches. We need to come up with a better way of coping with minor incidents and small setbacks in the wilderness, don't you agree?"

They decided the most logical solution was to have a little snack, go to sleep and hope that tomorrow would be a better day. The next day was, indeed, better. When they woke up, no one had even a trace of a headache. And during breakfast, the Voyageurettes agreed their grand and famous saying was much healthier and far superior to that of the voyageurs: *"On boit rarement, mais on mange souvent.* Seldom drink, but often eat."

Lorsqu'un mensonge et une vérité
sont prononcés dans un même souffle,
ils s'annulent l'un l'autre.

When a lie and a truth are spoken in the same breath,
they cancel out each other.

26

Marie Tricia and the Pink Flamingo

Early one morning the Maries were leaning up against the ledges at the beginning of the portage between Newfound and Splash Lakes with their heads bowed. No one said anything as they looked down at the three canoes and thirteen packs lying at their feet. Marie Ramona turned her head from side to side and checked out the other Maries. What she saw made her close her eyes and take deep breaths. Marie Candace could not carry anything that day because of a bad back. Marie Rebecca could hardly carry herself across the portage because of a pain in her hip, and Marie Sue was not in the best of shape because of sore rhomboid muscles. Poor Marie Ramona was the only Voyageurette capable of portaging all the gear that day.

As the other Maries rummaged through their packs looking for pain pills, Marie Ramona found a rosary. With the beads in her hand, she whispered, "Hail Mary, full of grace, may I get this stuff across this place." As Marie Candace rummaged through her pack, she muttered that on this trip the Maries sure could use a sherpa.

Right then, up paddled a smiling lady in a pink canoe. "Hello, there! Good morning! I am so glad to see you! Please accept my apologies for interrupting your portaging, but perhaps you can help me. I have come all the way from California hoping to meet up with a famous group of lady adventurers called the Voyageurettes. Would you, by chance, know of them? Have you seen them or know where I might find them?"

Now, the Maries were usually eager to identify themselves. Not because they liked to brag or be in the limelight, but rather because they knew it gave others genuine pleasure to meet such famous canoeists as themselves. But this particular lady they decided not to tell because of her pink canoe. They gave her a big Marie-smile anyway, hoping she would not detect their underlying suspicion and skepticism. Marie Ramona began to quiz the lady. She asked, "Are you the new Yvonne Lady?"

The lady just laughed and said, "No, I'm not a Yvonne Lady at all. I am a school teacher on summer vacation."

Then Marie Ramona said, "And just why is it that you happen to be paddling a pink canoe?"

The stranger answered, "Because I am from California where ladies paddle pink canoes which are very much in fashion there."

Marie Candace, Marie Rebecca, and Marie Sue were too busy rummaging through their packs to ask the lady any questions. Marie Candace was still muttering about sherpa porters when the lady said, "Well, I'd best get on my way and search for the Voyageurettes while it is still daylight. But before I go, please let me carry your gear across this portage for you. I just love carrying packs and canoes!"

Zoom, zoom she went and, in a flash, all the gear was at the other end of the portage. The Voyageurettes decided to disclose their identity and invite this bright, kind-hearted, delightful and charming person to join them before she got away. Their one mind told them they could forgive her canoe for being pink.

"We would be happy and proud to have you join us; however, there is one small obstacle. To become a true Voyageurette, your name must be Marie, Marie something."

She said, "That will not be necessary because my first name is already Marie. Marie is also my middle name! In fact, my full name is Marie Marie Baptiste!" She was going to fit in.

But when they started calling her Marie Marie, it was confusing because then two Maries were thinking they were being called at the same time. "Marie Marie," they said, "This is not working out very well. Would you object strenuously if we were to change your middle name to Tricia, so we can say "Marie Tricia" and not have two Maries answer?

She said, "Tricia is just fine! It suits me perfectly!"

So she was baptized Marie Tricia, making her an official Voyageurette. Marie Tricia could paddle hard and straight like Marie Sue and she could cook as well as Marie Ramona. She knew a lot about nature like Marie Rebecca and she could shop hard and lie big like Marie Candace. She had almost the grace of Marie Margot, an eye for stylish and colorful outfits like Marie Joyce and the wuuunderful personality of Marie Chris. She was, in fact, like all the Maries rolled into one.

The Voyageurettes were so pleased and proud of the newest Marie, they even let her take the lead position It was a sight to behold-two white and one brown Marie canoes following behind Marie Tricia in her pink canoe. She paddled with an iridescent pink paddle and wore a pink and purple paddlesuit to match. Her canoe was decorated with a bouquet of pink Dew Idiums painted on the stern and the words "Yvonne Lady— NOT" printed in bold letters just under the gunwales. Ah, it was a stunning sight to behold-beauty and class almost beyond comprehension.

Now, the voyageurs they met at the next portage were surprised when they saw a brand new Marie paddling a pink canoe. They reacted in typical voyageur fashion. "Hello there, Maries! And who is this new recruit with you? In a pink canoe, no less!"

Marie Ramona replied, "Please meet Marie Tricia who has just arrived from California where pink canoes are in style." The men rolled their eyes toward the sky and folded their arms across their chests when Marie Ramona told them about the pink canoe fashion in California. "Oh, no kidding," they said.

Marie Candace said, "Marie Tricia is really "Sis-ter Marie" and this sleek and fast, gorgeous pink canoe was given to her by the Pope himself."

The voyageurs took a second look at Marie Tricia and her canoe. "Really? Come on, Marie Candace, you're just making that up!" they said.

Then Marie Tricia bowed her head, crossed herself, folded her hands together in front of her and said, "Please forgive these voyageurs for being so rude. They know not what they are doing or saying. Amen."

This shut them up. Being good voyageurs, they knew enough not to fool around with a real Sister, especially one whose canoe was a gift direct from the Holy Father.

One may question whether the Maries had reverted to lying after they promised Father Jean Pierre Baptiste they would stop. Well, what the voyageurs were told was not a lie. Marie Tricia was, indeed, a sister - she had siblings. The part about the Pope may or may not be a lie, because they never did ask Marie precisely where she got that canoe. For all they knew, it did come from the Pope. Even if it were a lie, it was no problem. When the truth and a lie are spoken in the same breath, they cancel each other out.

Well, it was time to leave the portage. Marie Tricia got into her canoe and paddled off. Zoom! Off she went, leaving everyone else far behind and struggling to catch up. The men watched in awe. They knew the Maries were strong, hard paddlers and if the Maries had trouble keeping up with someone else, that someone must be an incredible paddler. When the voyageurs finally caught up to the Voyageurettes on the next portage, they said, "Marie Tricia, how is it that you can paddle so fast, faster even than Marie Ramona?"

Now, the Maries always stuck together. No way was Marie Tricia going to tell the voyageurs the truth, which was that she was not really paddling quite as fast as it seemed. It just looked fast because the other Maries were having to paddle so slowly due to their ailments. Not even for a second did she consider embarrassing her new sister Maries. So, instead of telling the truth, she did the next best thing. She lied hard. She could lie because she was not one of the Maries who made the promise to Father Jean Pierre Baptiste.

Marie Tricia announced, "It is because I paddle a pink canoe. Pink canoe paint has been scientifically proven to be the slipperiest of all paints. It enables canoes to go faster and better because of less friction and drag."

She said this so sincerely the men did not consider for even a moment that she just might be lying.

Then she said, "Didn't you read that article about the advantages of pink paint for canoes in last month's issue of Scientific North American newspaper?"

The men, not wanting to appear ignorant or uneducated, all said, "Yes, yes, we recall reading that article."

Then Marie said, "If you don't believe that article, just ask any woman. They all will tell you that pink canoes paddle best of all."

Since they were the only women around at the moment, the men looked to the Maries for verification. They all nodded their heads in agreement and said they were thinking of trading their canoes for pink ones so they could keep up with Sister Marie Tricia.

The men muttered something about having to hurry to the settlement and they all paddled off.

The next day the Maries went to the settlement for a hot shower. They noticed something going on in front of the canoe dealership. They decided to investigate, hoping a big sale was in progress. The poor canoe dealer was standing on the steps of his store, surrounded by a crowd of at least 250 people-all pushing hard to get near him, waving rolls of cash in the air and shouting to him. The Maries stood at the far edge of the crowd, scratching their heads, partly because of black fly bites and partly because they were trying to figure out what was going on. Pretty soon, everyone had placed orders and put down deposits. The crowd finally dispersed. The canoe dealer spotted the Voyageurettes standing off to one side of the dirt path and ran over to them carrying a fistful of hundred dollar bills.

He said, "Boy, oh, boy, am I ever happy to see you! Here Maries, please, please take this as a small token of my sincerest appreciation. It represents my advertising budget for the year and giving it to you is the least I can do for all the business you have brought me. You are truly marketing geniuses! You see, once the word got out about your new Marie with the pink canoe from California, Marie Wanna Bes from all over the North Country have been ordering pink canoes from me so they can be fashionable. Why, even the voyageurs have been buying pink canoes for their wives! Really, it's a, it's a MIRACLE, that's what it is!"

The Maries just shook their heads and smiled big smiles. They knew enough about voyageur lies to spot one a mile off. They knew the voyageurs were buying pink canoes for themselves, thinking they were the fastest of all canoes. Presents for their wives? Ha! "So! Jean Baptiste! What is a big strong voyageur like you doing paddling around in a dainty pink canoe, eh?" The teased voyageur would then say, "Oh, this isn't my canoe. It's my wife's. I'm just borrowing it while mine is in the shop."

The Voyageurettes thanked the canoe dealer for the cash and went on their way. Some people might think the Voyageurettes would stay in town and shop hard that afternoon. The truth was they did not shop at all. Marie Candace, Marie Rebecca and Marie Sue were much too stiff and sore to shop hard. Even an easy shop was too difficult. Now the Maries stuck together. They paddled together, they portaged together, and, when necessary, went doctoring together. It took all afternoon for the Maries to visit the doctor's office and then go to the apothecary's shop for pain powders and pills. By the time the Maries were all fixed up, all the stores were closed. So they went back to the outfitter's bunkhouse and sat around and pouted.

They were experiencing severe shopping withdrawal symptoms. Everyone with the exception of Marie Tricia, that is. She bounced around like a kangaroo on caffeine, looking at her pocket watch, then at the crystal rock and earpiece on the table. Then she looked back at her watch. Exactly one minute before nine she said, "Cheer up, Maries!" and began to count down the seconds. Five, four, three, two, one, zero! Then she fiddled with a cat's whisker on the crystal rock. On the earpiece, she heard a man say, "Welcome to the Home Shopper Service!" Marie Tricia was right. The Voyageurettes cheered right up. Marie Tricia chose a heavy-duty pink flamingo lawn ornament and a complete set of Sand Dune Boys' sheet music. Marie Ramona wanted a new dehydrator box and camp cook stove. Marie Rebecca picked out a newly revised bird identification book. Marie Candace chose a wind-up back rub machine, plus a rotating bar lamp. Marie Sue thought she would like the make-up kit with a mirror at no extra charge. Marie Tricia wrote all their choices on a little slip of paper. She rolled up the paper into a cylinder and sealed it with wax on both ends. Then she ran outside.

In the shed at the back of the bunkhouse were rows of boxes with small doors and perches on the front. Above the doors were signs that said, "To Grand Portage," "To the Place of Sieur deLuth," "To the Falls of St. Anthony, " "To Isle Royale," and "To Home Shopper Service." Marie Tricia opened the little door under the sign saying, "To Home Shopper Service," took out the gray bird that was inside and tied the paper cylinder to its left leg. "Now, Mr. Pigeon, go be a good messenger!" she said as she released the bird into the air.

By the following afternoon all the new purchases had arrived by super-fast overnight express canoe delivery and the Maries had packed them all up for their next adventure. Marie Tricia was especially happy, because with all their Home Shopper purchases, the number of portage packs went from thirteen to twenty-one. Just before they took off, Marie Tricia remembered her new pink flamingo ornament and fastened it to the bow of her canoe. Off they paddled. In the distance they saw a flotilla of pink canoes paddled by voyageurs they did not recognize.

When they came closer, the Voyageurettes called out, "What are big, strong voyageurs like you doing in those dainty, pink canoes?"

The men said, "Oh, these canoes are not ours. They belong to our wives! We are just using them while ours are in the shop. By the way, did you ladies know about the study written up in last month's Scientific North American newspaper? It's all about how pink canoe paint is fastest of all."

Marie Tricia and Marie Ramona said, "Yes, we have, indeed, heard of that article. We would be happy to put on a speed demonstration for you!" Zoom! Off they went. They went so fast, in fact, all anyone could see was a pink blur out on the lake. The men could not say anything. They just sat very still in their canoes with their mouths and eyes opened wide. When the two ladies came back after their demonstration, the men said, "Would you please explain why is your pink canoe so much faster than our pink canoes-oops, we mean our wives' pink canoes?"

Marie Tricia said, "It is because of this special heavy-duty, carved flamingo on the bow. Its beak cuts through the air. With this flamingo, my canoe is even more aerodynamic because of less frictional resistance." She then said, "Didn't you read about it in last month's issue of Aerodynamic Principles of Canoeing?" The men, not wanting to appear ignorant, said yes, of course, they recalled seeing that article.

The Maries were all of one mind. They wished the voyageurs "*Bon voyage*," turned their canoes around and headed right back to the settlement. They rushed directly to the stockbroker's office. All together they said the same words to him. "We want to buy stock in the company that makes pink flamingo ornaments." Knowing the voyageurs as they did, the Voyageurettes knew the pink flamingo stock dividends would totally finance their next adventure with plenty of money left over to shop harder than usual.

*Un verre de fort, ça fait que
les vies sauves valent
la peine d'être vécues.*

A strong drink can make saved lives worth living.

27

The Bad Bob Boys

The Maries drifted across the lake one hot and sunny day, all sprawled across the canoes. They were much too busy to even paddle. Their one mind was thinking hard about sun tans and how they were needing to even them out. Paddling would have only taken their mind off that job. Finally, they lazily floated up to a portage and started to unload their gear. Across the portage they heard weak moaning and groaning noises. Marie Candace said, "I am being a nurse and I am knowing those sounds are definitely the sounds of people needing medical attention." She grabbed her first aid pack and off she went running down the portage at top speed.

The rest of the Maries walked slowly across the portage, not wanting to run and risk tripping and getting hurt. They reached the end of the portage in time to see Marie Candace at work applying her medical skills to patients. First they stood back so they would not be in Marie Candace's way. She gave artificial respiration to three voyageurs. Then she sewed up gashes, bandaged wounds and applied air splints. The rest of the Maries just watched until the sight of blood finally made them decide they should all faint.

When they recovered sufficiently, the voyageurs told Marie Candace what had happened to them. It seemed they had been attacked by a group of toothless men who were all wearing worn-out bib overalls, no shirts and untied work boots. The strangers overcame the voyageurs, stole all their *pieces* full of beaver furs and rowed off in a leaking, green, flat-bottomed jonboat. Marie Candace asked the voyageurs if they had heard any of the strangers' names. One voyageur said, "Yes, I remember the names they used for each other. There was a Billy Bob, a Bobby Bob, a Bert Bob, a Jimmy Bob and a Joe Bob."

Marie Candace shook her head. She said to the voyageurs, "You were attacked by the Bad Bob Boys from the hill country far away. They are a bad bunch for sure."

The voyageurs said, "Please, please Maries! We are pleading with you to recover our beaver pelts for us."

Now the Maries were a soft touch for the beaten up robbery victims. It was possible they were still feeling just a wee bit guilty over the pink flamingo ornament trick they had played on the voyageurs, but they did not mention anything about that incident under the circumstances. Instead, they said, "OK, we will get your beaver pelts back for you."

Marie Candace saw that all ten voyageurs were well on the road to recovery. Then she said, "I am knowing these Bad Bobs and they are knowing me. It is best that I go alone to recover those valuable and stolen beaver pelts. The rest of you Maries stay here and keep an eye on our voyageur friends and make some tea and blueberry muffins for them. I will be back shortly."

Well, the Maries' one mind told them that Marie Candace knew exactly what she was talking about and could handle the Bad Bobs just fine on her very own.

Marie Candace could hold her own as far as tracking went. She hopped into her canoe and followed the trail left behind by the Bobs. Lucky for her, the water was as calm as could be and Marie just followed the trail of cigarette butts and empty chewing tobacco tins floating in the water. The trail led across the lake to the nearest campsite. Marie Candace landed at the campsite and saw all the Bobs gathered around drinking moonshine and counting stolen beaver pelts.

She said, "Howdy, y'all! Howdy, Billy Bob! Howdy, there Bobby Bob! How ya doin' there, Joe Bob? Say, what's up, Bert Bob? Hi there, Jimmy Bob! Y'all remember me?" She then spit and burped so they would accept her as a friend and one of their own.

Billy Bob, the spokesman for the Bad Bobs said, "Well, now, if it ain't Ms. Marie from the Backwoods Nursing Service. Been a mighty long time. Remember her, don't you Jimmy Bob? She's that nice nurse that took out all them shotgun pellets from your backside. And, Bobby Bob, ain't she the one what saved your life from that rattlesnake bite? Glad to see ya, Ms. Marie. What you doin' in these parts, anyhow?"

Marie Candace said, "Well, Bobs, I'm here to save your lives once again. You see, there is a turrable epidemic in these here parts. It's called Beaver Pelt Fever. It's carried by beaver pelts and it's mighty deadly."

Billy Bob looked scared and he said, "But we are all feelin' fine!"

Marie Candace answered, "Yup, I was afraid y'all would say that. That is the number one symptom of Beaver Pelt Fever. You feel so good, you just don't know you are even sick. Say, do you boys by chance have red dots all over your bodies?"

Billy Bob said, "Yup, sure do. We just figured them was skeeter bites."

Marie Candace shook her head slowly and said, "No, them what you got ain't no skeeter bites. Them is Beaver Fever welts. Bad sign. Real bad. Are y'all craving moonshine?"

Billy Bob, he said, "Well, yup, we always crave moonshine."

Marie Candace looked down at the ground and said, "Yup, that's how this particular fever goes. Makes you feel good, gives you red dots, and then it makes you crave moonshine so you will get drunk and not even know when the last, fatal symptom happens."

Billy Bob said, "What's that last fatal symptom, Ms. Marie?"

Marie Candace said, "You forgot what is the last symptom? Oh dear, that is a real bad sign. The last symptom before instant death is that you forget things and since you already forgot, I would say you boys are in real, real bad shape."

Billy Bob looked at the other Bobs and gulped, "Ain't there no cure to this here Beaver Fever?"

Marie Candace answered, "Grits! Grits is the only cure and the only place you can get decent grits is at Bessie Mae's Cafe back home. The quicker y'all can get there to Bessie Mae's, the better off you will be."

After hearing that, the Bobs all hopped into their green, leaking jonboat and rowed off as fast as they could go in a southeasterly direction, leaving Marie Candace behind at the campsite with big piles of stolen beaver pelts.

Marie Candace single-handedly loaded up the furs into her canoe and headed back across the lake. As she came close to the portage, she called out to the voyageurs, "Here are your beaver pelts!" The voyageurs all sighed in relief as they looked at the recovered pelts. Then they saw something in Marie Candace's hands. She carried two big clay jugs of moonshine that the Bob Boys left behind. The voyageurs stop sighing, stared hard at the jugs and started licking their lips. They said, "Hmm, are you Maries wanting those heavy and breakable jugs or would you be wanting us to take them off your hands for you?"

One by one, the Maries all shook their heads "no," they did not want any moonshine. When it came to Marie Sue, she was ready to say, "Yes, I'd like that!" Then she noticed the other Maries all giving her their special "say-'yes'-and-we'll-break-your-arm" looks. Marie Sue thought again and just said, "No, thanks," when she realized they were not talking about the moon making a shimmering path across the water at night. She had once heard about this other kind of moonshine and all the headaches it caused and decided the Voyageurettes had already had enough excitement in one day.

Marie Candace handed the voyageurs both big jugs of moonshine. One voyageur said, "Marie Candace, *mon cherie*, you have saved our lives with your medical skills and, now, by giving us this moonshine, you have made our saved lives worth living!"

The voyageurs all got busy at once. The healthiest one climbed atop the tallest nearby pine tree and chopped all the limbs off except for a tuft at the very top of the tree. Another voyageur carved the name "Marie Candace" at the base of the lobbed tree. The rest prepared a moonshine toast and a 21 gun salute for Marie Candace.

Lobbing a pine in honor of another person was the highest form of respect voyageurs could bestow upon another. From then on, everyone paddling near that lob pine was expected to stop and honor the very special and highly regarded person whose name appeared at its base.

If one happens to be paddling on Knife Lake and comes across the tree lobbed in honor of Marie Candace, one should make it a point to stop and pay homage and respect to the fine Voyageurette who saved the lives of ten voyageurs, single-handedly recovered all those stolen beaver pelts and who also made countless canoe trips safer by having rid the Canoe Country of the Bad Bob Boys.

Finally, the Maries and the voyageurs paddled off in separate directions. The voyageurs were, indeed, happy to be alive and to have two big jugs full of fine moonshine to celebrate the return of their stolen fur. The Maries were all very pleased and proud to be having a majestic "lob pine" named in honor of one of their very own. Marie Candace was especially happy to be away from the company of the Bob Boys and back with the Maries so she did not have to spit or burp anymore. It was thought by many that the Bob Boys were also very happy, indeed, to be headed back where they belonged and be forever cured of the dreaded Beaver Pelt Fever.

*Les voyageurs n'avaient jamais
vu de petite loups*

Voyageurs never see small wolves.

28

The Voyageurettes and "Le Colosse" (The Giant)

This old saying was indeed true. Voyageurs saw only big wolves, not because they were lying hard and bragging big, but because they were 'fraidy cats. Voyageurs were so afraid of wolves even small ones seemed big to them. The Voyageurettes were not afraid of anything, so to them wolves seemed small. It was the same with moose and bears. They all seemed small.

One day, however, they came across a strange animal. To them, it seemed small. Very small. That day the Maries had paddled thirty miles against the wind and made fifteen long portages. By noon they were a little tired and sore, mostly from sitting so long in the canoe. They found find a nice campsite and set up the Marie House. They were lying out on the smooth rocks at the water's edge sunbathing to even out their tans. That was when they heard something rustling around in the dense woods. It was headed in their direction.

The Voyageurettes all ran fast into the Marie House. It was not that they were afraid. They ran into the Marie House because each one of them happened to decide at the same time to get out of the sun's bright rays to avoid getting sunburned and overexposed to danger-ous and harmful ultra violet rays.

Pretty soon the rustling noise stopped. They heard something scampering around their campsite. Then they heard loud munching sounds. They peeked out of the Marie House and saw that something had opened their food pack and was eating their food. It was reddish brown, with black and white stripes upon its back. It was about two inches high and four inches long with an equally long tail which stood up straight in the air.

"Ooo," said Marie Margot. "Isn't that what Native People call *chetamon?*"

"Yes, they do," said Marie Rebecca. "It's *Tamias minimus*, the Least Chipmunk, one of two species commonly found here. The other is the Eastern Chipmunk, *Tamias striatus*, which is somewhat larger."

'What can we call it?" said Marie Chris. "The voyageurs always give things new names."

"How about The Giant One?" said Marie Sue. "You know how the men always twist names around, like calling the biggest voyageur in their brigade "Tiny." We can call this cute little tyke a giant!"

"Shh! While you are deciding what to call this invader, just look what he's doing!" said Marie Sarah. "He's already eaten half-way through our bag of trail snacks!"

Now, the Maries did not like the idea of any animal, small or big, eating up their food. Had it been a bear, they would have tried to shoo it away. This creature required a different tactic.

Marie Margot ran out first from the Marie House. She tried to grab the food pack away from The Giant One. She tugged and pulled to no avail. The rest of the Maries ran out to help. They grabbed on to Marie Margot and helped her pull. There were five of them and only one chipmunk. They pulled with all their combined strength, which was considerable. The Giant One pulled the other way with equally considerable strength. They pulled. They tugged. Their muscles were straining and burning. Blisters formed on their hands and on the chipmunk's paws. The tug of war went on for one hour. Then for two.

The chipmunk fell on his back in total exhaustion. Just as exhausted, the Maries fell over in a pile of arms and legs. They were all gasping and huffing and puffing for breath. The food pack just sat on the ground between them. It was a sight they were glad no one was there to see—the famous Voyageurettes unable to win a tug-of-war against a chipmunk. Of course, the chipmunk did not win either.

Finally, they all recovered sufficient strength to sit up. The Giant One crawled up on a log and sat there pouting. The Maries sat on another log facing him. They pouted, too. There were the Maries and the chipmunk staring at each other with the food between them. No one blinked. They just waited and watched for the other to dare make even the slightest move toward that food pack.

By now, the Maries were very hungry. So was The Giant One. His growling stomach sounded like faint and distant thunder. They decided to call a truce and to do the only logical and fair thing under the circumstances—share the food. The Maries found some beef stew in their pack. The chipmunk picked out rice, vegetables and some cracked wheat crackers. After they ate, they were all feeling better and were beginning to develop a little mutual respect for each other's strength and determination. The Maries brought out their kazoos and played a few tunes for The Giant One. He seemed to like their music. He twitched his tail in time to "Don't Fence Me In" and accidentally knocked over three hobble bushes. Then he entertained them by showing how fast he could scamper. Around and around the campsite he went in a big circle. The ground trembled as if an earthquake had struck, and the Marie House shook. The Voyageurettes were, indeed, impressed. Next, they showed him how they could skip rocks on top of the water. He showed them how he could crack nuts with his teeth and store them in his cheek-pouches. Then they modeled for him some of their color-coordinated outfits. He politely watched and patted his front feet on the ground. He showed how he could chirp loud and twitch his nose fast at the same time. They applauded him.

The Maries were becoming good friends with The Giant One. They popped a big batch of popcorn and shared it with him, one kernel for him and one for each of them, until it was all gone. Finally, it was getting dusk and well past the time for him to go back to his burrow among the rocks in the woods. It had been a most enjoyable experience for them all. When The Giant One looked at the Voyageurettes to say good-bye, he had a tear in his eye. They could tell he was as sad to leave them as they were sad to see him go. He stood up tall and put one paw behind his back and the other in front of his waist and, as a sign of friendship and respect, he gave them a most stately and chivalrous bow. The Maries honored him with their most dainty and graceful curtsies they had learned from Marie Margot. Then he was gone—scurrying off into the dense underbrush.

The Maries decided not to wait until morning. They quickly packed up and left that campsite. It was not that they did not want to see The Giant One again, but rather that they were thinking he might come back with his friends and relatives for a visit and they were running low on their food supply. By nightfall, they were several lakes away sitting around the campfire discussing the day's adventure.

Marie Sarah said, "Since The Giant One knew exactly how to unbuckle food packs and to bow and applaud, he has obviously been around canoe campers before."

Marie Chris agreed. "Don't you wonder why it is that no one has ever before told of seeing this Giant Chipmunk in the Canoe Country?"

Marie Margot said, "Oh, that is probably because people are scared that no one else would believe they had seen it and they would be teased."

Marie Sue said, "I can understand that! We Maries, too, should keep quiet about our encounter with the Giant One, especially the part about the tug-of-war that we could not win."

Marie Rebecca said, "No, no! We should swallow our pride, tell the truth, and be the first in the Canoe Country to admit seeing the Giant Chipmunk, *Tamias ginormous*. It is a truth needing to be told. Once we Maries admit to seeing The Giant One, others who have seen him will also come forth. Who is better to tell the truth first than the brave, courageous, greatly admired and respected, humble Maries?"

Marie Sarah said, "Just maybe we can gain something from this experience. We can make up nice commemorative Giant Chipmunk T-shirts and caps and sell them for a profit."

Well, they all pondered whether the Voyageurettes should be like all the others who have sighted The Giant One and keep quiet, or should be the ones to break the ice and tell of their encounter with that chipmunk. They voted. Marie Sue voted to tell the truth about seeing the Giant Chipmunk, but to lie and say the Maries won the tug-of-war. The other four Maries voted to tell the true and complete story.

From that moment on, the Voyageurettes always looked forward to seeing chipmunks at every campsite. They were never disappointed. Successive generations of the Giant One knew of the Maries' generosity in doling out tasty snacks well before nightfall. It was no longer necessary for chipmunks to have tugs-of-war with *les femmes du Nord* over food packs. And through the brisk sales of "I've Seen

The Giant One" T-shirts and caps, the Voyageurettes financed their canoe adventures for three more years.

Soon afterward there were many people admitting to having seen the Giant One. To this day numerous reports of additional Giant One sightings continue. And it is not unusual for people to get Giant One pictures — just as they do of Bigfoot.

Un travail bien fait porte sa propre récompense, que la renommée s'ensuive ou non.

Good work is its own reward. Fame will follow, or not.

29

Undercover Drug Agents

One day the Maries were paddling along, fighting a 53 mile an hour wind on the South Arm of Knife Lake. They were each working too hard at paddling to even talk much. Being of one mind, though, they did not need to say many words in order to communicate. They just knew what the others were thinking.

Marie Candace started off by thinking, "It's a nasty business, that's for sure. Ruining the health of the younger generation, destroying families, undermining values, corrupting communities and leading to the downfall of our society."

Marie Sarah added, "Yes, it is and we Maries should do something about it."

Marie Chris said, "Ah, it would be dangerous, but we can handle it."

Marie Margot chimed in, "Marie Rebecca can be in charge of the training."

Marie Rebecca thought she could handle it. With that, they turned their canoes around and headed for a campsite to begin their new careers as undercover drug agents.

Marie Rebecca started a condensed, fast-track training session. She taught the Voyageurettes all they needed to know for their new job assignments. They learned how to spot drug dealers, how to spy on them and how to apprehend them. After two prolonged hours of intense training, the Maries appointed themselves Official Volunteer Undercover Drug Agents and were ready to go, and none too soon either.

Marie Ramona spotted suspicious activity on the other side of the lake. Canoe after canoe paddled up to a tent on a small, wooded island. They stayed only a few minutes and were gone. Marie Rebecca said it was probably a drug dealer's crack cocaine tent they were looking at. They got out their spy glasses and sure enough, the paddlers got out and handed what looked like money to the man in front of the tent. Then they all went into the tent for a couple of minutes and left, carrying a small packet.

The Voyageurettes quickly covered their faces with soot from the fire grate, cut thick reeds big enough to breathe from and swam underwater to the drug island. They climbed ashore at the back side of the island and darted zig-zag from tree to tree until they came within earshot of the tent. What they saw and heard stunned them. All of them stood with their mouths open, too shocked to even say one word. The drug dealer they saw was Father Jean Pierre Baptiste.

Right then, along came a canoe. Three people got out. Father Jean Pierre Baptiste greeted them and invited them into the tent for confession. When they gave Father some money, he put it into his little wooden box, folded his hands and said, "Thank you very much for your contribution to the Children's Mission School. As a token of my appreciation, please accept this little gift in return." He then handed out packets with rosaries inside.

Well, the Maries were greatly relieved to find it was religious activity rather than drug activity. They decided to sneak back to their camp. Not that they did not want to contribute to Father Jean Pierre Baptiste's school, but having to sit through another confession with Father Baptiste was at the absolute bottom of their list of preferred things to do that day.

Just then, Marie Margot went, "AH CHOO!" very loud because she had caught a little sniffle from the swim in the cold water. Father spotted them. He was very happy to see the Voyageurettes, even though their faces were covered with soot and they were all dripping wet.

He said, "Oh, dear, dear Maries, it's you! How can I ever thank you for suggesting I relocate my mission and meet people at the point of their need? Can you believe all these new parishioners? Bless you for dropping by to make a contribution to my mission school and for coming to make confession again so soon!"

They were caught. They dug into their pockets for some shiny new coins and put them into the box by the tent. Father gave each of them a beautiful "thank you rosary" in a little leather pouch. The Voyageurettes knew just what to do because they remembered what Marie Sarah had taught them about saying the Rosary. Out came the beads and the cross on a string. Click, click click went the beads as the Maries' fingers flew top speed around the string. They did not leave out anything as they said all the prayers silently to themselves. They remembered the happy, sad and glorious Mysteries and did not skip even one word of the "Apostles' Creed," the "Our Father," the "Hail Mary," the "Glory Be To the Father," and the "Hail, Holy Queen" prayers or forget to make the sign of the cross. Saying the Rosary helped. Their prayers were immediately answered. A canoe full of nuns paddled up, right at the moment Father was ready to usher them into the tent for confession. Father was beside himself with happiness to see a whole boatload of religious colleagues.

The Maries said, "Oh, Father, you must go greet your friends and spend time with them talking about important things. Don't worry about us. We'll just be on our way. Catch you later!"

Father Jean Pierre Baptiste said, "Oh, Maries, blessings upon you dear souls! You are so considerate and thoughtful."

They quickly headed back to their camp to dry out around the fire. They did not say anything to each other. Their one mind was telling them their first drug bust was, indeed, a bust. They were not discouraged. They decided what they needed now was a drug-sniffing dog.

Off they paddled to the nearest settlement of two cabins where there were plenty of dogs. They picked out a big black one named Shaman with a large nose for sniffing. They headed out - six trained Official Volunteer Undercover Drug Agents and one drug-sniffing canine. Drug dealers beware! They knew they were on a roll now. It wasn't ten minutes before they came across a party of canoes. As they paddled near, the dog went "sniff, sniff." Then he went, "bark, bark." Ah, ha! Drugs for sure!

Marie Chris said, "What those drug dealers won't do to disguise themselves. Look, they are all dressed up like girl guides."

Marie Ramona had been a leader of girl guides and knew all about them. She was livid. She said, "I'm just livid. Drug dealing is bad enough, but to hide behind girl guide uniforms is even nastier."

They paddled up to the canoes, ready to identify themselves as Official Volunteer Undercover Drug Agents, when they spotted what the dog had sniffed. It was a little white and brown dog sleeping in the bottom of one of the canoes. The dog had not found drugs at all. He had found a sweetheart. Lucky for the Maries, they had not identified themselves so they did not have to weasel out of an embarrassing situation. They said, "Cute dog you have there," and quickly paddled off.

An hour or two later, they came across two rough-looking men. Drug dealers, for sure. They followed the two men to the next portage. As they carried their canoe across the portage, the men left one of their packs unattended. It was sitting on the shore patiently waiting for the men to return. The dog walked over to the pack. "Sniff, sniff," he went and then started ripping into the pack with his paws and teeth. The Maries ran over to see the stash of drugs the dog had uncovered. But they did not move fast enough. The pack was a food pack, now minus a slab of bacon that was already in the dog's stomach. The Maries did manage to save a package of salt pork.

Just then the men came back. The Maries said, "Halloo, gentlemen! We just rescued most of your food from this dog of yours. Too bad, we could not save your bacon."

The men said, "That dog is not ours. He must be a stray. Thank you so much for saving our food!"

The Maries said, "Oh, the poor dog. A stray, eh? Perhaps we will take him with us and try to find him a good home."

The men give the ladies a gift of the salt pork for saving their food. They left with the men thinking they were very noble to rescue their food as well as being kind-hearted enough to try to find a good home for a stray dog. Another drug bust gone bust, but still the Maries are not discouraged.

Off they paddled once again in search of drug dealers. They hit the jackpot late that afternoon. It was the last portage of the day. On the portage were two seedy-looking men. Drug dealers, for sure. They even had scruffy drug dealer beards and squinty eyes. The dog went "sniff, sniff," then "bark, bark." He grabbed their pack and ran off into the woods with the Maries chasing after him and the two drug dealers chasing after them. They all caught up with the dog. The pack flopped open. Out came small bags of dried mushrooms, white powder and crushed leaves and seeds, funny-looking pipes and a set of scales. In a flash, the two men were face down on the ground with their hands tied up with basswood string. One man said, "You ladies have made a big mistake. We are both undercover agents! These drugs and paraphernalia are evidence for a big case we're working on!"

Ha! The Maries did not fall for that one! Marie Rebecca said, "OK, show us your ID."

The men each pulled a card and badge out of their pockets. Marie Rebecca said, "Well, they do look authentic, but they could be just good fakes. To prove you are really drug agents, you wouldn't mind answering a few questions, would you?"

The men said, "Fine, ask away."

She ask, "OK, who is the Constable in this county?"

The men said, "Well, that is Jean Melvin Baptiste. We are good friends of his. In fact, in April we were at his office for a meeting with him.

Then Marie Margot ask, "Did you go to the Agents' Convention at Fort Detroit last December?"

Both men said, "Yes, we were there."

Marie Margot said, "What did you do there?"

The men said they attended seminars and one night all the agents got free tickets for "The Nutcracker."

The Maries had heard enough. They got into a huddle to discuss what to do next. Marie Rebecca said, "I think they are telling the truth. We know Constable Jean Melvin. Marie Margot agreed. She said, "Last December I was lead ballerina in "The Nutcracker" and do remember putting on a performance for the Agents' Convention."

The Maries decided the men were telling the truth and let them go. The men were not angry. In fact, they are very happy that they were finally believed and that the Maries had not tied them up too tightly.

Then one man said, "Maries, I have something serious and important to share with you. Being a drug agent is very dangerous work. Not that you can't handle it. But did you ever think what would happen if you were involved in a paddle-by-shooting? Marie Tricia, your pretty pink canoe would be filled with holes. Marie Margot, what would happen if some drug dealer busted your kneecaps? You could no longer do beautiful ballet dancing. Marie Sue, if something happened to you, who would guide the Maries back to the settlement? All you Maries, if something happened to you, who would be around to rescue children, advise priests and do all manner of good things for other people?

Well, the man did have did have a point, but not enough of a point to discourage the Maries. Then the other agent said, "You are all trained, sure. But you do not have the proper drug agent equipment. You see, we have steel-plated canoes. We have bullet-proof life jackets. We have real identification cards with real badges, not like yours made of silver-colored paper. We even have a secret smoke signal system to call for backup."

The men were trying their best, but it was still not enough to deter the Maries from their commitment.

Then one agent said, "OK, Maries, the bottom line is this. If you continue being undercover agents and catch all the bad people, the two of us will be without jobs. We both have wives and eight children each. Without work, we could not feed, clothe and educate our children."

Those words touched the hearts and mind of the Maries. Right then and there, they decided to give up undercover work. They could not bear the thought of two desperate wives and sixteen hungry, uneducated children in rags. They told the men they were no longer drug agents and they could relax.

Everyone walked along the portage together, except for Marie Margot. She carried a canoe and leaped from rock to rock, with an occasional twirl, ahead of everyone else. She got to the end of the portage first. By the time the agents and the Maries caught up with her, she was bent over a strange man who was lying face-up on the ground. Marie Margot was shouting, "Wake up, sir."

Everyone rushed over to see what was happening. The man was just regaining consciousness, when one of the agents said, "It's him! It's him!"

It seemed Marie Margot had twisted her ankle on a rock while carrying her canoe. The canoe went flying through the air and landed right on the head of that poor man, knocking him out cold. The man, it ended up, was one of the drug cartel leaders on the agents' Most Wanted List.

The Voyageurettes decided to let the agents take full credit for the arrest instead of them, since they were now retired. With this major arrest, the two agents were very likely to be promoted and receive a nice salary increase which they both needed with all those children to support. The agents were both very happy to get full credit for successfully resolving this case. The Maries were happy, too, especially since the bust was an accident.

That evening, the Maries sat around cooking supper and reflected on their one big day as Official Volunteer Undercover Drug Agents. They participated in the capture of a leading drug dealer and helped two agents get promoted. They each got a nice new rosary from Father Jean Pierre Baptiste and, at the same time, successfully eluded another confession. They also got a gift package of salt pork. And they had a nice dog to accompany them for a few days until they could find him a suitable new home.

They decided they should take the following day off and paddle to the L'Spurr Convenient Trading Post down the river. Perhaps one might think they wanted to get steel plating for their canoes and bullet-proof life jackets. No. The truth was they wanted to go to L'Spurr for a "fix." Their stressful day as drug agents had caused them to develop slight tremors and deep-seated cravings that they could not ignore. They were going to L'Spurr for chips and dip, pop, cupcakes, chocolate candy and, if there were any in stock, gourmet ice cream bars.

*Prenez garde aux ours 'roses'
dans les bois.*

Beware of pink bears in the woods.

30

The Purse-snatching Bear

One day, while they were paddling on Lake Insula, the Voyageurettes were happily following along behind Marie Sue in the lead canoe. Being a proud leader, Marie Sue was not at all inclined to let the rest of the group know what was on her mind.

"Why ruin their happy mood?" she thought.

So she just paddled along, acting as if she knew exactly where she was going. After a couple of days, the other Maries grew suspicious.

They said, "Marie Sue, could it be we are a little turned around?"

Marie Sue said, "No, I know exactly where we are." That was the truth. Marie Sue did know. They were on a lake between two islands. Where the islands and the lake were on the map was beside the point.

Three days later the Voyageurettes asked, "Marie Sue, show us exactly on the map where we are."

Marie Sue said, "I can not do that. Where we are going is a surprise."

The Maries asked no more questions. They would paddle anywhere, for any length of time, for a surprise. Marie Sue was hoping if they paddled long enough, she might just see something familiar. So they paddled and portaged for another day.

Late that afternoon the fog rolled in. The Maries made camp on a small island. While they were busy collecting firewood, purifying water and fixing their supper of turkey jerky, Acadian coush-coush, boudins (blood sausage), stewed apricots, strawberry cheesecake, sugared tarts and pralines, they got the giggles-loud, raucous and uncontrollable giggles.

From out of the fog bank a voice called, "Marie Sue, is that you?"

Marie Sue answered, "Yes, and that voice of yours, who is it belonging to?"

The voice said, "E-laine Mil-ler!"

Marie Sue could not believe her ears. She whispered to the rest of the Maries, "Elaine Miller, you all know of her because I am always talking about her and saying what a wuuunderful person she is."

Yes, the Maries knew of her and had been waiting to meet her for a long time. They were excited and called through the fog to her, "Elaine, come on over and have supper and giggle with us."

Elaine called back, "I'm on the porch of my cabin. Why don't you come over here instead?"

In a flash they packed up and paddled toward the voice. On the way to the cabin the other Maries said to Marie Sue, "So, this was the surprise-a trip to Lake Vermillion to see Elaine Miller. How nice!"

Marie Sue could have lied and said, "Yes, I have been planning this visit all along!" Or she could have told the truth, which was that she was lost and stumbled upon Elaine quite by accident. She did neither. All she said was, "Let's paddle faster."

The Maries landed and found all was not well with Elaine. Her leg was broken. But in her usual spirit, she said, "Well, at least I can hop on my good leg."

And how she did hop—down to the dock, up the steps, and around her cabin. So well did she hop, in fact, the rest of the ladies had trouble keeping up with her.

Elaine told the story of her predicament. She paddled home after babysitting with her grandchildren. At the dock, she had been mugged. A 375 lb. bear grabbed her purse, pushed her down hard and ran off, carrying her favorite deerskin purse and all her important papers. On her good leg she hopped after him, but after a four mile pursuit through the woods, the bear escaped. Hop, hop, home she came, just in time to hear the Maries giggling through the fog. She was very lucky they were nearby.

Their first thought was to go right then after that bear, but Elaine was all hopped out and needed immediate medical attention and rest. So the Maries spent the night to help Elaine. First, they fixed up her leg with a walking cast. Then they helped chase off a beaver that had been chewing on her mailbox post. They dusted her cabin inside and out, swatted mosquitos and helped her eat up the food in her cabin.

The next morning about 4:00 a.m. a brigade of twenty-eight voyageurs came to the door. They dropped in to visit with Elaine who was a good friend of all the voyageurs and always had coffee and caramel rolls ready for them. The Voyageurettes could not hold themselves back. They had to tell the voyageurs what was going on.

"You must listen to this! Elaine got mugged yesterday by a rogue bear. He pushed her down hard on her own dock and she got a broken leg out of the whole deal. Besides, he got away with her purse. We've got to do something about it!" they said.

The voyageurs thought the Voyageurettes were teasing and did not believe a word. Ha! Of course, Elaine verified the story. Her, they believed. Everyone knew Elaine Miller was completely, totally and 100% truthful—a unique quality among the voyageurs and Voyageurettes of the Canoe Country.

When the voyageurs realized what had really happened to Elaine, they clenched their fists and their faces turned red. Then they growled, which was a sign that they were, indeed, very angry. They said, "Dear Elaine, you stay right here. Don't hop around. And do not worry. We will spread the word of what has happened to you to all the voyageurs from Montreal to Lake Athabasca and from the Gulf of Mexico to Hudson Bay. That purse-snatcher won't get away with this! Especially not with all 5,000 voyageurs out looking for him!"

The Maries were already packing up to go on the bear hunt. Then the voyageurs said, "OK, Maries. We are needing you to form a search party on Lake Insula. You must know that area well by now. We heard you spent all last week paddling in circles around that place. If we did not know any better, we would think you were lost, ha, ha."

The Maries and Elaine all looked at Marie Sue, waiting for a reply. Marie Sue would not say anything. She just gazed up at the ceiling and hummed Christmas carols to herself. Then she stuck her pointing fingers in her ears. The other Maries and Elaine were of one mind and that one mind was telling them Marie Sue was in no mood whatsoever to discuss the subject any further.

All the Maries did not go hunting for the bear that day. Marie Sue stayed with Elaine on Lake Vermillion, which was the right and proper thing to do. Someone had to watch Elaine and make sure she did not over-hop.

It did not take long to locate the bear. Within an hour, the Voyageurettes had followed its tracks through the woods and found it sitting quietly at the base of a jack pine, amusing itself by pawing through the contents of Elaine Miller's special deerskin purse.

The Voyageurettes called out, "OK, guys, you can come out now, it is safe! We have caught the bear red-pawed! Maybe you big and strong cavalier voyageurs, who have been following us through these dark and scary woods for five miles, could help us get this bear back to the cabin."

Twenty-eight voyageurs peeked out from behind the trees and rushed over to help. They put the bear in a wire cage they had brought with them and carried it back to Elaine. They brought the bear up on Elaine's porch so she could see him up close.

She said, "That's the one, that's the one! I'd know him anywhere!"

The voyageurs said, "Elaine, would you like us to make this bear into a bearskin rug or do you want to do it yourself?"

The bear shook his head, "No, no."

Elaine said, "No, that punishment is too harsh and a bit premature. I have a better idea. I will do something simple to distinguish that bear from all others."

The bear shook his head, "Yes, yes."

Elaine found an aerosol can of paint on her pantry shelf and sprayed that bear as pink as Marie Margot's ballet slippers, except for his nose. She left that part black. Then she spoke sharply, "OK, you rascal! Now you are the only pink bear in this vast expanse of woods and water-ways. If I ever hear of a pink bear snatching purses or taking anything which does not belong to it, I will know it is you up to your old tricks. I'll get the word out far and wide and you, my furry friend, will be caught once again. Then we will see how you like spending eternity as a pink bearskin rug in front of someone's fireplace!"

The bear ran off fast, never to be seen again, at least not that anyone has heard. But just in case, in the meantime, it would be wise to follow the maxim: "*Prenez garde aux ours 'roses' dans les bois.* Beware of pink bears in the woods."

Le chemin le plus court pour atteindre la coeur d'une personne passe par l'estomac.

The fastest (quickest) way to a person's heart is through her stomach.

31

The Cajun Marie

Early one morning Marie Sue heard the other Maries muttering something about wanting to revisit Lake Insula for a bowl of steaming hot oatmeal. Marie Sue immediately decided to hop into her canoe and paddle off quickly before the other Maries could firm up their plans. The other Maries followed her, thinking she was paddling fast over to Lake Insula for a nutritious, stick-to-the-ribs, oatmeal breakfast. They did not know Marie Sue was headed due south, leading the Maries far, far away from Insula. The truth was Marie Sue did not originally intend for the Maries to go quite as far south as they actually did, but going so fast, they were not able to stop. A few days later the hardy band of Voyageurettes found themselves in the bayous of Louisiana.

By that time, the other Maries were too hot in the 105 degree temperature with 98 per cent humidity to be wanting any hot oatmeal for breakfast. They were far too preoccupied by looking out for alligators to feel sad that they were not on Lake Insula. Marie Sue was thinking the heat, humidity and alligators were nothing compared to having to eat oatmeal on Lake Insula.

As the Maries were taking a short break, sitting on a grassy hummock swatting mosquitos and taking a short break, a nice-appearing

Cajun lady came walking by. Everyone was impressed. Even from far away, the Maries could not help but notice the seven full shopping bags the lady carried effortlessly in her arms. As she came closer, they saw her wide pleasant smile and a twinkle in her eyes. All of the Voyageurettes smiled back. She stopped in her tracks in front of the line of resting Maries and said, "Hi, there! My name is Tina. Are y'all lost?"

Marie Sue answered, "Oh, no, we are not lost at all. It is just that we overextended our destination by a few thousand miles."

Tina, the Cajun lady said, "Y'all must be from up north. I can tell because of your accent and funny way of talking."

The Maries told her they were, indeed, canoeists who came from far up north and introduced themselves, one by one.

Tina said, "I've always wanted to go paddling up north. The only problem is that I haven't done much canoeing; but, I can lie hard, shop hard and I don't eat dogs."

All of the Maries knew at that moment that Tina would fit right in and decided to invite her along on their summer voyage and introduce her to the Canoe Country Wilderness up north. She packed her bags fast, hopped in the canoe and they all paddled up the Mississippi River together. The Voyageurettes began to like this Cajun Tina very much.

Now when they arrived in the Northwoods, Tina underwent a period of adjustment. She was not used to the Northwoods at all. She was used to the Southwoods with armadillos, alligators and poisonous water snakes. It took the Voyageurettes a few days to teach her the difference between the two woods. She said, "Y'all sure have a lot of lazy armadillos around here." She did not know that what she saw were just shiny brown rocks.

She said, "Y'all have some pretty weird ducks up here with crazy voices." She did not yet know about loons.

After carrying heavy packs and canoes across a rough 180-rod portage, Tina said that she did not know about having to make such a strenuous walk in the woods. "I heard them talking about a 180 rod portage this morning, but I had no idea they would be crazy enough to actually take it!" she said.

But Tina learned fast. She learned that rocks are rocks and not lazy armadillos and loons are not weird ducks and that 500 rod portages are not portages with 500 paces. She learned that when she paddled in the bow of the canoe and Marie Candace said, "Paddle backwards, Tina," that did not mean for her to turn around in the canoe seat and paddle forward while sitting in a backwards position.

After only two days in the woods, the Maries' jobs as teachers for Tina were over. Tina had become a true Timber Savage Outdoors Woman. She was able to spot loons from far across the lake, watch for signs of bears and moose and tell the difference between rocks and armadillos. She soon acquired the skill of making the paddle work right and doing the "J", "C", sweep, pry, draw and bow rudder strokes. She learned to portage the canoe. She found out how to make the camp stove work, how to purify water, find the way with a map and compass and check out good places to camp and pitch the tent. She became knowledgeable about all the ways of the Canoe Country. After a few days, the Voyageurettes proudly baptized her Marie Tina Marie. The Marie tacked on after the Tina part was because Marie was already her real middle name.

Once she became a full-fledged Marie with all the privileges and liberties going with that title, Tina began to act like a true Marie. She began to taunt the rest of her fellow Voyageurettes for their ignorance of important things, like Cajun ways. She told the Voyageurettes they needed lessons on how to talk right and keep their eyes open for all wildlife, not just armadillos. She also said the Maries need to learn to eat right.

Lessons in speaking correctly were not difficult for the Maries seeing that the Cajuns are also of French descent. They practiced saying "Dew Saw," for Marie Tina's former hometown of Duson, Louisiana. The Maries practiced saying Cajun words that Tina taught them, words like "french fries" and "french toast". She had them practice their "y'all's" over and over again until they got it right. Then one night Marie Tina Marie said it was time for the Voyageurettes' to learn to eat crawfish, or in Cajun words, "mud bugs." Now, the Maries' acquaintance with food from the water consisted of just plain fish; for example, walleyes, northerns, lake trout and bass. To them, crawdads were something to put on the end of their fishhooks instead of in their mouths. While Marie Tina went off hunting for crawfish, the rest of the Maries conferred about this serious matter of soon having to eat crawdads with little pincers, skinny legs and crunchy bodies. They decided that since Marie Tina had made such a successful effort to learn their ways, they should, perhaps, make the same effort to learn some of her Cajun ways.

Marie Margot said, "I will eat the crawdads and, if they taste bad, maybe I will put a clothespin on my nose to kill the taste and just tell Marie Tina that is the way I always eat seafood."

Marie Candace said, "Eating crawdads will not be hard for me because I am a great lover of almost anything edible."

Marie Rebecca said, "Eating crawfish will be easy for me because I think of them as petite lobsters."

Marie Sue said absolutely nothing. She quietly harbored a deep thought. A big bowl of oatmeal did not sound too bad after all.

Soon, Marie Tina Marie came back to camp with three pounds of crawfish. She picked out the meat from the tails and cooked it in a special sauce of secret ingredients. She poured the crawfish and the secret sauce over cooked fettucini. The Maries watched carefully as Marie Tina took the first bite. They watched and waited for her to grab her throat and keel over in a state of unconsciousness. Instead, she smiled her big happy smile and made her eyes sparkle and said, "Y'all dig in and eat!" They'all did! After just one bite they found out that crawfish prepared Cajun-style was the best food they had ever eaten. The only things that tasted better were the second and third helpings they'all had.

When the Maries first started their voyages many years ago, they were Midwesterners with Midwestern speech and Midwestern cultural tendencies. Then, with the influence of the Eastern Maries, the Voyageurettes assumed a slight New England twist to their speech and thought patterns. Now, with the addition of Cajun Marie Tina Marie, they were a multi-cultural group. Next summer when the Maries gather for their adventure, they will be having a big Fourth of July Celebration at their campsite. The afternoon will be spent looking for armadillos. For suppah, they will be having Cajun-style crawfish, New England style baked beans and bannock with pure maple syrup, and for dessert, some bars made from a recipe out of the Prairie Farmer cookbook. When it gets dark, they will light up some sparklers.

*Derrière chaque grand homme,
il y a une grande femme.*

The Great White Father may do some good,
with guidance from great women.

32

The Voyageurettes Go to Washington, D.C.

The Voyageurettes had just finished their lunch and were taking a short mid-day break on a small island in Rainy Lake. They unfolded their woven reed sit-upons, put them on the bare granite ledge and stretched out on their backs.

"Too bad the sun is shining so brightly," said Marie Sue, "or I could be using my sextant to determine our longitude and latitude and keep track of our progress in my journal for posterity. I know the stars are out there somewhere."

"We will have to be gazing at something else besides stars this time of day," said Marie Chris. "We can always try to figure out what shapes the clouds are making. You know, that one right above us looks like the face of an old man!"

Their rest period was interrupted by the sound of shouting coming from across the lake. The shouting got louder and louder. Ma-rie! Ma-rie! Yoo hoo, Ma-rie!" Soon the Voyageurettes could see a whole brigade of voyageurs, about one hundred of them, paddling at top speed toward them.

"Halloo, wuuunderful ladies! We are so 'appy to see your big smiles and the rest of you, too!" said the *avant*. "We need your help for a ve-ry special reason. I am telling you all about it."

He explained that all the voyageurs had just been requested to go to Washington, D.C. as soon as possible. A man called James had invited them. His father's name was Mr. Smith, so they called him "Smith's son." James had a warehouse in Washington. It was huge. For James, it was like an attic where he kept his own treasures and the treasures and artifacts of just about everyone else. Around Washington it was a landmark that people called "Smith's Son's Place." It was a real institution. James was planning to have a big gathering to honor living legends. Already Mr. Smith's Son had invited native people, explorers, frontiersmen and voyageurs to come for seminars and a special ceremony to receive the first annual, "Shaping of North America" Award.

Jean Emanuel Baptiste, the *avant*, explained that the voyageurs simply could not go. It was the height of their busy season. Also, they were not sophisticated enough to go to festivities with powerful and influential people.

"Oh, *Monsieur l'Avant! C'est pas correcte!* That is not true! You voyageurs are so handsome, charming and beguiling! Of course, you can go to this place and mingle with the people and you would get along just fine!" the Voyageurettes protested.

He said, "No, no, Maries! Just look at me. Both of my front teeth are missing because of a fight. Look at Ignace over there with part of his nose bitten off and back there is Gabriel. He is missing an ear from fighting. Please Maries, would you go as our representatives? You have time on your hands and are not afraid to say what is on your mind. We would be too shy in that situation. So, if for us you will go, we will be very grateful."

The Maries looked over their beloved voyageur friends. They looked at Jean Emanuel and his missing teeth, and his voyageurs with bitten off noses and ears and agreed that they might not make the absolute best impression among Washingtonians. The Voyageurettes looked at their pleading big brown eyes. It is well-known that the voyageurs were great charmers and, for that brief moment, the Maries were not immune to the spell they cast. After all, they were friends. They always teased and pestered each other at every available opportunity. But, when either was in a real pinch, there wasn't anything in the world they would not do for each other. This time the voyageurs were in a pinch.

The Voyageurettes agreed to go. The very next day, they paddled off to Washington, D.C. as fast as they could. They made one very long portage over to the Mississippi River and south they went. They turned left and went up the Ohio River and kept going until they came to the

Monongahela and followed it upstream to the very end. Then they portaged up and down many hills and valleys until they found the beginning of the Potomac River. Down the Potomac they paddled until they came to a place called Mount Vernon where a friendly white-haired man waved them over to the boat dock. He gave them good directions. They paddled downriver for a few minutes longer and portaged their canoes one more time to a little pond not far from a white house in the middle of a large green pasture. The Voyageurettes set up their Marie House and made themselves comfortable.

The next morning the presidential carriage took them to the event over at Mr. Smith's Son's Place where a crowd had already gathered. The President and the First Lady were there in the front row along with members of Congress and some other men wearing black gowns. Regular people made up the rest of the audience.

Panel discussions were first. The panel members had to introduce themselves and tell where they came from and what their life back home was like. Panel members all agreed that the places where they lived and roamed were the most beautiful and interesting of all. The native people described the woodlands, prairies, rolling hills and high mountain country that they knew so well. They called the earth their mother and everything in it their brothers and sisters. The explorers and frontiersmen captivated the crowd with descriptions of immense river systems which were perfect for getting from one place to another. They told about all the wildlife they had seen in their travels. They said this huge continent may look a little empty at the moment, but it held great potential for the future. When it was the Voyageurettes' turn, they told about the voyageurs' role in the fur trade and how that was important in strengthening the economy. They told how the voyageurs helped explore, chart and settle the great North Woods and how they sometimes fought along with soldiers in a few wars. They explained that the voyageurs were strong, brave, tireless workers and, if other people followed their example, there was no challenge or problem so great that could not be overcome. Then the Voyageurettes made a special request of the President, members of Congress and the men in black gowns. They asked them to not ever forget the way things are in this beautiful, immense land. Parts of it deserve to stay wild, untamed and special, as it is now. And could they please do something about it before it was too late. The audience was spellbound.

Next came demonstrations. The native people demonstrated a sampling of their many special skills: shaping arrowheads and spear points, constructing shelters and houses out of natural materials and skins. Frontiersmen demonstrated their expertise in hatchet-throwing and musket shooting. The Voyageurettes showed the Washingtonians a thing or two: how to paddle in formation and how to carry 90 pound packs and run at the same time.

Next came dancing. Men of the frontier danced jigs and the native people showed the audience their ceremonial hoop dances. On behalf of the Voyageurs, Marie Margot did an enchanting rendition of her famous "Danse du Nord" with a canoe on her shoulders.

At last, the potluck supper was ready to be served. The native people had fixed beans, corn, squash, pumpkins, hominy and wild rice, which everyone liked. There were platters of corn bread, dried fish, venison pie, stewed pigeon, bison *boudin*, (which everyone liked until they found out what the ingredients were), and pots of rabbit stew. The voyageurs' favorite, *rubbaboo*, with beavertails and turtle meat added for extra flavor, bubbled in a kettle over the fire.

The evening featured the participants and audience singing together around the campfire accompanied by fiddles and harmonicas. The frontiersmen did a cappella numbers about two of their own, Davey Crockett and Daniel Boone, plus a beautiful rendition of "The Bear Went Over the Mountain." The native people presented chants accompanied by flutes and drums and the Maries sang "A La Claire Fontaine" and "En Roulant Ma Boule" with Marie Jackie playing the kazoo.

The closing ceremony featured the presentation of a "Shaping of North America" plaque to every group. Then the President himself gave a gold Itty Bitty flashy light to each participant.

After the ceremony, the people of Washington wanted everyone to stay for a few more days so they could show them around town. The President graciously invited the Voyageurettes to stay over as special guests at the White House and to teach him and the First Lady how to paddle a canoe the next morning. The Maries hated to disappoint the fine folks of Washington, but they had been away from the Canoe Country long enough. They needed to get back. But before they left, the Maries asked the President for a special favor.

"Could we please have 5,000 more Itty Bitty flashy lights engraved to take back for our friends and kindred spirits, the voyaguers? Engraving would be easy," they explained to the President. "Just make up 5,000 under a government contract and write the name Jean Baptiste on half of them. We will take care of personalizing the other half."

Early the next morning, the Itty Bitty flashy lights were delivered to their Marie House and the Voyageurettes went on their way. Once they got back to the North Woods, the voyageurs were so very glad to see them. The Maries presented the bourgeois with the coveted "Shaping of North America" plaque and gave each of the voyageurs his very own engraved light. Their eyes filled with tears. They said, "Maries, we are forever in your debt. Please tell us how we can repay you?'

The Maries' request was simple. "You can not pester or tease us for one full year! How about it?"

The voyageurs groaned and shook their heads. A whole year without teasing? Finally, they said, "Can we talk about this? How about agreeing to "many days" or "a long time" without teasing? We could go along with that." The voyageurs stuck to their promise. It was a nice quiet two weeks for the Maries.

Legend has it that the voyaguers always carried their prized possessions in leather bags tied around their waists with strings. It is well-known that they carried such things as rosaries, packets of tobacco and other valuables inside. This is true. The bags also held their Itty Bitty flashy lights.

Adventurers from all over the world come to the Canoe Country. Many parts of this vast land and waterways are now designated as parks and protected wilderness areas. People often say that this came about because of the efforts of environmental activists and forward-looking people. This is indeed true. The Voyageurettes would like to think their good-will trip to Washington on behalf of the voyageurs played a small part in setting aside and preserving special places for the enjoyment of everyone. It is possible that the Great Father in Washington may do some good, with inspiration and guidance from great women.

Il ne peut pas y avoir beaucoup de femmes canoêistes dans le Grand Nord.

There cannot be too many lady canoeists
in the North Country.

33

How the Voyageurettes Hear of Other Lady Canoeists

The Maries paddled out of the wilderness into the nearby settlement. They checked into their favorite outfitter's bunkroom, which they call "The Hilton on the Alley." Suddenly very friendly face appeared at the door. The face belonged to Gail, a long-time friend of Marie Rebecca and Marie Sue's. These three had not been together in one place for many, many years and were overjoyed to see each other again. All the other Maries did not know Gail, but being of one mind, when they saw their two sister-Maries jumping for joy, they all jumped for joy, too, when they met Gail. They found out that Gail lived in the settlement near St. Anthony Falls. The minute she heard the Maries were in the area, she paddled several days to the north in hopes of meeting up with them. The Voyageurettes also found out that Gail was the Bourgeoise for another group of well-known lady canoeists who paddled out of Grand Marais every summer.

The Voyageurettes were shocked, dismayed and frightened to hear of another group of ladies who are canoeists. Knowing Gail as a fine and honorable person, they were not worried about her at all. It was the other ladies in her group who caused concern. The Maries were already very familiar with three groups of voyageurs — those from the North West Company, the American Fur Company and the

Hudson's Bay Company. The Maries had first-hand knowledge of the high tension and fierce competition among the three companies. They were afraid that perhaps Gail's brigade might have the competitive and fierce nature of men voyageurs.

After meeting and becoming acquainted with all of the Maries, Gail said, "You will get along famously with my group. No problem!" But the Maries are not convinced at all. They kept thinking about the voyageurs. They vividly remembered witnessing one canoe race between two rival companies. It lasted a full forty-eight hours and was finally called off after one voyageur fell asleep, tumbled out of his canoe and almost drowned. The Maries also remembered fierce fights they had observed between groups of voyageurs that left some of the combatants with parts of their noses or ears bitten off. They were more than a little concerned that Gail's group of lady canoeists may be like the mens and not take kindly to the presence of another company of Voyageurettes paddling the Canoe Country. Not that they were afraid, but they were quite fond of and attached to their noses and ears and did not relish the thought of a forty-eight hour canoe race either. The Voyageurettes were happy to learn that Gail's group of lady canoeists would not be coming to the Canoe Country until later on in the summer. For the time being, at least, their noses and ears would be safe from harm.

That summer's adventure ended without encountering Gail's group of lady canoeists. With fall coming on, the voyageurs had begun to split up from their brigades and head to their own remote posts for the winter to continue trading by dogsleds. The Voyageurettes decided it was time to head back to their home settlements and spend the winter months with their husbands and families. Marie Candace and Marie Rebecca paddled east to New Hampshire. Marie Chris paddled west to her home beyond the big mountains out in the West. Marie Tricia headed to the Pacific Northwest. Marie Sarah headed south to Atlanta. Marie Margot paddled off to Fort Detroit and Marie Ramona, Marie Sue and Marie Joyce headed south to the Rock River Valley. Marie Tina paddled down the Mississippi River to her home near the port of New Orleans.

Marie Ramona and Marie Sue were home by mid-September. Early in October, they were fishing for catfish along the banks of the Rock River when a trapper paddled up to them. He said, "I am looking for a Marie Sue and a Marie Ramona. Who might you be?"

The two Maries were very happy to inform him that he had,

indeed, found them. He had a note with him from one of Gail's Brigade — a lady named Corita from the trading center of Eau Claire to the north.

The note said, "Hi Maries. I heard about you from my bourgeios, Gail. She told me you live in the Rock River Valley which isn't too far south from my settlement at Eau Claire. She also said that our canoeing brigade has a lot in common with yours. I am a famous ballerina, just like your Marie Margot. In fact, I own my own dance studio and am a professor of dancing at the local gathering place for higher learning. Gail said that you Maries paddle pink canoes. We, however, paddle plain colored You-Know-Now canoes because we are loyal to Minnesota where they are made. We are fast paddlers, just like your group. Last summer, we out-paddled a raging forest fire, in fact. I would very much like to meet some fellow lady canoeists like you. There are so few of us, you know. Can we perhaps get together sometime this fall before winter sets in?"

"Hmm," said Marie Sue after reading the letter. "Do you realize, Marie Ramona, that this Corita person brags even worse than we do? Everything we do, she seems to do better."

"Yes," said Marie Ramona. "I think we better plan a little paddle up stream to meet this Corita person face to face and check out our competition."

They sent a note back with the trapper. It said, "We will be coming to meet you in person in a few weeks. Please make reservations for us at a local wayside inn for November 1. Signed, Marie Sue and Marie Ramona."

The two Maries fully anticipated that Corita would challenge them to a marathon canoe race and began to prepare themselves. They began exercising their sternocleidomastoideus muscles and every day they diligently practiced reducing the angle of the power side of their blades by 3 or 4% on their offside strokes. Marie Sue collected documentation and artifacts of past Voyageurette adventures - the original and authentic scientific drawings of the record-breaking muskie they caught, pictures of the famous Marie Margot giving her best ballet performances, the special trophy they were awarded for making the fastest 1,000 mile journey to Nome, official certificates of appreciation for their numerous heroic deeds and also the golden Itty Bitty flashy lights they brought back from Washington, DC.

By the end of October, they were ready. Marie Ramona and Marie Sue got into their fastest canoe and paddled north to Eau Claire, half-expecting a cool reception. They were not often mistaken; however, this time they were. They paddled upriver and as they rounded the bend into the center of the settlement, the shores of the Chippewa River were decorated with hundreds of beautiful and magnificent pink flamingos. Their breath was taken away. The high school band played fine paddling music. The riverbank was lined with thousands of people waving red and blue bandannas. Signs and banners saying "WELCOME MARIES!" were posted everywhere. Little girls dressed in pink tutus twirled and pirouetted all around. Marie Sue and Marie Ramona were stunned and overwhelmed by this fine reception. To help offset the expense of the Maries' trip, the Eau Claire residents stood on the bridge and tossed paper money down to Marie Ramona and Marie Sue. Lucky for them, they brought a fish net and captured the floating money. The mayor greeted them personally and presented them with latch keys to the settlement. Marie Margot was, of course, not along on this trip, so Marie Ramona stood in for her and made a finely executed curtsy from the middle of the canoe.

They had not yet met Corita in person because she had to teach late at her dance studio. By nightfall, the two Maries had signed thousands of autographs. They were tired and went straightaway to the wayside inn. As they entered their room, Marie Sue and Marie Ramona found that Corita had been there before going to work and had left a pink paper flamingo for each of them, plus a plate of homemade chocolate chip cookies and a fruit basket. A three piece polka band was in the lobby to provide evening entertainment for them. The two Maries were flabbergasted by the warm reception. Just about 10:00 p.m. they heard a knock upon the door. They expected to find a stranger at the doorway, but instead, they were greeted by a friend they had not ever met. They did not even get formally introduced to each other. They immediately recognized each other and instinctively knew they were kindred spirits. They talked late into the night. Corita told Marie Ramona and Marie Sue about her trips and they told her about the Maries' adventures. They all felt that both lady canoeist groups were in the same circle and, unlike the voyageurs and no matter who was the bourgeoise, all are of one mind and spirit. Paddlers of the Canoe Country are indeed lucky that at least two groups of lady canoeists are paddling through the Canoe Country, one from the east and the other from the west. Now the chances of meeting up with a group of famous lady canoeists have increased by 100%.

Les deux choses qui disparaissent les plus rapidement sont l'argent et les amis, n'est-ce pas'.

Money and fools are soon parted, eh?

34

The Voyageurettes Learn about Papillons

A fter they met Corita, Marie Ramona and Marie Sue were relieved not to have to prove themselves by getting into a forty-eight hour canoe race with her or risk losing parts of their noses or ears in a big fight. That was especially reassuring because none of the Maries are fighters like the voyageurs. Ramona and Sue now felt that they had been long-time friends with their new kindred spirit. She invited them to her cabin to meet her husband, Jean Claude Baptiste, her two cockatiels and three papillons.

Marie Ramona and Marie Sue paddled along, following behind Corita in her canoe because she knew the way to her cabin. Marie Ramona and Marie Sue whispered to themselves, wondering about papillons. They did not know quite what a papillon was, but were hesitant to ask Corita for fear she would think they were not very smart Maries. They pretended to know exactly what papillons were in front of her. But since they paddled out of earshot of Corita, Marie Ramona said, "Marie Sue, what are these papillons we are about to meet?"

Marie Sue responded, "Beats me."

Marie Ramona said, "Maybe they are some sort of creatures and we should try to be extra careful and not stomp on them."

Marie Sue said, "We should be careful because papillons may be full of germs and infect us with papillonitis."

Then Marie Ramona hoped out loud that maybe papillons were something delicious to eat. Marie Sue wondered if they might be Corita's three children. Sue and Ramona decided to be cautious in regard to this meeting of three papillons and searched through their packs for a variety of devices just in case they were needed to protect themselves from these papillons.

Since they did not know exactly what they would be encountering, they brought a variety of safety items: running shoes, water guns, and a bag of cookies. They stuffed these things into a day pack to take into Corita's cabin just in case they were needed. Just then, Marie Ramona squealed with delight, "Oh! Oh! I just remembered what papillons are! Forget the protective devices! Papillon is French for butterfly! Corita must have butterflies!"

Marie Sue said, "I have never known anyone who has butterflies for pets."

Marie Ramona concluded that Corita was an artistic, creative person and that artistic and creative people tend to have artsy, creative pets, like butterflies. That made sense to her.

Marie Sue thought there was a correlation between Corita's being a ballet teacher and an affinity for graceful butterflies. They both were hopeful that Corita did not like unique and graceful pets such as rattlesnakes or poisonous spiders.

Finally they pulled up to Corita's cabin which was enclosed by a big high fence. This added to their nervousness as it appeared that her papillons were a vicious, unfriendly variety of butterfly and must be kept confined. They went into Corita's house and were greeted by a series of "Hello, Maries!" from Corita's very friendly, polite and gracious cockatiels. Next, they came to three medium-sized cages. Corita slipped open the latches and released the papillons.

"Here are my darling papillons," she said to Marie Sue and Marie Ramona.

She was right, they were, indeed, darling little things. However, they looked more like dogs than butterflies to Marie Ramona and Marie Sue. But they were polite and did not say to Corita what they really wanted to say, which was, "Corita, we are sorry to inform you of this, but your three butterflies are not butterflies at all—they are really dogs."

Ramona and Sue just kept that thought to themselves. Instead they quietly said, "We think they are really cute papillons, indeed."

The truth is they were cute, but they did look a lot like dogs. They had four legs, long black and white hair, dog-like noses and whiskers. They also barked. Sue and Ramona believed Corita when she said they were papillons, since she knew a lot more about papillons. They knew enough about biology to remember a few evolutionary tricks of butterflies. They knew that Monarch butterflies are nasty-tasting to birds and that other butterflies, like the Viceroy, mimic the Monarch's coloring in order to make themselves less attractive to birds for food. They figured that this dog-like species of butterfly had evolved to look and sound like dogs in order to protect themselves from birds and cats and other such butterfly predators.

Marie Ramona and Marie Sue fell in love with the papillons' sweet personalities, which were more like a butterfly's personality than a dog's. They licked faces just like a dog, sat on laps and also fetched balls. By far, they were the very most interesting and entertaining butterflies Marie Ramona and Marie Sue had ever met.

Finally the time had come for Sue and Ramona to head back south to the river on the prairie. They bade a fond farewell to Corita and her cockatiels and three papillons. In fact, they were thinking that they should get papillons for all the other Maries as a present. On the way home they stopped at the pet shop and said to the clerk, "We would like ten of your very best papillons."

The clerk said, "Well, papillons are a very rare breed and we don't have any in the store right now. I can order them for you, but they will require a $400 pre-payment for each one."

Marie Sue quickly got out her pocket abacus and multiplied $400 times 10. $4,000, not including tax. She told Ramona the bad news. They pooled their resources and found that they were a little short— $3,950.97 short, in fact. They told the clerk they were sorry, but they had changed their mind. They looked around the store for a few more minutes and found just what they wanted—ten butterfly nets on sale for $2.95 each. They bought all of them— one for each Marie. Ramona and Sue figured out that for a savings of $397.05 each, the Maries could use their new nets and catch their very own papillons.

The next spring right after ice out, Marie Sue and Marie Ramona left their wintering post and paddled back up north to Knife Lake to rendezvous with the rest of the Maries who had wintered in their own remote posts. The Maries were all delighted to see each other again and spent the afternoon sharing stories of their winter adventures.

Marie Ramona said, "Well, Marie Sue and I learned all about papillons this winter. Do any of you know what papillons are?"

Marie Candace answered, "Sure! Papillons are dogs."

Marie Ramona and Marie Sue stood in stunned silence. All they could manage to say was, "Dogs? Not butterflies?"

"Of course!" said Marie Candace. "They are little black and white dogs with great big ears—ears that are shaped like the wings of a butterfly!!

Marie Ramona thought to herself though, "You fool, Marie Ramona. How could you ever confuse dogs with butterflies?"

Marie Sue said to herself, "What are we going to do now-stuck with $29.95 worth of obsolete butterfly nets that the rest of the Maries do not need or want?"

After five hours of non-stop conversation, the Maries were worn out and they laid down in the sunshine and all began napping—all except for Marie Ramona and Marie Sue. They grabbed their ten butterfly nets and hustled to the closest portage where they set up a little booth. Before long, a brigade of voyageurs came across the portage. As the men got within earshot, Marie Ramona, in her loudest and fastest voice, began, "Todayisyourluckyday. Ihave-herethefinest, Isayfinest, buyofthecentury! Itisamultipurpose-net. Youcanputitonyourheadanditkeepsthefliesandmosquitoesfrombitingyourfaceandneck."

With those words, Marie Sue put the net over her head, smiled and nodded her head in agreement with Marie Ramona's fast, non-stop words.

Marie Ramona, without even taking one breath continued, "Youcanalsouseittocatchminnowsforfishingbait."

With those words, Marie Sue ran to the shore, dipped the net into a school of minnows and proudly displayed them to the voyageurs. Marie

Ramona continued without hesitation, "Youcangive-thenettothelittlewomansoshecancatchbeautifulbutterfliesforherbutterflycollection." Marie Sue ran gracefully around with the net, pretending to catch beautiful butterflies.

Marie Ramona continued talking fast, still without taking even one breath, "Yesmyfriends,allthisfortheunbelievableIsayunbelievablepriceof only$25!" Before she could say another word, the men had snatched up all ten butterfly nets and handed Marie Ramona bags full of coins.

After the voyageurs had all left, Marie Ramona and Marie Sue were counting their money, "247, 248, 249," when a second brigade of voyageurs came down the portage.

"Bonjour, mes Maries," said Jean Paul, their bourgeois. "My, that is a lot of money you are having. Might you be interested in doing a little trading with us?"

Marie Ramona replied, "Oui, we would!" What do you have to trade?"

Jean Paul said, "Well, we have a whole canoe full of fine, beautiful woolen Hudson's Bay Point blankets that we might part with."

Marie Ramona said, "Hmm, how about trading us fifteen blankets for $250?'

Jean Paul countered, "Five blankets for $250."

Marie Ramona answered, "Ten for 250!"

Jean Paul said, "Traded, ten blankets for $250."

Marie Ramona and Marie Sue made it back to the rest of the Maries just as they were waking up from their nap. "We have for each of you a present." Marie Ramona said. The rest of the Maries had big smiles on their faces. The Maries just love getting gifts. "We have for each of you a nice, woolen Hudson's Bay blanket."

The Maries all squealed in delight at the thought of having a Hudson's Bay blanket of their very own. Marie Ramona looked at Marie Sue. She winked and whispered, *Les deux choses qui disparaissent les plus rapidement sont l'argent et les amis, n'est-ce pas'.* Money and fools are soon parted, eh?"

Il vaut mieux en avoir moins que plus.

Less is more.

35

The Voyageurette Method of Gear Management

One day the Maries were on a long portage feeling very tired, which was unusual for them after having paddled only 31 miles and taking seven other portages so far that morning. Marie Tina Marie helped pass the time of day as the Voyageurettes were carrying their heavy loads across the steep and rocky portage path. Marie Tina Marie talked enthusiastically about the advantages of using credit coupons designed to make days of hard shopping even easier. She said she had a dream of going shopping with no worrying. She would have her husband, Jean Butch Baptiste, worry and pay for everything. She suggested that all the Maries could try her new idea, too, since it made shopping such a care-free experience. The other Maries were busy thinking as they portaged along that when they had the next shopping opportunity, they might just do that. Considering the size of Marie Tina's shopping bills, five more Marie-bills added in would not make that much difference. It was not that the Maries were greedy or opportunistic or interested in having Jean Butch pay their way. Instead, they felt that generosity was a well-known virtue. They wanted Jean Butch Baptiste to experience the great satisfaction of being well-known for having such a fine, admirable trait. Marie Margot thought that Jean Butch would probably be glad for her to have new boots. Marie Candace thought Jean Butch Baptiste would probably be happy for her to have a new, lightweight sleeping bag. Marie Sue pondered getting a new Angry Creek Sunskipper canoe and how that would please Jean Butch. Marie Rebecca thought he would want her to have a waterproof tissue container and a new waterproof sleeping bag cover because she had just accidentally rolled both her bag and the Voyageurettes' tissue supply into the lake.

As the Voyageurettes mulled over these admirable, generous and comforting thoughts, their silence was interrupted by a distant "tap, tap, tap" sound. Marie Margot said, "Hmm. I am hearing what sounds like tap dancing. In fact, that sounds like someone doing the "Buffalo Shuffle!"

Sure enough, around the bend in the portage came a lady tap dancer. "Tap! Tap! Tappety, Tap!" her feet went lickety-split as she double-packed two huge canvas packs. As she passed by, she took off her silver sequin derby hat and waved it Al Jolson-style. "Hi, Maries," she said as she quickly tap danced right past the thunder-struck Maries, went around the next bend and out of sight in a flash before they even knew what had happened or recognized who it was. The Maries were stunned! Marie Margot in particular. She was very excited to think another professional was dancing her way across the Canoe Country Wilderness. Marie Margot missed the networking and bonding that goes on between professional dancers. Just as she was preparing to run after this tap dancing lady, the Voyageurettes spied another lady quietly strolling down the portage carrying a huge, honey-colored, 18 and a half foot canoe. How she was able to walk along so casually under that load was too much of a shock for the Voyageurettes to believe. She walked with the canoe balanced on her shoulders. One hand held a short length of basswood cord tied to a thwart. The other hand fluffed up her hairdo.

Now the Maries, they, too, made difficult jobs look easy, but their way was nothing compared to this lady's. The Maries, also like this lady, were always striving to have their hairdos look nice, but not when they were carrying heavy canoes. Their thoughts were generally not on hairdos at that moment. Rather, theirs were more basic and primitive survival thoughts — like how to endure intense suffering and pain and how to live long enough to take the next step. As this lady strolled closer to the Voyageurettes with her canoe on her shoulders, they suddenly recognized her as the famous Canoe

Country explorer and guide, Gail.

Gail said, "Oh, Maries! I am so glad I found you at last! I heard you were up here and thought I could try to track you down. In fact, I've been following your scent trail of S'Fantastic insect repellant for over an hour. By the way, have you seen my tap dancing friend, Corita, anywhere around here?"

The Voyageurettes acknowledged that, indeed, they had seen a tap dancer, but she was tapping so fast that she had passed by before they even recognized who it was or had a chance to ask her to stop and chat. That was how all the other Maries met up with Gail and Corita on the water. The two joined the other Maries for the rest of their voyage. It was a fine experience for all of them to paddle and portage together. Gail and Corita acted and thought just like all the other Voyageurettes, having been kindred spirits for many years. After paddling a few days together, the Voyageurettes officially baptized them into their ever-expanding circle. The cedar branch and water baptismal ceremony for Marie Gail and Marie Corita brought tears to everyone's eyes.

The Maries were happy to learn all sorts of things from Marie Corita and Marie Gail. Marie Corita taught the very experienced Marie Margot some new dance steps and moves. She introduced Marie Sue, Marie Candace and Marie Tina Marie to the basics of tap dancing. Marie Gail shared her secrets of making a water-proof, fool-proof, very sharp and impressive-looking rain tarp, making flavored gelatin in the cold lake water, playing tunes on the harmonica and quickly rescuing binoculars that fall into the lake with such speed that they did not even get wet.

The Maries had a voyage full of laughter, friendship and serious geological discussions about how glacial erratics can be shaped just like buns belonging to people. They exchanged recipes and camping tips, sang songs and told tales of their wilderness adventures. They had a wuuunderful trip. It was wuuunderful until they paddled past a group of voyageurs who spotted the Marie flotilla and began pestering them. The voyageurs called out across the water to the two new Maries, "Now, really, ladies, aren't you embarrassed to be traveling with the chronically over-packed Maries? Just look at all those bulging packs!"

The voyageurs were teasing. They said the Voyageurettes must have everything except the kitchen sink in those big packs. Unknown to them, Marie Rebecca did have one tucked away in the bottom of her pack, but the Maries did not offer to tell the voyageurs everything they knew. The two new Maries, in true Voyageurette spirit, stuck up for the others. They did not agree with the pesky voyageurs and did not join them in poking fun at their fellow Maries. Instead, they thought fast and told the voyageurs the Maries were actually making big bucks transporting essential trade goods into the Canoe Country and running a portable discount trading post.

The men suddenly became interested in the Voyageurettes' hidden treasures. "How about showing us your stuff?" they asked. The Voyageurettes agreed to stop at the nearest island, unpack their gear and display their trade goods.

Marie Margot's new pink tutu did not interest the voyageurs. However, they were very excited to check out Marie Tina Marie's fine T-shirt selection. She sold them Cajun Country Club T-shirts with alligators playing golf on the front. She sold her stylish, boy-designed T-shirt to one of the voyageurs who bought it as a gift for his own son. Marie Rebecca sold half of her supply of peppermint schnapps and Marie Candace, who had lost one of her ear rings, sold off the remaining one for two beaver pelts to a voyageur with a pierced nose. Marie Rebecca sold her bird identification book because she no longer needed it to tell the difference between adult ospreys and immature bald eagles. Marie Tina Marie brought out her see-through bag of dried moose droppings and passed it off to one rather unenlightened voyageur as a bag of extra large malted milk balls. Marie Gail managed to unload six of her seventeen harmonicas, figuring that she could struggle along for the rest of the trip with only eleven. Marie Corita sold off her whole supply of homemade chocolate chip cookies to a bachelor voyageur who had no wife at home to bake for him. Marie Margot sold one of her extra pairs of pink ballet shoes to a burly voyageur. She convinced him they would fit his size 14 feet just fine and would look très chic. Marie Candace pulled out her neat light that displayed the correct time onto the tent walls at night and auctioned that off for $35.

Marie Sue was the only one who did not make any profit that day. In fact, she lost money. She paid five dollars to one hungry voyageur to take the Maries' 25 extra packets of oatmeal off her hands. It was well worth the five bucks for her not to worry about having to eat oatmeal again for the rest of the trip.

In all, the Voyageurettes had unloaded 27 extra T-shirts to the voyageurs plus the six harmonicas, a pair of ballet slippers, the time display light, two quarts of booze, 25 packs of oatmeal, 14 boxes of cookies, two folding camp chairs, one spare tent, two pulleys, four rolls of duct tape, eight pairs of sweat pants, four short, skinny paddles, eight pounds of cheese, three quarts of vegetable oil, one mini-microscope, Marie Corita's extra pair of tap shoes, a spare gold derby hat and matching dancing cane, one 10' x 12' extra-heavy canvas tarp, 14 bottles of Epidermis-So-Smooth, seven pink flamingo lawn ornaments, 56 packets of hot chocolate, one inflatable kitchen sink, three spare butane hair curling irons, one portable hand-operated fan, ten pounds of trail snacks which had became totally unacceptable for the Maries to eat after one of them had mined out all the coated chocolate bits, plus one fish net and seven fish poles, reels and tackle boxes since the fish weren't biting.

They also sold all of their Blue Light Specials for the day—camp-made coffee cakes, scones, blueberry muffins, banana bread, double chocolate brownies, chocolate cake, strawberry cheesecake, raspberry tarts, and pineapple upsidedown cake from their Way-Out-Back-Oven Bakery Department.

The Voyageurettes sold so much of their spare gear and supplies that they were also able to peddle their now-empty 25 foot cargo canoe and one dozen empty packs.

It has been said that the Maries were known to exaggerate at times, but this is the true, perhaps even conservative estimate, of the profit they made that day from selling just their spare supplies and extra gear. They were ashamed to tell anyone precisely how much money they took in, but it was enough to promptly replace all the sold gear with brand new gear, plus purchase a few new items when they got back to the settlement. It was also enough for them to finance Voyageurette trips for the next seven years. All this was due to the fast thinking of the two fine and loyal new Maries and also to the other Maries who, on the rarest of occasions, may have tended to ever-so-slightly overpack.

*Mieux vaut mourir heureux
avec un estomac plein.*

Die happy with a full stomach.

36

How Marie Jackie Beat a Bear at Its Own Game

The Voyageurettes were thinking about expanding their numbers and heard of a possible new recruit named Jackie. Now there were a few things about Jackie that were not known at that time, but the Maries soon learned that she had spent time living at several forts and military encampments. Marie Sue, as Bourgeoise, was all ears. She was well-aware that such a person would be familiar with the concepts of the chain of command and would know how to maintain strict discipline within the ranks. She concluded that a person with exposure to the military was likely to be very bossy and have a directive and controlling management style. Marie Sue was worried that Jackie would have both of her eyes on Marie Sue's bourgeoise job and that Marie Sue might soon end up being demoted to potato peeling duty or, even worse, cleaning latrines.

Marie Sue kept close track of this Jackie person. Marie Sue figured she had two choices: Either she would soon be replaced or she would simply have to out-boss the new recruit. She decided on the latter.

On her first day in the Canoe Country, Marie Sue announced, "Jackie, I have something to explain to you. First, I am the Bourgeoise, which in Army language means I am like a general — a Five Star General, in fact. You are like a private and you must obey me because I am the one who gives the orders here. Is that clear?"

Jackie sat up at attention when Marie Sue said that to her. Marie Sue explained that the first day on a Voyageurette trip was similar to basic training and part of basic training was learning to carry a canoe and a pack at the same time while running across a portage.

At the very first portage, Jackie jumped out of the canoe, stood at attention and saluted, grabbed the two heaviest packs and put them on her back and front, threw a canoe on to her shoulders and went down the path at a fast trot. The rest of the Maries stood watching in amazement. Marie Sue was very quiet because she knew the rest of the Maries would not have approved of her heavy-handed tactics. At the far end of the portage the rest of the Maries immediately baptized Jackie as Marie Jackie, making her an official Voyageurette. Marie Sue had hoped to hold off on that ceremony until after the 309 rod portage toward the end of this journey. This was because she instinctively knew that once Jackie became an official Marie, she would not listen to Marie Sue's orders any more than the other Maries ever did. For a few brief moments Marie Sue had secretly relished the idea that she might not always have to carry the heaviest loads over long portages.

Now that she was officially baptized, Marie Jackie, being of one mind with the rest of the Maries, joined them in telling Marie Sue that since she was the Bourgeoise, she should do several things. Marie Sue should be the one to run out into the rain to put up a tarp for the rest of the Maries to sit under, make hot chocolate for them to drink while they sat under the tarp, carry the nastiest packs over the portages, clean out the fire bowl and do all the other unpleasant jobs no one else eagerly volunteered to do. But Marie Sue did not mind that kind of talk one little bit. She was used to it. Besides, she was growing to like this new Marie very much.

Most of the time the Voyageurettes were confident they already knew just about everything worth knowing. However, there was one area in which they were not so confident. It had to do with bears. Marie Jackie was not at all hesitant about what to do when a bear came into their camp during the supper hour. All the other Maries shouted and yelled, blew their whistles and banged pots and pans together. Marie Margot threw stones in the bear's direction to convince it to go away. All the Maries jumped up and down in fear, except for Marie Jackie, who calmly remained standing straight up with her dinner plate close to her face. She shoveled food into her mouth with such speed that a person could not tell if she were using a fork or a spoon. It was simply a silver blur.

The Maries said, "Marie Jackie, why are you just standing there eating fast while the bear is threatening us with extinction?"

She said, "I have concluded the bear is here for one of two reasons: First, he is hungry for food. Second, he is vicious and wants to attack us. I figure if he is hungry, I want to eat my supper quickly before he can get it. If he is vicious and attacks, I want to die happy with a full stomach. Either way, that is why I am eating my supper so fast."

The rest of the Maries nodded their heads. They were embarrassed because they had not thought of that before. The next night, when another bear appeared during supper, they all quickly ate their food, following Marie Jackie's clever and innovative example from the previous night.

On that particular trip, the Voyageurettes had two small portable cloth houses. Maries Jackie, Rebecca and Margot were in one portable cloth house and Maries Candace, Tina and Sue were in the other.

In the middle of the night, Marie Jackie was awakened by a strange and very annoying grinding and munching sound from just outside her portable cloth house. She called out, "Who is out there munching?" She heard an answer from the other portable cloth house. "It is simply a bunch of sawyer beetle grubs chewing inside a log next to your portable cloth house. It's OK, you can go back to sleep now".

She was just about asleep again when she heard the sawyer beetle grubs say, "Oh, boy! There are coated chocolate bits still left in this bag of trail snacks!"

Normally, Marie Jackie would have known immediately that something suspicious had occurred, especially since sawyer beetle grubs do not speak; however, in the middle of the night, her thinking was not particularly acute. Then she heard the grubs again. They said, "Yum-my! Chocolate cookies! Munch, munch!"

Marie Jackie's sleepy, sleepy mind woke up with a start. It told her she should get up and check out this talking grub phenomenon. She crawled out of her sleeping bag and discovered three Maries from the other Marie House sitting around an open food pack with guilty looks and cookie crumbs on their faces. "Exactly WHAT are you doing?" she asked.

Now the Maries were quite capable of lying hard; however, at other times they could be completely truthful. On this particular occasion Marie Tina said, "We have heard a bear just now in the woods. We did not want to wake up the other Maries and scare them. We felt it was best to eat up all the food immediately so the bear would not be getting it."

This way of thinking made sense to Marie Jackie, especially because it was her idea in the first place. By now, the other Maries in camp were wide awake. They instinctively gathered around the food pack. All six of them sat down and finished off six loaves of bread, two jars of peanut butter and jelly, eight packs of cookies, seven mugs of hot chocolate and four gallons of fruit drink, two apples each, eight bagels with cream cheese, four pounds of trail snacks (only one pound of which had any blue coated chocolate bits left in it), three pounds of cheese and five small salamis. All that remained in the food pack was part of one loaf of bread which had a lovely green mold culture growing upon it. They returned it to the food pack and left it for the bear, who was not as sophisticated an eater as were the Maries. Before long, the Maries retired and went to sleep. Sure enough, the bear came calling in the night and ate that partial loaf of moldy bread, but the Maries were in no condition to care if the bear ate the last of their food or not.

With a dose of pink Peppy Bismuth Tummy Medicine each, the Maries were all ready to head out in the morning without any breakfast. They were not the least bit interested in eating lunch or supper that day or breakfast the following day. By lunch time on the second day, they were only slightly hungry, but that was not a problem because it was their last day out on the water and they would soon be in the settlement in plenty of time for the Tuesday Special at the tavern.

On their very last portage, they meet up with a group of very sad and hungry voyageurs who had lost all their food and special beverages to a bear on Sunday. The Maries felt sorry for them and carried all their canoes and packs across the portage without being asked. They told the voyageurs that a bear had stolen their last bit of food, too, that same evening. The poor voyageurs were so debilitated and totally out of steam with only enough energy left to think how tough and brave the Maries were to have gone more than one full day without any special beverages and still be so utterly cheerful.

The Voyageurettes knew there were many people who looked to them for advice. One big question was what to do about bears. And this is what the Voyageurettes tell them: We will tell you exactly what to do in case a bear is coming into your camp. We know you have been advised to hang your food packs from high branches, blow whistles, bang pots and pans together, throw rocks to scare the bear away and use pepper gas spray as a last resort. Some experts will tell you to cover your food packs with a tarp and hide them far away from camp. The advice of the Maries, however, is to forget all that. Just camp out right next to your food pack with a spoon, fork and knife under your pillow ready to get at quick, in case a bear comes. When you hear a bear come close, open the food pack and start eating quickly until all the food is gone. Speed is important. Don't worry about using napkins or chewing each bite 27 times before swallowing. This new bear-proofing technique was invented by Marie Jackie and successfully field tested by the famous Voyageurettes, so you can be having utmost confidence that it works.

Leave bear ropes, pulleys, whistles, sirens, firearms, firecrackers and pepper gas canisters at home. Simply remember to bring a container of pink Peppy Bismuth Tummy Medicine along on your next adventure into the Canoe Country.

Les bonnes tentes font les bons amis.

Good tents make good friends.

37

"A Night Chez Marie"

The Marie House was an essential part of the Voyageurettes' outfit. It was second only to the cooking kit, which was the very most important piece of equipment in camp. The Marie House was a tan-colored six-person expedition size tent with a vestibule. Sometimes people were curious to know how many and what size tents they took on their voyages. The answers were simple. One, but that depended. If there were more than six Maries on a given voyage, then they must take one six-person and one four-person tent. Sometimes people asked why they usually all stayed together in one tent and did not spread out and use two tents all the time and have more room. Marie Sue always gave the same answer: "We Maries, we all stick together. If a big storm blows trees down on us or the bear comes in the night to hurt us, then we will all go together."

The Marie House had been around for a long time. It had been on more voyages than any of the Maries, except for Marie Sue. She had been on more than seventy trips and the Marie House had been on many of them. The Marie House was showing its age. The floor was patched with duct tape to cover many holes made by rocks and roots and the seams needed to be sealed tight every summer. On their most recent trip, the right side of the front door zipper would not work any more. It would not stay closed, but instead popped open about a foot all by itself right after any Marie thought she had zipped it up tight. A very smart and observant scout-mosquito found out about the broken zipper and told all of the other Canoe Country mosquitos about it. Most of them came inside the Marie House. Marie Sue and Marie Candace used up a whole roll of duct tape trying to keep the hole shut up tight. Unfortunately, the other Maries were always on the wrong side of the door when Sue and Candace did their repair job, and everyone else was either taped inside or taped outside of the Marie House. The Maries all had to enter and exit the Marie House by unzipping the bottom horizontal part of the door and squeezing themselves through the slit-like opening one at a time. It was not a pretty sight to see the proud Voyageurettes waiting in line for their turn to roll on the ground to get inside or out of the Marie House.   The Voyageurettes had a pattern and regular routine of in-tent behavior. When it got dark and the bugs began to sing and bite, the rain came, or there were spooky noises in the woods, the Maries got ready to go to bed. There were three rules:

1) Big packs, they are banished from the tent and stay out in the vestibule.

2) Smelly wet boots and polypro socks are not permitted inside the tent, and

3) No food, gum or candy can be inside to attract bears.

The Maries took their last peek at the stars, moon, aurora borealis or other interesting things they might like to look at, made the last run to the hover-spot, and finally almost got ready to zip up the mosquito net door of the Marie House. All the Maries got busy finding things all at once. They found their ditty bags full of important things. They got out bug dope, lip balm, after-bite medicine and other useful items. They rummaged through all of the packs inside the vestibule. They found their sleeping clothes and lights. They brought in their journals and books for writing and reading, and dry socks and knit hats for keeping warm on cold nights. Then they let air into their sleeping mats, fixed up their sleeping bags and pillows and got into their sleeping clothes. They put things back into the packs in the vestibule and put their blue Marie hats in the overhead gear loft. They made small piles of things at the head and foot of their sleeping bags so they were available in the night and in the morning. Marie Sue's jar of firecrackers was put by the door in case the bear came.

Then, it was time for Bug Patrol. Out came the Itty Bitty lights. One or two Maries stood up and tried not to step hard on the other Maries who were already lying down inside their sleeping bags.

"OK, mosquitos, you've had it now! Here we come!"

"Euugh!"

"You got 'em!

"There's one over there."

"OK! Got 'em."

"Yes!"

"Oops, missed that one."

"See the one on the ceiling? No, behind you your head.".

"Here's one. Just roll 'em over."

"Yep! Got it."

"And one here, by the light!"

"Any more?"

"Yes! Three more on the ceiling!"

"One's buzzing by my head, can you see it?"

For five minutes and maybe more this went on until most of the bugs were nothing more than little brownish-red spots on the inside of the Marie House.

Now the Maries could do other things they liked to do in peace. Marie Candace and Marie Tina wore their glasses and read their books. Their lights went back and forth on the pages of their books and shined on the side of the Marie House. Marie Margot wrote notes in her journal.

"Does anyone have a spare mini-candle? My light, it does not work any more."

Marie Rebecca dumped everything out of her ditty bag and found two mini-candles, just in case.

Marie Sue said, "Does anyone have a back ache?"

Marie Sue had found her trigger-point therapy activator-zapper. She gave back rubs and she also used the zapper. "Snap! Snap!" went the zapper.

"Oww, Marie Sue!"

"Did that hurt?"

"Yes, but it hurts so good that now I feel better."

Then, one Marie might say, "Let's do "Singing Lights!" Right away, they all stopped what they were doing. They thought a song to sing. They all turned on their Itty Bitty lights and pointed them at the far wall of the Marie House. They had long ago figured out that when they twisted the ends of their lights, the light-spots on the wall got bigger or smaller. To the Maries the light-spots looked like little mouths opening and closing. When they sang their songs, they twisted the lights and made the mouths open and close along with the words. This worked best when they sang "Home, Home On the Range" and "She'll Be Comin' 'Round the Mountain." It was especially impressive when the mouths made big "O's" when they sang the words "hooome," "buff-a-looo," and "roooam" and moved open and shut quickly when they went "whoo, whoo" for the train whistle sound.

Sometimes Marie Corita read them funny stories. She put great expression into her voice and they all laughed at the right times. At least once on every voyage they got a spontaneous case of contagious giggles and could not stop laughing for five minutes. By the end, they were all out of breath and had tears in their eyes and, for the life of them, they could not remember what it was that made them start giggling and laughing in the first place. Then they laughed some more.

Marie Sue read serious stories out of her nature-writing books and, other times, if they asked her nice, she would tell the Maries stories about her adventures on canoe trips a long time ago. And sometimes they talked about other important things, things they were doing when they were not on voyages and what they would like to be and do when they grew up. They were all trying to be good listeners and thinkers and make a real effort to understand and give good advice and ideas to each other.

Marie Gail played her harmonica just about every night. She played songs like "Sentimental Journey," "Don't Fence Me In," "Red River Valley," and "Somewhere Over The Rainbow." This made Marie Ramona feel dreamy and sleepy. Pretty soon, her eyes closed and she made little purring noises into her pillow.

Finally, one Marie would say, "Goodnight, Marie; good night, Marie; good night, Marie; good night, Marie; good night, Marie" to everyone else. At least thirty times, "Good night, Marie" was said out loud because each Marie must bid good night to every other Marie and not forget anyone. But, that was not the end of it.

Even after all of them said "Good night" to each other, rolled over and closed their eyes, other things happened. In the night, some of the Maries tossed and turned in their sleeping bags because it is too hot, or woke up because they were chilly. Sometimes a bug might wake them up or there might be a noise outside that made them sit up straight and their eyes get big. There were other reasons for the Maries to wake up, like checking to see what time it was, listening for loons or waiting for the sun to come up so they could begin a new day of fun together.

Not long ago they were thinking up suggestions for a perfect Marie House design if they ever had to get a new one. Their new Marie House should have two big doors, front and back, and maybe two vestibules. It should have a thickly padded root and rock-proof floor, accommodations for at least nine Maries at the same time, an attic for added storage, a skylight, a sundeck, an emergency night-time exit and a bear alarm system.

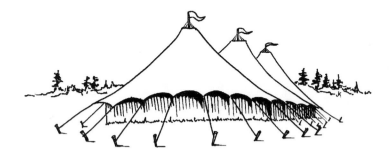

Ne te laisse jamais tracasser par des choses qui ne revêtent aucune.

Don't ever let the little things in life bother you.

38

The Flying Pests

One cloudy warm day the Voyageurettes took time out from their business appointments and hectic travel schedule to catch up on their chores, write in their journals, nap in their hammocks, and browse around websites in the woods in search of marbled orb weaver spiders (*Araneus marmoreus*). In fact, they decided to spend a couple of days at a campsite by an inlet near a portage.

Marie Sue immediately occupied herself with her own very important project. She sat on a flat rock ledge over-looking the water, patiently waiting with a canoe paddle at her side. She watched and listened carefully. Soon she heard a faint humming in the distance. It got louder and louder, until suddenly she saw a gray cloud the size of a huge pumpkin fly toward her and hover over her head. As quick as a wink, she swished the paddle in figure-eights, round and round like a sword cutting through the air. When she stopped waving the paddle, the flat rock around her was almost all covered by a layer of mosquitos. They were not humming or moving any more; instead, they were lying on their backs with their little feet sticking up in the air. Marie Sue neatly arranged the mosquitos in rows of ten and counted them. Forty-two rows and seven left over.

Within a few minutes, Marie Sue saw that her right pant-leg was totally covered with small black dots. The dots had teeny wings folded up along their sides. The dots bent over and looked as if they were trying to bite through Marie Sue's pants. Whack, went the paddle! Marie Sue arranged the black fly dots by tens on the paddle blade and counted out twenty-one with three left over.

It wasn't long before Marie Sue heard buzzing. Along came a line of big deer flies straight toward her. The deer flies landed on her bare arm one at a time. Smack, went her open hand! Smack, smack, smack! After awhile no more flies landed. Marie Sue lined up the flies and counted five rows of ten with six left over. She made some quick calculations using her very useful new math skills.

Marie Sue was pleased with herself. She found some birchbark on the ground, took a piece of charcoal out of the firepit and made a sign. When Marie Sue finished writing, she tied the piece of birchbark to a tree down by the portage path.

The sign said:
"Marie Sue killed 427 with a sword
and whacked 213 with a blade.
Then she smacked 56 with only one hand."

While she was down by the water's edge, Marie Sue noticed a skinny stick about nine and a half feet long on the shore. A beaver had chewed off all the bark, leaving it smooth and white. She took the stick back to the rock ledge and tied a very long thin basswood string to one end. Marie Sue looked down at the ground and spotted an acorn cap that looked like a little eye. With her knife she made a hole in the middle and tied the eye to the other end of the long stick. Next, she put the basswood string in the hole, pulled it all the way through and tied a small hook on the very end. When that was finished, Marie Sue scooped up all of the mosquitos and flies she had swatted into a big pile. Carefully she tied one of the deer flies to the hook with a strand of her hair.

"Szzz! Szzz! Szzz! went the basswood string as Marie Sue moved the beaver stick forward and back in the air. Then the small hook and the deer fly landed gently in the water. Marie Sue twitched the string and waited to see what would happen. Right away she caught three fish in a row, big enough to feed six people.

"Oh, Marie Sue! Where are you and what are you doing?" called Marie Ramona.

"I'm over here fishing. I know fish like to eat bugs, so I am bug-fishing. I harvested so many bugs, I thought it would be good ethics not to waste any, but put them to good use by feeding the fish." said Marie Sue. "And I have already caught and cleaned enough fish for our lunch!"

"So you have! But to be perfectly accurate, that is not a bug on the other end of your string, it is a fly!" said Marie Ramona. "So you must be fly-fishing."

"Whatever." said Marie Sue.

In just a few minutes Marie Ramona had cooked the fish and it was time to eat. The Voyageurettes all gathered around on the rocky ledge where they could enjoy their lunch and watch all the comings and goings on the portage at the same time. Right away there was something to see. Along came two voyageur canoes with their crews of eight men each. The Maries recognized seven of the voyageurs as *hivernants* they had met on other journeys. The rest were strangers. From their vantage point up on the rock ledge, the Voyageurettes could see that every one of the strangers had short hair and their ears looked puffy. Their faces were covered all over with small red spots. One of the strange voyageurs, the shortest one, was redder than all the others.

"Shhh! The voyageurs do not see us 'way up here," whispered Marie Candace. "Oh, look! Some of them must be very young, judging from all those red dots on their faces. Maybe they are *mangeurs de lard* (pork-eaters) just arriving from Montreal for their first full season in the *pays d'en havt* (high country)."

The voyageurs unloaded their canoes. One of voyageurs noticed the birchbark sign on the tree and stopped to read it outloud. "Now, this is something!" he said. "I know this Marie Sue very well. She's the leader of the Voyageurettes and hardly the type to kill anyone or any thing. But 696 at one time? I wonder what's up!"

All the voyageurs looked around. They peeked behind trees and checked the bushes for any sign of the dangerous Marie Sue. Seeing no signs, they prepared to take part of their cargo down the portage path.

Marie Sue could not remain silent. *"Salvuut, nos gens! Fa va?"* ("Halloo there, fellows! How's it going?") she said. With that, the voyageurs stopped in their tracks. Then they turned around and spotted the Voyageurettes up on the ledge. Seven of the men broke into wide smiles and their eyes twinkled.

"Alors, mes filles! How pleasant it is to see you once again! It makes us feel that the sun is shining upon us," said Jean Claude

Baptiste. "Marie Sue, *ma cherie* may I ask you just what is this sign all about? My crewmen are all on edge because they worry what you might do to them."

"Jean Claude, you know it is the season of peak abundance for those who have acquired a taste for human blood and delight in causing substantial annoyance!" said Marie Sue.

"Yes, that is exactly what my men are fearing! What ever has come over you since last we met? Have you turned yourself into a were-wolf or some other fearsome creature?" he asked.

"Oh, no, Jean Claude, my good friend, there is nothing to fear from me!" said Marie Sue. "I have just spent the morning killing pesky mosquitos, black flies and deer flies, not voyageurs like you! I am totally harmless!"

"Yes, that is what all women say, Marie Sue! We sure would have been happy to have had you with us at our camp last might, especially our "Big Guy," said Jean Claude as he patted the smallest new voyageur on the shoulder. "Jean Rene, here, who sleeps under the *canot*, he woke us all up in the middle of the night. He was having the big nightmare of a giant crayfish claw coming to bite him. In the light of day we could tell he had been chewed by many biting gnats or midges, the "no-see-ums." See how he is suffering?"

The Maries could see. They felt badly for young Jean Rene and wanted to help him, but by then, the voyageurs were trotting down the path carrying most of their goods on their backs and were soon out of sight.

"I understand exactly what that young man is going through," said Marie Margot. "But soon his hair will grow as long as the *hivernants'* and his ears and neck, at least, will have some protection. Hopefully, the other men will remind him to wear his *toque* while he sleeps."

"We can help our voyageur friends with some hot tips for dealing with annoying insects in the wilderness!" said Marie Ramona. "They could always make up some oatmeal with milk and brown sugar to attract mosquitos and when they swarm around to eat it, the men can smack them."

"That might work, but the voyageurs don't usually fix oatmeal. Besides, mosquitos and all those other biting pests are after blood! Who among them is brave enough to volunteer his own blood as bait?" said Marie Candace.

"All I know for sure is that swatting takes a lot of energy," said Marie Sue. "I would like to try trapping thousands of these flying biters in a huge bag. If we tied a stout rope to the bag and hung on tight, maybe they would fly up into the air and give us real lift."

"Traps sound pretty good to me," said Marie Margot. "If the voyageurs hung a very small piece of meat on a string a couple of inches above a pan of water, the bugs would fly or drop into the water, get caught and drown. I just had another thought. Don't the voyageurs already coat themselves with bear grease to keep the bugs away?"

"Bear grease?" said Marie Rebecca. "And just how do they go about convincing a bear to give that up? Wouldn't it be easier to keep the little nuisances out of their hair in the first place? They could drape a huge piece of finely woven bobbinet or cheesecloth over their canoes at night. Actually, it might be better for them to make see-through veils long enough to cover just their heads and necks and tuck the ends into their shirt collars. If the insects get too bad, the men could wear two layers of netting around their heads and also wear gloves."

"Would mud work as a deterrent?" asked Marie Margot. "Mud is more readily available than bear grease. And after awhile, it might also work like a facial treatment and make their faces feel smooth and soft."

"I heard that mosquitos and flies are attracted to dark colored clothing," said Marie Rebecca. "How about wearing light colors to keep them away, like light blue or white, for instance?"

"Right," said Marie Candace. "Can't you just see the men going about their work for eighteen hours a day with mud all over their faces and wearing white clothes? You know how they enjoy doing laundry!"

"You would think that the voyageurs' campfires, smudge-pots of smoldering pine needles and humus, and their pipe-smoking would keep the bugs away at night." said Marie Sue. "On the other hand, maybe little Jean Rene hasn't mastered using his white clay pipe yet, since he's so new."

"Well, frankly, I think we should share our special insect repellant with them," said Marie Ramona. "You know, the bottles of fly dope we made up with three ounces of pine tar, three ounces of vaseline, one ounce each of citronella and pennyroyal with a little camphor mixed in? At least we know what works for us."

Just then, the voyageurs came tromping back down the portage for their canoes and the rest of their gear. "Hey, Marie! Who has been fishing? We could see all those nice big ones you were having for your lunch. What are you using for the bait?" asked Jean Henri.

"I caught them," said Marie Sue. "The bait was dead mosquitos and flies. Marie Ramona is calling my new technique "fly-fishing." What do you think about that?"

The voyageurs laughed and laughed. "Why that is the silliest idea we have ever heard — fishing with little dead flies, ha, ha! That is just beginner's luck and this fly-fishing of yours will NEVER catch on!"

"OK, gentlemen, gather around! Before you depart," said Marie Rebecca. "we have a little something to keep insects from biting you. It's our special old timey fly dope recipe, made up for you in this bottle." She handed the bottle to Jean Claude Baptiste with a big smile.

"So how does this work?" he asked. "Do we put it on our faces, hands, heads and ears?"

"Nooo, Jean," said Marie Rebecca as she turned and winked at the other Voyageurettes. "Insects love this stuff! What you do is sprinkle it someplace where you are not, like on a tree stump, instead of on yourselves. Then the bugs fly over to the stump and stay there. They do not come near you."

"Thank you, Maries, ever so much! We're off! *Bon voyage!*" called Jean Claude, as he and his men waved cheerily and trotted out of sight with their heavy burdens.

The Voyageurettes looked at one another and smiled demurely. They did not have to say one word because they all knew what they had learned that day: "*Ne te laisse jamais tracasser par des choses qui ne revêtent aucune importance*. Don't ever let the little things in life bother you."

*Après le couchant, le sage évite
les discussions oiseuses.*

It is wise never to speak of certain things
after the sun goes down.

Stories of the Night

It was the magic hour in the Canoe Country. The sun had gone into hiding for the time being behind the black silhouettes of the trees on the other side of the lake. A thin line of shining silver made its way across the meeting place of water and land along the far shore, as if someone had drawn it with a pen. It was quiet and peaceful.

Suddenly it was not so silent any more. Across the water came four voyageur canoes making a bee-line for a campsite nearby. The men were singing "*Nous etions trois captaines.*"

"My goodness," said Marie Margot. "They're still wound up, listen to their song! Sometimes I feel sorry that they have to work hard all day and half the night. You'd think the voyageurs would be really tired after all they've been through for the past eighteen or twenty hours."

"Maybe it's just as well that they do work so hard and sleep so little when they're out here on the water." said Marie Candace. With all that extra energy of theirs, who could keep up with them around a cabin all summer?"

"Yes, just like children." said Marie Sue. "Wear them out during the day with lots of physical activity and they will sleep better at night. The only problem with voyageurs is that they are bigger and older and they take longer to wear out!"

The singing voyageurs beached their canoes on the end of a long island within sight of the Maries. In no time the men had unloaded their canoes and begun to set up their camp. The Voyageurettes could soon see the faint glow of their campfire in the twilight. Their voices and laughter echoed across the water. It was a comfortable feeling to know the men were near and going about their routine evening chores and were not still out on the water after dark by themselves.

"After awhile, let's go over and see what the men are up to," said Marie Ramona. "Maybe they would like to play cards or something. We might even get some of them to play checkers!"

"Well, cards might be better," said Marie Rebecca. "I can never figure out why their checker boards have 12 rows of squares instead of eight."

As it grew darker, the Voyageurettes paddled over toward the voyageurs' campsite to see what was happening. They could see the bourgeois' tent was all set up, the four *canots du nord* were flipped over and covered with oilcloth and the men were hanging around the campfire smoking their pipes and not doing much of anything, or so it seemed. The Voyageurettes paddled closer.

"Heavens, it's hot, or is it just me?" said one voyageur. "This heat is terrible, and the bugs are biting wicked! I say it's necessary to refresh ourselves! OK, Friends! Pour me some of that!"

Marie Rebecca said, "I think they are getting into their cups!"

"They might be," said Marie Candace. "They are drinking rum. And lots of it! They probably will not want to play checkers after all."

The Voyageurettes let their canoes drift along the shore in the dark. They heard the voyageurs' voices a little clearer. They heard one, Jean Joseph, say, "Draw near, you five or six little pork-eating new boys on the crew! If you are ever wanting to say proudly, *"Je suis un l'homme du Nord!"* (I am a man of the North) then there are some things you must know. And I am the one to be telling you."

"That guy is blowing smoke!" whispered Marie Rebecca.

"Yes, he is," said Marie Candace. "But, then again, all the men are puffing away on their pipes and drinking down their toddies in good shape. They are probably getting around to telling stories."

"Stories? I like stories!" said Marie Ramona. "Do you suppose they tell about scary things?

"What's scary is the voyageurs!" said Marie Sue. "What they eat is real-ly something. Did you know they put turtle eggs and bird eggs into the 'rubbaboo' they ate for supper? I think they would eat eggs so nearly hatched that the chick could almost peep. That is scary! And their manners are frightening. Once I saw a voyageur pour stew into his hat and..."

"Shh!" said Marie Ramona. "Come on! They are telling stories, let's listen in!"

Jean Joseph began to speak in his deep and quiet voice.

"Here in this place, you must be careful and keep your eyes and ears open for the Giant Beaver that lives nearby. The Giant Beaver rules these woods and is to be feared, for he is very powerful. His jaws are like a vise and his teeth are even bigger than the largest axe-head you have ever seen. When he wishes to cut a tree, it takes only seconds and down it can crash on your head if you are not paying attention. And when the Giant Beaver walks through the woods in search of a tree for his food or his dam or lodge, the earth rumbles and shakes.

"I know the Giant Beaver lives very near. In fact, there is evidence of his presence just above your heads. Look up, lads, and see for yourselves if you do not believe my words," said Jean Joseph as he pointed to the deep gouges and marks fifteen feet up on the birch tree beside him. He did not say even one word about how deep the snow gets in this place every winter. He did not mention that sometimes in the winter or early spring the beaver must cut trees for their food.

All the voyageurs looked up at the tree. They saw the gouges. They saw other trees that had been gnawed and cut off by the beaver very high off the ground. Some of the older voyageurs put their hands over their mouths.

"Aiee! Jean Joseph, I can see the marks on the tree from where I am sitting!" said one of the new voyageurs. "I will volunteer to stay up all night to be watchful and alert for the arrival of this Giant Beaver and wake everyone in camp so they can protect themselves!"

"Good boy!" said Jean Joseph. Then he continued his stories of the night:

"In the great North Woods there lives a creature that you cannot see. It may be invisible, but it is always on the move. It slips by as fast as the wind. And it can roll through the grass or slide across the snow to catch it's prey. This dangerous and very bad creature, it is called the Windigo. The Windigo is always hungry. In fact to live, it must eat seven times its own weight in food each day. So you must watch out, for the Windigo is happy to have human flesh when it cannot find other things to eat. I have heard the hungry Windigo can rush over lakes so fast that it strips fish out of the water for a meal. If anything to eat is left out anywhere, the Windigo is sure to steal it when no one is looking. So, do not hide your lunch behind a tree to save it for later or leave your traps untended for very long. And do not let small children play alone outside if you are not watching them. The Windigo will surely come. And if you ever hear the sound of the Windigo rushing by, there is only one thing to do. You must offer the Windigo something to eat and it will leave you alone and you will be safe, at least for a short while."

The Maries watched as two or three of the new voyageurs reached into the leather bags tied to their waists. They broke off small pieces of something that was either a cookie or a biscuit and flicked them into the woods when no one else was looking.

"And now, my comrades," said Jean Joseph. "There is one more important thing you should always remember. It is something else that can happen to you in the wilderness. Your mind can be easily lost, if you are not careful. There is an entity called the "Folly of the Woods." It is well-known for stealing men's minds and never returning them. This is what happens..."

"Well, at least he's not talking about something that steals women's minds! Maybe that's why we are still so smart If we leave now, before we find out how men lose their minds to this Folly, maybe our minds will stay with us a little longer. If it's OK with you," whispered Marie Margot, "can we please go back to our campsite now?"

The Voyageurettes paddled right back to their campsite and immediately headed for their Marie House. They did not sing or giggle or write in their journals. They just changed into their sleeping clothes and quietly went to bed. All six of them stared at the ceiling of the Marie House in the dark. Each one breathed in and out very slowly and quietly on purpose. They did not twitch one muscle, move one inch or blink one eye. After awhile, each Marie knew the others must be asleep, so she tried hard not to wake up anyone else.

Marie Ramona thought she heard something go whooshing past the back window of the Marie House, but she was not sure. Marie Chris knew she heard small sighs and little feet padding on the ground. Marie Margot was convinced she heard twittering and scratching noises near her head. Marie Candace thought she heard crunching and rustling in the leaves nearby and a tiny rattling of the pan out by the firepit. Marie Sue heard deep croaking noises coming from the water and even louder squeaks coming from the trees back in the woods. Marie Rebecca detected faint howling, yowling and snorting in the distance. Then for awhile, the silence was deafening. Each Marie listened to her own heart beat, thump-thump, thump-thump, thump-thump. Then she felt the pulsing arteries in her neck getting bigger and bigger. Each Marie counted out seconds and kept track of minutes in her mind. Then hours. Now the Maries were not doing this because they were afraid of anything. It was because they were excited. They were anticipating the dawning of a new day of grand adventures out on the water, or maybe it was because of something they ate for supper, it was not entirely clear.

The next morning, when she had finished baking the cranberry muffins, Marie Ramona took one little pinch out of a muffin and tossed it into the woods. Then she turned to the other Voyageurettes and quietly said, "Take it from me, ladies, in the future, *"Après le couchant, le sage évite les discussions oiseuses.* It is wise never to speak of certain things after the sun goes down."

*Prends le temps de respirer
l'odeur des nénuphars!*

Take time to smell the water lilies.

40

The Voyageurette Nature Guide

In the Canoe Country there are numerous and varied species of plants and animals. One common species which might be encountered walks upright on two legs and talks. This is Homo sapiens, or the human being. The Maries have spotted them in several varieties - male and female, adult and child versions. They can be dressed in anything from scout uniforms to fancy B.B. Legume apparel to more causal, worn-out jeans and shirts. Men wearing suits and ties and women in dresses and high heels are rarely encountered. Almost all humans in the Canoe Country are friendly.

If a black, furry animal about the size of a human being is sighted, it is probably a black bear. It should be avoided. If it sniffs around the campsite or tears apart food packs with its large claws, it is definitely a bear. Mice also sniff around camp and help themselves to the contents of food packs, but they are much smaller than bears and have pointed noses and long, long tails. With just a little practice, one can tell them apart, especially when they make noise. Bears snuffle, growl and snap their teeth together. Mice squeak.

Moose and deer are also seen in the Canoe Country. They are a little harder to tell apart. Whatever the species-deer or moose, if it has antlers, it is a male. If not, it is a female. Deer tend to be tan or reddish-brown in color and are less than half the size of moose. Moose are dark brown or black and are bigger than deer.

If someone says, "Look at that cute, little graceful four-legged animal over there," it is probably a deer. If they say, "Look at that really big, dark brown, clumsy and ugly four-legged animal that looks like a horse over there," it is probably a moose. If two animals look quite a bit alike, except one is a smaller version of the other, they are a mother deer or moose and her baby.

There are many fuzzy little animals that are frequently observed running around campsites. Chipmunks have stripes. Squirrels are larger and are rusty-red or gray. They do not have stripes. Both squirrels and chipmunks have fluffy tails and are very cute and are, indeed, fun to watch. Neither are big enough, or with sufficient meat on their bones, to be caught and eaten for supper.

There are several weasely-looking creatures in the Canoe Country. If they are very small and run through the woods, they are least weasels. If they are medium-sized and run around the woods, they are regular weasels. If they are big and playfully swim in the water, then they are otters.

Beavers are one other frequently observed mammal. They are brown furry animals that are bigger than mice and smaller than moose, unless they are especially tiny beavers or especially large beavers. Most are about the size of a small dog. They are easy to identify by their teeth, which look very much in need of an orthodontist or dental hygienist, and also because of their tails, which are large and flat. They look very much like muskrats, except that muskrat tails look like fat rat tails. If the animal is swimming in the water far away and a person is not able to see its tail and cannot tell if it is a beaver or a muskrat, it is safe to identify it as a beaver since no one else will know the difference. Beavers do not make good house pets. They are very hard on wooden furniture and they like to hog the bath tub and plug up drains. Even though they are very cute, it is best to leave them in their proper wilderness habitat.

Timber wolves live in the Canoe Country. Dogs are found in the Canoe Country also, but they just are visiting there with their masters. Dogs are easy to tell from wolves. They usually have collars and some might even wear red bandannas around their necks. If they are black dogs with red bandannas on their necks they are probably black labs. If they are reddish or tan colored, they are either Irish setters or golden retrievers. If the dog is little and white with painted toenails and bows tied to its ears, it must be a poodle. If a person needs to know precisely what particular species of dog it is, simply pose the question to the owner, who is usually at the other end of the leash from the dog.

Wolves look different. They do not have owners and they do not wear collars or bandannas. Their noses are pointed. At night, both dogs and wolves are vocal. If barking or howling is heard at night, assume it is a wolf. It is much more thrilling in the wilderness to think of hearing wolves howl rather than dogs making noises.

There are hundreds of birds in the Canoe Country. With patience, any observant person should soon be able to identify them all. Some swim. If a bird is black and white and swimming, it is a loon. If it is brown and swimming, it is a duck. Mallard ducks and black ducks have round heads. Mergansers have pointed heads. The points on merganser heads face backwards. If a bird is white and swimming or if it is white and dive-bombing a canoe or campsite, it is a gull. If the swimming bird is being followed by several miniature fluffy things, the fluffs are its babies.

If a bird is huge and standing along the edge of the water on long, skinny legs, it is a heron. If a canoe is paddled closer and closer and the heron does not fly away in alarm, it is a skinny tree stump.

In camp, if a grayish-brown bird about the size of a blue jay flies up close and takes food out of a person's hand or off a plate, it is a Canadian jay, sometimes called a "Whiskey Jack" or "Camp Robber." If it is blue, it is a blue jay. Both birds make loud squawking noises.

Woodpeckers are called that because of what they do. Some nature experts say they peck into wood and bark in search of insects or grubs. The Voyageurettes think differently. They know these black-and-white birds peck on trees because they find it amusing to make irritating pounding noises in an otherwise peaceful and quiet environment.

Because they both are big, eagles and osprey look a lot alike, but they are easy enough to identify. Eagles have white heads and tails, brown wings and legs and look like eagles. Osprey look more like osprey. They have white legs. If there is a really big bird soaring high in the sky and it is difficult to tell for sure what it is, just declare it an eagle because, for some people, eagle sightings are more rare and exciting than osprey sightings.

All other birds can be scientifically categorized into two general, but very separate species:

1) Big birds that go "tweet" or
2) Little birds that go "tweet."

For those wishing to be more specific, two more species may be added: little birds that chirp and big birds that chirp.

If a big bird that fits neither category is detected because it goes, "caw, caw" or "hoot, hoot" instead of tweeting or chirping, it is a crow or an owl.

Other things that live in the water are very important to know about also. If it has a shell, it is likely to be a turtle. If the turtle has a thick neck and an ugly, rough shell with spikes, it is a snapping turtle. Walk fast away from snapping turtles. Do not run or other people will think you are not brave. Other turtles that are smaller and have smooth shells are likely to be painted turtles.

If you are fishing and catch something, it is either a turtle or a fish. Fish are easy to spot because of their fins, scales and smell. Fish common in the Canoe Country are northern pike, walleye, bass and trout. They are all very hard to tell apart. If you look closely, and the fish has sharp, wicked-looking teeth, it is probably a northern. If its eyes bulge, it is a walleye. Bass do not have sharp teeth or bulging eyes. It is called a trout if it does not fit in the bass, northern or walleye categories. No matter what the species, all fish from the Canoe Country are safe to eat, unless it was not moving or was floating on the water when you caught it. If you have a fine stringer of fish and are not sure what kind you have caught, simply announce, "Look at this!" If you want to be more specific, you can categorize fish as being "little," "big," or "really big." If it is a "really, really big fish" you have caught and the fish has sharp teeth, quickly toss it back into the water before it bites. Officially, this is known as "catch and release."

If you are walking in the woods and see a fat, ugly, gray, rat-like animal with a shell on its back, try to examine it more closely to see if it is, indeed, a rat wearing a turtle shell. If it is not, you had better check your map and compass carefully because you are probably lost and have paddled far south of where you think you are. You are looking at an armadillo. Armadillos are harmless, but more than likely, alligators, crocodiles and water moccasins are in the vicinity also. Head your canoe north and paddle fast!

Yes, there are snakes in the Canoe Country. They are neither poisonous nor dangerous, except to frogs, insects, worms and mice. They are no pleasure to look at, however, and should be avoided at all costs. Luckily, most snake sightings are false. What you are seeing is just a piece of rope left by another canoe-camper or it is a twig or a stick. Twigs and sticks in the Canoe Country are known to mimic snakes. It is best not to stick around long enough to determine if what you are seeing is a real or a false snake sighting. Just follow the regular snake-sighting protocol. First, gasp and grab at your heart. Next, yell "SNAKE!" Then, run in the opposite direction. Chances are high that no one else will want to venture to the site of the reported snake sighting. If, however, you have a brave and inquisitive person in your group who checks it out and discovers a snake-like piece of rope or stick and says, "Ha, ha, look, it is only a piece of rope, ha, ha!" You can always say, "Well, there was a snake right next to that piece of rope; however, I scared it away." Then, at least, the others in your group will thank you for performing such a brave and useful deed.

In the Canoe Country, you will see bugs. Many, many, many bugs. None of them are big enough to eat, except for deer flies, but they are not very tasty. There are three general bug types in the Canoe Country:

1) Pesky bugs that bite
2) Bugs that do not bite, and
3) Big, ugly bugs

Pesky biting bugs can be handled in three ways: swatting, shooting and escaping into the tent. Small biting bugs can be swatted with your hand or a fingers. Big ones should be swatted by your canoe paddle or shot with a hand-held anti-aircraft missile. There are four major varieties of biting bugs - all easily identified by sound. If they hum, they are mosquitos. If they buzz, they are flies. No-see-ums and black flies are both silent.

Bugs that don't bite you probably will not even be noticed because you are busy dealing with those that do. You can just forget about those bugs.

Big, ugly bugs that don't bite are another matter. They are just too big and ugly to ignore. Since they do not bite, you will not have to worry about them, except for their ugly looks. The Voyageurettes strongly urge you to feel sorry for these bugs because of their appearance. Just walk away from them without feeling obligated to even identify them. They should be pitied, not scorned.

Proper identification of flora is quite difficult, indeed. There are just so many different plant species in the Canoe Country and they all look basically alike, except for trees, which are big. Generally speaking, if there is a plant that has a flower on it, it is called a "flowering plant" and probably is a "wild flower." If it is a pretty wildflower, one can say, "Oh, look at this pretty little wildflower." Proper etiquette would be for all members of a group to come and look at it and all take turns smelling the pretty flower. If the wildflower is not a pretty one, ignore it. Probably it will not smell very nice, either.

Making up names for unknown species is perfectly acceptable in the wilderness. One very authentic-sounding, make-believe flower name is Dew Idium. Dew Idiums, for instance, can come in blue, pink, white, red or yellow. Feel free to declare any color of Dew Idium as being very rare, indeed. Names such as "Gossip flowers", "Land-lilies" or "Violettas" also sound very authentic to people not knowing that such plants do not exist.

Most wilderness canoeists love to gaze into the sky at night. It is, indeed, an awe-inspiring and pretty sight as well as a challenging task to locate and identify planets, moons and constellations by their proper names. In the northern sky, there is a constellation that looks like a spoon. Legend has it that a Voyageurette of long ago was left with the after-breakfast chore of washing the oatmeal pot and the long-handled spoon used to dip out the oatmeal. She cleaned out the pot, but was so disgusted by the sticky contents, that when no one else was looking, she flung the big, gooey spoon into the sky where it became known as the "Oatmeal Dipper."

Just to the east of the "Oatmeal Dipper," there is a constellation which looks like an upside down letter "W." Some people mistakenly identify this arrangement of stars as Cassiopeia, the Queen, sitting upon her heavenly throne. Actually, it is Marie Chris sitting in her camp chair. Officially, this constellation should be called, "Marie Reading a Book."

To the west of the "Oatmeal Dipper," almost at the top of the summer sky, are several stars in a semi-circle. Some people call this "Corona Borealis," thinking it has the shape of a crown. Others say it appears to be native people sitting in a council circle. The truth is that it is several Voyageurettes from long ago, sitting around a bowl. The proper name for this constellation is "Maries Eating Popcorn."

To the west of "Maries Eating Popcorn," is a constellation which looks like a lopsided rectangle. This is not actually the constellation Hercules, as many think. It is named for the famous Marie of long ago. Some say she was the fastest paddler ever known and in her hand is a bent-shaft paddle. Others feel that this Marie was the best angler the world had ever known and in her hand is a fishing pole. It is unclear which version is true. Whichever it is, she was, indeed, very important because a constellation is now named for her. This constellation is called either "Paddlin' Marie" or "Fishin' Marie."

In the summer sky there are three very bright stars known as the "Summer Triangle." It consists of the stars Deneb, Vega, and Altair. Deneb is also part of a cross-shaped constellation known by some as "Cygnus, the Swan" or Northern Cross. The Voyageurettes have always called this constellation "The Giant Mosquito." It is definitely not a swan. The Voyageurettes all agree that the Summer Triangle symbolizes the three most necessary items of a wilderness canoe trip; however, they sometimes argue about what those items are. Some Maries steadfastly maintain they are breakfast, lunch and dinner, while others are convinced, without a doubt, that the three most important items are a canoe, a paddle and a Duluth pack.

Si on devait renaître, on serait encore des Voyageurettes.

If we had our lives to lead over again,
we would lead them as Voyageurettes.

41

Journey's End

The Voyageurettes' journey had come to an end for another season. They paddled to the landing, beached their canoes, and unloaded their packs for the last time. Quietly, they stood together at the water's edge, not wanting to leave, but knowing they must.

A tall, young, blond outfitter's helper came over and looked down at their well-used outfit lying there on the sandy shore. He noticed the faint scratches on the bottom of their resin canoes, the worn grips of their bent paddles, and their faded packs standing upright, side-by-side. And he studied their faces for what seemed like a long time. Finally, the boy asked,

"You ladies been out on the water before?

"A few times," they said.

"What do you ladies do when you go out?" he asked.

"The same thing everybody else does. "

"Anybody go with you?"

"No, just us."

"Weren't you ladies afraid to be out there all alone?"

"We were not alone. We went together. All of us."

"So you got along all right, out there, then? "

"Yes, we got along just fine."

Then the boy thought he heard them say, "Ah, yes, the life of the Voyageurettes is hard. It is a dangerous life. But it is a happy life. We would not trade this way of life for any other. If we had our lives to lead over again, we would lead them as Voyageurettes. And that is why we will return to the wilderness another day, as the voyageurs did, and go to the lakes and rushing rivers in the land we have never seen." And that is the truth.

Back row left to right: Jackie, Becky, Tina, Margot
Front row left to right: Candace, Sue

The Real Maries

Initially, there were only four of us: Sue, Becky, Margot and Chris. After our first week-long trip together, we returned to Ely, Minnesota, the town nearest the BWCAW Canoe Country. A local voyageur re-enactor, Mike Hillman, was sitting outside a store front in downtown Ely, entertaining the town's many tourists. We visited with him, asking him historical questions about the French voyageurs of long ago. He never broke character, claiming to be Jean Baptiste, a common name among the real voyageurs of long ago. It was then we decided that we too could play a role. The name for our group, The Voyageurettes, seemed appropriate. Unfortunately, we did not know any French and were unable to easily come up with four French women's names. We asked Jean Baptiste what his wife's name was. He said he had several wives-all named Marie so we all just took that name for ourselves. We were all Maries, Sue, Becky, Margot and Chris. As time went along, the number of Maries grew. There are now 14 of us. We became the female counterparts to the male French voyageurs.

The real voyageurs exaggerated their skills, lied about their accomplishments and bragged constantly. They were, however, fiercely loyal to each other, worked well together and were mannerly and polite to visitors and outsiders. In this spirit, the stories of The Voyageurettes were written. Each story has absolutely no guarantee of any truth to it.

Meet "The Maries"

Each of the Maries does indeed exist. Actually, that is not entirely true. It is more accurate to say that most of the Maries are real people. Marie Bambi is a total fabrication.

In real life, SUE is a Physical Education teacher in Rockford, IL. She is considered the bourgeois simply because someone has to be in charge and she organized the first trip. Over the years she has lead many groups of teenagers into the BWCAW and the Quetico. Sue does, in fact, get lost on Lake Insula, has a real aversion for oatmeal and once did get attacked by a grouse on a portage and mistakenly thought it was a wild turkey.

BECKY is Sue's older sister. Both grew up in Rochelle, IL. Becky now lives in N.Haverhill, NH and is an amateur naturalist. A former college dean, elementary school teacher and educator with NH Fish and Game Department, Becky has written articles for newspapers, outdoor magazines and compiled a cookbook. She is presently a court security officer. She is married to the Grafton County Sheriff.

MARGOT is an elementary school teacher in the Detroit, MI area. She and Becky are long time friends, having met years ago at summer camp. It is true that on her very first trip, Margot did take a tumble while carrying a canoe across a portage. She executed the fall so gracefully that we dubbed her, "The Ballerina". She does know many folk and camp songs and is an accomplished kazoo player. She gets up early each morning and tries very hard to figure out how to light the one-burner Coleman. We are confident that someday she will finally figure it out so she can make morning coffee for the rest of us.

JOYCE is indeed a very pretty lady. She always looks very clean and well-groomed in her color coordinated attire. Her hair always looks perfect because she brings along a small butane hair curler in her pack. The rest of us look as if we belong on a wilderness trip. Not Joyce. A Boy Scout troop passed us on a portage one year and one of the boys just stared at Joyce. With admiration in his eyes, he said, "You are so pretty. You look like you just stepped out of a L.L. Bean catalogue." After that, we dubbed Joyce, "The Model". A few years ago, we were beginning a portage at the moment a wind shear hit the area. Joyce was carrying a canoe and a large tree fell across the path, missing her by inches. It was a very sobering and frightful experience for us all. Joyce also did have an allergic reaction to no-see-um bites. Her ears swelled up, not quite as large as "Dumbo ears," but, then, the Maries do tend to exaggerate at times.

CANDACE is Becky's husband's cousin. She joined the Maries several years ago after hearing stories of the Marie trips. Candace and her husband Bill are avid sailors. When she is not canoeing, she can be found in their sailboat, cruising the east coast. Candace is presently a school nurse in southern New Hampshire. In her early years as a nurse, she worked for Kentucky Nursing Service in the Appalachian mountains of Eastern Kentucky. On N. Hegman Lake, drops of water were trickling down an overhead cliff into the lake. Candace did, on purpose, paddle up to that trickle of water just so the drips would hit Sue on the head. In the Marie stories, that little trickle turned into a raging water fall.

RAMONA is truthfully a very competent canoeist and camper. She has taught camping and canoeing skills to hundreds of Boy Scouts and Girl Scouts and their leaders in Rockford, IL. Ramona is very proud to have received a high honor among Boy Scouts-the Order of the Arrow and the District Award of Merit. She is married to Dick who is also an avid canoeist. They were among the co-founders of the Midwest Voyageurs, a canoe club in Rockford. They have six grown children and several grandchildren.

SARAH is a court reporter in Atlanta, Georgia. She met Becky while working at the Grafton County (NH) Superior Court. Prior to joining the Voyageurettes, Sarah had never camped or canoed before, but having grown up on a dairy farm in Vermont, she was used to doing hard work outdoors. On her first trip, she picked up paddling and portaging skills in a snap. Putting up the tent, however, was another matter. She put it up; however, it fell down several times in succession. The Maries found this highly amusing.

TRICIA, another elementary school teacher and NH Marie, lived in Candace's home town. She joined the Maries on one trip and has subsequently moved to the Pacific Northwest. Tricia originally came from California, where she did actually own a pink canoe at one time. The Maries were impressed to think that one of us actually owned something as classy as a pink canoe. On the trip Tricia also wore a very striking pink and purple paddling outfit. The Maries fondness for pink things-pink canoes and pink flamingoes can be directly attributed to Tricia.

CHRIS was one of the original Maries. She is a learning disability teacher who taught at the same school with Sue. She is an avid reader and outdoors person. Until the first Marie trip, Chris had never been to the Canoe Country. She fell in love with wilderness canoeing and participated in many Marie trips until she relocated to California. The Maries delight in pestering poor Chris when she reads her books. She did once tell three of us that we were "skewed to the lower end of the Bell curve" in math.

GAIL is an experienced BWCAW trip leader, having lead many groups of youth and women from her church over the last 25 years. Gail and Becky attended Hamline University in St. Paul, MN during the 1960s. Gail still lives in St. Paul with her canoeist husband Jack and canoeing daughter Amy who is now a student at Brigham Young University.

A few years age, CORITA went along on one of Gail's women's trips. They have been good friends ever since. Corita lives in Eau Claire, Wisconsin where she owns a ballet/tap/jazz dance studio. She also teaches dance at the University of Wisconsin in Eau Claire. She is married to Claude and they have three grown children. Corita met up with the Maries via computer. Gail and several of the Maries had been exchanging e-mail with each other and Corita joined in. She and Ramona, having had met her only through e-mail, drove north to Eau Claire one weekend to meet Corita in person. They also met Claude, their three very cute little papillon dogs, and two cockateil birds. The following summer, she joined us on a Marie trip and became an "Official Marie."

TINA is another Marie who we met via the Internet. Tina's husband, Butch, had been e-mailing Sue in search of information about taking his Boy Scout troop on a BWCAW trip. Tina soon joined in the e-mailings and got connected with the other "online" Maries. Before long, we had her convinced to join us on a canoe trip. Quite bravely, she flew up to Rockford to meet these canoeing strangers and joined us on our canoe trip. Tina, even though she is a Cajun and lives in Louisiana, fit right in with the Maries. By the end of the trip she was hooked by the Canoe County. We knew she liked us when she offered to let us use her ATM card ("Butchie can pay for it," Tina said). It took Tina a few days to get acclimated to the northwoods-she just couldn't believe that we don't have any armadillos "up north". We just can't help but tease Tina about her having mistaken a rock for an armadillo. We can't tease her about her Cajun cooking, however. Her secrete crawfish dish is spectacular.

KAREN went on just one Marie trip. She is now very busy, married to Mark and mother of Hanna. Karen is a nurse at a major Chicago hospital and enjoys such uncitified things as canoe camping, snow skiing and sky-diving. On the Marie trip, Karen hoped that we all remained healthy. She said, "I am on vacation and don't want to go to work as a nurse." She then pulled out a t-shirt that said "Off Duty" printed right on the front. That was just enough ammunition with which to tease Karen. She heard more than once from one Marie or another that they, too, were "off duty" in regard to unpleasant camp chores like doing the dishes.

JACKIE is the Director of Patient Services at the Cottage Hospital in Woodsville, NH. Her nursing career spans more than three decades, including service in Viet Nam. She and her husband Bill live in Lisbon, NH. They have three grown children and one wonderful grandson. The other Maries consider Jackie to be their "bear magnet." After making at least eight wilderness excursions without having even one up-close-and-personal encounter with a bear, things changed dramatically the year Jackie joined us for the first time. That year, three individual bears visited us at three separate campsites on three successive nights. During one evening mealtime, a particularly assertive bear made threatening displays of a full up-right posture, snorting, growling and snapping its teeth at us. Throughout the experience, Jackie maintained her composure, kept her priorities straight and calmly continued to enjoy her supper. After the bear finally retreated into the underbrush and headed toward another campsite, Jackie shared her secret. The way she handles stress is to go into a state of full denial.

Anyway, that's the Maries. We are not psychologically imbalanced people with dual personalities, a real personality and a "Marie" personality. Rather, we are multiple people with one personality. The Maries are all of one mold. We have paddled, portaged and camped together for so long that we know what the others are thinking. We are all of one mind. Since we are of one mind, we never get confused as to who the others are at the moment-their "real" self or their "Marie" self. We just know. We do paddle hard, portage hard, lie hard, sleep hard, shop hard (when we have the money) and we don't eat dogs. And this is the truth.

Glossaire (Glossary)

avant
bowsman; "first mate" (often the guide, *guide*, m.)

aviron, m. (also pagaille, m.)
paddle (not an oar); used by the NWC canoes

bourgeois(e), m/f
boss, team captain; add "e" for a woman (used both for the boss's wife and for a lady boss)

brigade, m.
flotilla, canoe brigade

canot express, m.
express canoe, 18-22' long, used by couriers at speed

canot(s) de maître, m.
freight (war) canoe, 36' long, used on Great Lakes-Montreal run and east of Superior

canot(s) du nord, m.
North canoe, 26' long, used west of Superior to Athabasca

castor, m.
beaver (see also *peau de castor*)

Chez Marie
the Marie House

colosse, m.
colossus, giant (often used to mean the opposite)

femme du pays (sauvage)
(wild) woman of the North Country

gouvernail, m.
steersman (lit. governor); "captain" (but not the *bourgeois*)

habitant(e), m/f
farmer; one who stays home in Montreal

hivernant(e), m/f
wintering partner; one who has passed one winter west of Superior

les femmes (du pays)
ladies (*mes femmes* when addressing)

ma chérie
my dear (woman)

mangeur du lard, m.
new voyageur, greenhorn, rookie (lit. pork-eater); usually a *milieu*

milieu, m.
    middleman; "private" (in a freight canoe, the horsepower)

mon chéri, m.
    my dear (man)

ours, m.
    bear

pays d'en haut, m.
    North Country or Far North (lit. high country); begins west of Superior to Athabasca District

peau(x) de castor, m.
    beaver pelts; basic unit of fur trade currency. Use for $100 bills (or any money; one beaver = $50)

peltries, f.
    pelts, furs

petites filles, f.
    little girls

rame, f.
    oar (not a paddle); used for a York boat by HBC

rat-mousqué, m.
    muskrat

raton-laveur, m.
    raccoon

tant pis!
    too bad!

tout le temps
    all the time

vite (vite)
    quick (quick)